"This humorous cozy is framed by life in small-town Iowa and teems with quirky characters."—*Booklist*

"A charming story and a fun summer read."
—*A Book for Today*

"This is such a fun book to read. It was hilarious and had me laughing out loud many times. Highly recommended for cozy mystery fans and fans of those storage unit auction shows on TV."—*Daisy's Book Journal*

ANTIQUES KNOCK-OFF

"An often amusing tale complete with lots of antiques-buying tips and an ending that may surprise you."
—*Kirkus Reviews*

"Quirky . . . Throw in a touch of Mafia menace, a New Age hypnotist with a herd of cats, a very tasty recipe, and some smart tips on antique collecting, and you've got yourself a sure-fire winner." —*Publishers Weekly*

"If you like laugh-out-loud funny mysteries, this will make your day. Place your bets on this screwball comedy cozy where the clues are thick and the mother-daughter dynamics are off the charts."
—*Romantic Times Book Reviews*, **4.5 stars**

"Stop shoveling snow, take time to chuckle: *Antiques Knock-Off* is a fitting antidote to any seasonal blues, putting life into perspective as more than a little crazy, and worth laughing about."—*Kingdom Books*

"Great reading, very funny. In fact, the first page of this book is so funny and so well done that I just had to stop reading for a while and admire it. Highly recommended."—*Bill Crider's Pop Culture Magazine*

"Scenes of Midwestern small-town life, informative tidbits about the antiques business, and clever dialog make this essential for those who like unusual amateur sleuths."
—*Library Journal*

ANTIQUES BIZARRE

"Auction tips and a recipe for spicy beef stew enhance this satirical cozy."—*Publishers Weekly*

"If you delight in the absurd and enjoy manic humor, you'll treasure the Trash 'n' Treasure mysteries."
—*Mystery Scene*

"Genuinely funny . . . another winner! The *Trash 'n' Treasures* books have to be the funniest mystery series going." —*Somebody Dies*

"I love the books by 'Barbara Allan.' Great characters drive this series, and the research about the antiques really adds to the story. It's fun reading and the mystery is terrific."—*Crimespree*

ANTIQUES FLEE MARKET
"Lively…this bubbly tongue-in-cheek cozy also includes flea market shopping tips and a recipe."—*Publishers Weekly*

"A fast-paced plot, plenty of tongue-in-cheek humor, and tips on antiques collecting will keep readers engaged."
—*Library Journal*

"Top pick! This snappy mystery has thrills, laugh-out-loud moments and amazingly real relationships."
—*Romantic Times Book Reviews, 4.5 stars*

"This is surely one of the funniest cozy series going."
—*Ellery Queen Mystery Magazine*

"Marvelous dialogue, great characters, and a fine murder mystery."—**reviewingtheevidince.com**

"Very engaging, very funny, with amusing dialogue and a couple of nice surprises. Next time you need a laugh, check it out."—*Bill Crider's Pop Culture Magazine*

ANTIQUES MAUL
"Charming. . . a laugh-out-loud-funny mystery."
—*Romantic Times* (**four stars**)

ANTIQUES ROADKILL
"Brandy, her maddening mother, her uptight sister, and all the denizens of their small Iowa town are engaging and utterly believable as they crash through a drugs and antiques scam on the Mississippi. Anyone like me, who's blown the car payment on a killer outfit, will love the bonus of Brandy's clothes obsession."—**Sara Paretsky**

Also by Barbara Allan

ANTIQUES ROADKILL
ANTIQUES MAUL
ANTIQUES FLEE MARKET
ANTIQUES BIZARRE
ANTIQUES KNOCK-OFF
ANTIQUES DISPOSAL
ANTIQUES CHOP
ANTIQUES CON
ANTIQUES SWAP
ANTIQUES FRAME
ANTIQUES WANTED
ANTIQUES SLAY RIDE (e-book)
ANTIQUES FRUITCAKE (e-book)
ANTIQUES ST. NICKED (e-book)

By Barbara Collins

TOO MANY TOMCATS
(short story collection)

By Barbara and Max Allan Collins

REGENERATION
BOMBSHELL
MURDER—HIS AND HERS
(short story collection)

Antiques
Frame

A Trash 'n' Treasures Mystery

Barbara Allan

KENSINGTON BOOKS
http://www.kensingtonbooks.com

KENSINGTON BOOKS are published by

Kensington Publishing Corp.
119 West 40th Street
New York, NY 10018

All Kensington titles, imprints, and distributed lines are available at special quantity discounts for bulk purchases for sales promotion, premiums, fund-raising, educational, or institutional use. Special book excerpts or customized printings can also be created to fit specific needs. For details, write or phone the office of the Kensington Special Sales Manager: Attn. Special Sales Department. Kensington Publishing Corp., 119 West 40th Street, New York, NY 10018. Phone: 1-800-221-2647.

Kensington and the K logo Reg. U.S. Pat. & TM Off.

ISBN-13: 978-0-7582-9314-5
ISBN-10: 0-7582-9314-3
First Kensington Hardcover Edition: May 2017
First Kensington Mass Market Edition: April 2018

eISBN-13: 978-0-7582-9313-8
eISBN-10: 0-7582-9313-5
First Kensington Electronic Edition: May 2017

10 9 8 7 6 5 4 3 2 1

Printed in the United States of America

For Mary Minton,
who is nice enough to love these books

Brandy's Quote:
Each betrayal begins with trust.
—Phish, "Farmhouse"

Mother's quote:
O, beware, my lord, of jealousy;
it is the green-eyed monster
which doth mock the meat it feeds on.
—William Shakespeare, *Othello*, Act III,
Scene III

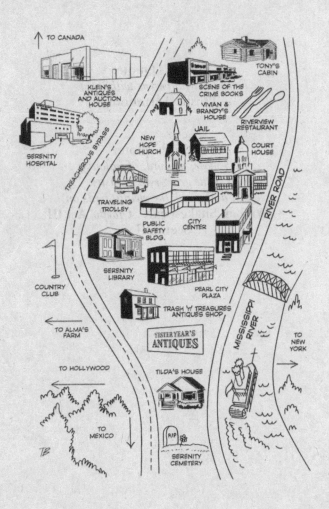

Tinseltown Reporter

Antiques Sleuths, that new reality-TV series now airing—currently shooting its final episode of the first season—opened to high numbers, pleasing network executives. But lately episodes have gone soft in the ratings.

The show features two amateur sleuths-cum-antiques dealers, a mother-and-daughter team, who have solved a number of real-life murder mysteries in their quaint hometown of Serenity, Iowa—uncovering the mysteries behind the strange and unusual antiques and collectibles that are brought into their shop.

Mother is Vivian Borne (age undisclosed), a widowed local theater diva with a nose for sniffing out murder and mayhem. Daughter is Brandy Borne, a thirty-three-year-old divorcée who plays reluctant Watson to her mother's zealous Holmes, with the help of an ever so cute shih tzu named Sushi.

But the murder mystery aspect of *Sleuths* is nowhere to be seen on their series, other than the occasional interview segment. Bad choice?

Producing is cinematographer-turned-show-runner Phillip Dean, who stepped in to replace the late reality-show guru Bruce Spring (*Extreme Hobbies* and *Witch Wives of Winnipeg*) after Spring's tragic death last year. *Antiques Sleuths* is Dean's first foray

into the reality-show biz, and this
Tinseltown reporter deduces it will be his
last—unless he can boost the ratings with
a killer first-season cliff-hanger.

—Rona Reed

Chapter One

Lights, Camera, Auction!

Dearest ones! It is I, Vivian Borne (aka Mother), who—for the second time in our enduring, endearing series—has found herself in the position of having to begin a book, or risk missing our publishing deadline.

Let us be clear! It is not without a pang of guilt—or, at least, a ping—that I must usurp Brandy's usual opening chapter. But the poor girl is in the doldrums, in spite of—or is that despite? (the difference eludes me)—her daily dose of Prozac.

The reason for Brandy's melancholia—and since she won't tell you, I fear I must—is the sudden and unexpected arrival in town of Camilla Cassato, the estranged wife of Serenity's chief of police, Anthony Cassato, who happens to be Brandy's significant other.

(For newbies or those needing a refresher course, read on. All others may feel free to skip to the paragraph that begins "But now, with the return of Mrs. Cassato . . .")

Tony arrived several years ago from the East (not the Orient, but rather the eastern USA) to take the top cop position in our sleepy little Mississippi River town . . . and for a time was a man of mystery, until things got lively. By lively, I mean when an assassin came after our chief at a secluded cabin where he and Brandy were enjoying each other's company.

Seemed a New Jersey godfather had taken a contract out on the chief (a murder contract, not home improvement), who had testified against a certain crime family in those environs (*Antiques Knock-off*). Tony and Brandy managed to duck the hitman's bullets and flee, but the chief was forced to disappear into WITSEC (the United States Federal Witness Protection Program), his situation heating up just as he and Brandy were really warming to each other.

A subsequent mother-and-daughter trip to New York to sell an original vintage Superman drawing at a comics convention (*Antiques Con*) afforded me, sans Brandy, the opportunity to drop in on this New Jersey godfather (name withheld) and reason with him. My warmth and charm (and some take-out ziti) convinced him to void the contract, which allowed for Tony to return to Serenity . . . and to Brandy's arms. A happy ending! Or happy middle, at least.

But now, with the return of Mrs. Cassato, the couple's happiness has once again been derailed.

Seems Tony had assumed that divorce papers sent to him by Camilla's lawyer, and signed and returned by him, had been properly filed; but recently Camilla informed Tony she had had a change of heart and had never followed through with the filing . . . or the divorce.

Though Tony had rebuffed Camilla's efforts to resume cohabitation, the idea of a married boyfriend has not been sitting well with my sensitive child.

And, to complicate things further, Camilla has set up a rival antiques shop just a block from ours, popping up at various auctions around town, outbidding us in a mean-spirited attempt (I can only assume) to get back at Brandy.

So Brandy has had to put her relationship with Tony on hold until his marital status with Camilla is resolved. This is sensible but takes an emotional toll.

Now that all of you are up to date, I wish to address several criticisms that have been coming my way via e-mails, tweets, and blogs. Some of you accuse me of (as we say in the writing game) telling, not showing. Had I *shown* the above, we'd be on page fifty. Do you really think that's efficient?

Also, those of you who do not like my digressions, I refer you to thousands, nay, tens of thousands, of satisfied readers who find my little side trips every bit as rewarding as the journey itself. Besides, those who accuse me of such digressions are exaggerating my tendency toward such.

By the way, do you know what *really* irks me? People who end every sentence as if it were a question! Here is an example: "The other day? When I went to the grocery store?" Uptalking, I call it. Some strange remnant of Valley Girl that has infiltrated the mother tongue (but not this mother's tongue!).

This distortion of our language seems to be spreading everywhere. Even television newscasters do it, and not only women, but men, as well. Might I suggest forming an organization against this abomination? We could call it People Against Uptalking, or PAUT. Well, admittedly, that's not very catchy. Citizens Against Uptalking, or CAUT. No better? How about Down with Uptalking, or DWUT? I like the wordplay of "down" and "up," although as an acronym, DWUT comes out perhaps too close to "duh." The Anti-Uptalking League has a certain ring, although AUTL sounds a bit like "ought'll." As in, "We ought'll stop uptalking?"

Please send your suggestions, care of our publisher, to Vivian Borne.

Oh, one more thing. If you need to use a stick to snap a "selfie," for pity's sake, just have someone else take the darn picture!

All right. Enough's enough.

Brandy stepping in, taking over for Mother after her well-intended effort to get this narrative aloft. I only hope we didn't lose too many readers in Mother's opening pages. On the other hand, Vivian Borne does have her fans, not to mention if she hadn't stirred me to action, this book may never have gotten started.

Because I have been, for the reasons Mother shared, down in the dumps of late. Not to worry! Fun will ensue. So will a mystery.

A rather unseasonably mild November settled in during the filming of season one of our reality series. Even though we were mostly shooting inside our Trash 'n' Treasures antiques shop—which took up an entire small house at the end of Main Street downtown—we did produce the occasional segment outdoors. Locations included flea markets, estate sales, storage-locker auctions, and the like, as Mother and I gathered stock for the shop. Not having to stand out in inclement weather was appreciated, the Indian summer occasionally giving way to some crisp fall temps that weren't bad at all.

My role in our show was a snap—playing second banana to Mother, and sometimes third banana, since Sushi, my shih tzu, quickly caught on to the filming process ("Mr. DeMille, I'm ready for my incredibly cute close-up") and began upstaging Mother to the point where Phil had to limit the little fur ball's screen time. (For those who don't know, Sushi, once blind, after an operation can now see, although she still has diabetes.)

I have to admit that our producer/director, Phillip Dean, who was also running the camera, and his pared-down crew—camera assistant Jamal Jeffers, soundman Steve Ballard, and assistant director Jena Hernandez—were doing a bang-up job not only at handling Mother, but also at finding unusual objects for us to identify, brought into our shop by "colorful" locals, customers we personally selected from a weekly cattle call. Many of those we selected, naturally, were locals Mother and I knew and often owed favors to.

While our dialogue was strictly ad-libbed, ours was like any other reality show—carefully scripted, shaped, and staged.

This Sunday morning (we usually filmed on Sundays and Mondays, when our shop was normally closed), the "customers" who just "happened" to stop in were Heather Conway, a former police dispatcher now with the forensics department, who, in exchange for a promised shot on our show, gave us sensitive information that proved vital in *Antiques Swap*; Matilda "Tilda" Tompkins, Serenity's New Age guru, who also helped us in previous cases, giving Mother gratis regression sessions (did you know Mother was first handmaiden to Cleopatra, and Cleo's head asp wrangler?); and Joe Lange (an old pal), a former marine, a confirmed bachelor, and a local institution (in the sense that he'd been institutionalized several times). Joe worked part-time at the shop, but Phil wasn't using him as a regular, and I thought it would give Joe's morale a boost.

Heather—midthirties, with auburn hair and red glasses—brought in an object with four cylinder-shaped wire holders attached to a six-inch-by-two-inch piece of wood. This Mother correctly identified as a tool once used by teachers to draw straight lines on a blackboard.

Tilda—late forties, long golden-reddish hair, freckles, and dressed in hippieish attire—came into the shop bearing a set of eight T-shaped tools, which I identified as being used for fixing a horse-drawn wagon wheel. (After the first take, soundman Steve told Tilda to remove her armful of clanking bangles.)

Finally came Joe, tall, loose limbed, with short hair and pleasant if slightly off-center features, slim in desert camouflage utilities. I might mention that I was taking a chance using him on the show, since he'd only recently gotten back on his meds after a drug holiday, but Joe did all right, even though he spoke mostly in military jargon.

Joe brought in a mechanical contraption that itself had a vaguely military look to it (it was used to put gunpowder in bullets), but according to our script, neither Mother nor I could identify it, and the gizmo was relegated to a section of each show where home viewers could call in their guesses (informed or otherwise) to an 800 number, with the correct answer being revealed in the next episode.

That was this morning. This afternoon Phil wanted to shoot Mother and me (minus Sushi) at yet another storage-locker auction, but Mother had other plans.

"Been there, done that, dear," she told our muscular producer, a handsome forty-something with thick dark hair and a salt-and-pepper beard.

We were standing in the living-room area of

the shop/ house as Jamal, Steve, and Jena were packing up for the move. The show did not provide our wardrobe, and Mother was wearing her favorite emerald-green velour pantsuit. I was in black leggings and a gray silk tunic, with a David Yurman necklace I'd snagged on eBay.

Mother was saying, "I have a far more interesting segment—something to entice the male audience."

Phil—in his traditional plaid shirt, jeans, and Nikes—frowned. "We could use more male viewers. What do you have in mind, Vivian?"

"A farm-tool auction."

Phil's frown deepened. "Good idea, Vivian, but we'd need a full crew for that, including another camera."

"Pish-posh," she retorted. "It's a small event at the O'Grady farm, exclusive only to a local antique tool club, fifty people, tops. It's not been advertised, and I only found out about it yesterday through the grapevine."

The vines of Mother's grapes twined everywhere.

Phil was stroking his beard. "I don't know. . . ."

His eyes went to soundman Steve Ballard, a good guy of maybe thirty-five, with an oval, lightly pockmarked face.

Shrugging, Steve, in a voice ravaged by cigarettes, said, "No problem on my end."

Phil looked at first AD Jena Hernandez—in her early twenties, attractive, clad in a black leather jacket over a white T-shirt, and tight jeans—who nodded. "I like the idea. Shouldn't be any problem handling a small crowd."

Still, Phil hesitated.

Jamal said, "We can cover it, boss. Nobody's better at handheld than you."

To that, Phil smiled and nodded.

I spoke up. "I know the farm, and it's a really picturesque place. Should make for good coverage."

Actually, I'd never been to the O'Grady farm, but I just didn't want to go to yet another storage-locker facility.

"All right," Phil granted. "Who should I contact to say we're coming?"

Mother, eyes gleaming behind her large-framed glasses (themselves collectible, if not quite antique), said, "I've already called Mrs. O'Grady, in anticipation that you would see the wisdom of this change of venue. She's thrilled to her toes, of course, and pledges cooperation in any way possible."

Phil didn't bother being irked with Mother; he'd long since learned not to waste the energy. "Well, all right, then. Where's this farm?"

While Mother gave him directions, I had a little talk with Sushi, whom we'd be leaving behind at the shop.

"Now, be good," I said, placing her in the leopard-print bed behind the checkout counter. "We'll be back in a few hours."

She looked up at me with her lower teeth jutting out in a pout, which said she was not pleased. And, despite my warning—or is that in spite of? (I don't know the difference, either)—I knew I'd have to search the store later for any cigar-shaped symbol of her displeasure she might have bestowed.

While Phil, Jamal, Steve, and Jena finished packing up their gear—they would follow in the equipment van after locking up the house— Mother and I got our coats and bags, then headed out into a cool yet sunny day, where our Ford C-Max hybrid waited at the curb.

With me behind the wheel, and Mother riding shotgun—she had lost her driver's license for various infractions too numerous to mention—we were soon tooling out of town, heading west on a two-lane highway, harvested fields gliding by on either side.

I knew darn well that Mother had a secondary reason for wanting this afternoon's shooting schedule changed—though a better venue than a storage-locker auction was plenty—and I said, "Smart ploy."

Mother turned her head. "Whatever do you mean, dear?"

"You know what I mean. Good move."

A wicked little smile appeared on her still pretty Nordic face. "I'm glad you agree. This should throw her well off the scent."

Mother was referring to Camilla Cassato. The *Serenity Sentinel* had been publishing a daily schedule of where *Antiques Sleuths* was shooting, and the nasty woman had been using that information of late to disrupt our location segments. It gave me great pleasure knowing she'd be showing up at that storage-locker facility this afternoon, and we wouldn't be there.

Mother was asking, "Are you in touch with Tony?"

"We talk on our cells about once a week."

"And he knows what *Mrs.* Cassato's been doing?"

Mother made "Mrs." sound like a swearword.

"Yes," I said. "And he's asked her to stop bothering us, hounding us . . . but she's told him it was none of his business, and she wasn't breaking any law."

Mother's chin went up. "It's blatant harassment, dear. Stalking!"

I shook my head. "I'm afraid it isn't, Mother. Camilla's merely showing up at auctions and outbidding us. And she *does* have her own antiques shop to run."

Mother harrumphed. "It sounds like you're defending the vile creature."

"Just stating the facts."

I turned off the two-lane onto a gravel road, the Ford's tires kicking up dust. I was glad I'd procrastinated about washing our ride.

Mother ventured, "Do we know anything about the current status of the Cassato divorce?"

"Not really." That came out harsher than intended, so I added, "Just that Tony says Camilla refuses to even discuss it."

"Well, she was certainly ready to divorce him *before*."

"Before I came along, you mean."

We fell silent for a few moments.

Then Mother said, "Tony could take matters into his own hands—although such an action might not sit well with the good people of Serenity and could hurt his career."

"There's that."

Mother reached over and patted my knee. "Where there's a will, there's a way, dear."

The great Vivian Borne, reduced to dispensing homilies.

I said, "The only way *I* can think is . . . nothing."

"You mean, if the woman should . . . pass away?"

"Mother!"

"Well, you must admit she'd relinquish her hold on your beau, in that case. And there'd be a will. The reading of?"

"Don't uptalk, Mother. Doesn't become you." To get off this subject, I asked her about Mrs. O'Grady, one of countless friends of hers whom I knew nothing about.

"Well, dear, Alma has been a widow for several years and has decided to put the farm up for sale—along with its contents—and move to Arizona to live closer to her daughter and grandchildren. The daughter lives in Phoenix. Or is it Scottsdale? Anyway—"

That's all I can report of that, since I stopped listening, just glad to have her off the subject of Tony and his wife.

Alma O'Grady's farm was down a long dirt lane, a neat white clapboard two-story with latticework and a wide front porch, with an adjacent red barn complete with rooster weather vane. Turned out I hadn't been lying: this *was* a picturesque location, worthy of a heartwarming Thomas Kinkade print over your hearth.

The private auction would not begin for another hour, but already a dozen or so cars were parked on the still-green lawn, among a few bare fruit trees and beds of hardy fall mums that had somehow survived the frosty nights.

I found a spot for the car, and we got out. Suddenly a diminutive woman came rushing toward us, her apple-cheeked face flushed. She wore an autumn-theme dress festooned with plump pumpkins and fallen leaves that might have made a nice Thanksgiving tablecloth.

Mother turned to me and said softly, "Our hostess."

The small figure grabbed Mother's hand and began shaking it up and down like it was an old-fashioned water pump. "Vivian, I can't *tell* you how exciting this is! To be on your show, I mean. Just imagine!"

"Think nothing of it," Mother granted regally.

Mrs. O'Grady, releasing Mother's hand, turned to me. "You must be Brandy. We haven't met."

"I must be," I said pleasantly, "and now we have." I pressed my hands to my breast in hopes of avoiding the pump-handle handshake. "Thank you so much for allowing us to film here today, and at such short notice."

I thought it should be said, since Mother apparently wasn't going to.

"My pleasure!" The tiny woman gestured to the

barn; her eyes were a little wild. "Come along and I'll introduce you to the tool club. Most of our members are here by now."

I followed Mother and Mrs. O'Grady to the barn, its heavy wooden double doors opened wide, revealing a rustic interior. Folding chairs had been arranged in rows on the dirt floor and faced a card table on which a bidding gavel rested.

In the chairs sat a dozen or so people, waiting for the auction to begin. Another dozen or so bidders were on their feet, viewing the various items displayed along a long workbench—vintage tools for sale.

Mrs. O'Grady clapped her hands. *"May I have everyone's attention, please?"*

The little woman had summoned a big voice.

Heads swiveled our way.

"I have a wonderful surprise! Many of you may know Vivian and Brandy Borne from Serenity's very own reality show, *Antiques Sleuths.* . . . Well, they are going to be filming our auction this afternoon."

A murmuring rolled across the crowd, which mostly consisted of men over fifty, with a few wives scattered in, but, basically, no one seemed overly excited about us being there, one way or the other.

Which I could tell irked Mother (the white was showing all around her magnified-behind-her-oversize-glasses eyes). Didn't these hayseeds know they were in the presence of a star?

So I took her hand. "Let's go have a look at the tools and decide what we want to bid on."

Bidding was expected of us as part of the TV show. The precedent in other on-location segments was that we each would be featured bidding on something at an auction or buying something at a flea market, swap meet, estate sale, or the like. We had a budget of a thousand dollars per episode and were able to keep whatever we bought and sell it in our shop, but we had already used six hundred of this episode's budget that morning on the items Joe and the others had brought in.

So if we bid over four hundred dollars on antique tools, it would come out of our own collective pocket.

With this in mind, Mother and I skirted around the folding chairs and headed for the long workbench where the tools were neatly arranged, each having a lot number tag attached. A second tag gave a brief description of the item.

Mother started at one end, and I at the other. I walked slowly along, taking in the hay knives, hand rakes, coupling hooks, horse hoof picks, cowbells, turnip choppers, branding irons, and barn lanterns, each highly polished. Then my eyes fell on a rare (according to its tag, anyway) corn husker, which (again, according to the description) removed the husks from ears of corn. The hand tool looked like a wicked oversize wrench with razor-sharp teeth and a spike with which to hold the corn.

Even though a sign was posted to remind everyone not to pick up the tools, I discreetly did so with this one in order to gauge the metal and determine its heft, the corn husker being cast iron. Then I quickly put it back.

Mother, having determined what she wanted to bid on, came rushing over, any thought of being taken for granted by the crowd long gone now.

"I'm going for the bushel and peck!"

She meant two wooden measuring buckets sold as a set.

Then Mother began to sing the Frank Loesser song from *Guys and Dolls*, which she'd directed and starred in some years ago at the Serenity Playhouse, including every last "doodle oodle." And at least now she got some attention from her audience.

Phil, Jamal, Steve, and Jena arrived, hauling in their equipment, preventing Mother from continuing with "A Person Can Develop a Cold" (aka "Adelaide's Lament," her *Guys and Dolls* character's other big tune), and we went to join them.

Phil, taking in the surroundings, said to us, "I like it. Very manageable, even with a small crew. Good call, Vivian. There's enough natural light coming in the barn doors that we don't need anything else." Then to Steve, "Where do you want to set up?"

The soundman gestured to an out-of-the-way spot. "How about there?"

Phil nodded. He turned to Jena. "Got the release forms?"

"Right here." She patted a messenger bag slung over one shoulder.

"All right, let's do this. . . . Jamal, put the

camera on sticks just over there. We'll move to handheld later."

Jamal nodded and set about doing that.

While Mother and I stood awaiting our marching orders, Phil strode to the front of the now seated crowd, positioning himself behind the auctioneer's card table.

"Hello, everybody. I'm Phillip Dean," he said affably. "And I'd like to express my gratitude to the Serenity Antique Tool Club for letting us shoot here this afternoon. I want to assure all of you that we'll be as unobtrusive as possible. Just pretend we're not even here. I only ask that you don't look at the camera. Oh . . . and we request that you sign the release form that Jena—she's the attractive young woman with the clipboard there—will be passing among you, getting permission from you to use you in the show." He paused. "Does anyone have any questions?"

A middle-aged woman in the back asked, "When's this going to air?"

"Sometime in January. Anyone else?"

A grumpy guy up front said, "What if I don't feel like bein' on TV and don't give you permission? I got as much right to be here as anybody."

"Yes, you do. And if you don't sign off on appearing, you will appear, anyway, as a bunch of scrambled pixels. And I don't think the grandkids'll wanna see that!"

General laughter and even a smile from Grumpy Gramps.

Phil slow-scanned the audience. "Anyone have anything else?"

No one did.

An arrangement was made with the auction-eers—husband- and-wife team Gerald and Loretta Klein—to move the items Mother and I would be bidding on to the front of the schedule.

The Kleins had been at this for a while. Both in their midforties, Gerald was skinny, with shaggy white hair, a leathery tan, and cowboy boots and hat; and Loretta was of medium height, big boned in a curvy way, with brassy blond hair and heavy make-up that stopped just shy of clownish, and a dress with petticoats straight out of a square dance.

For years, the pair had run an auction house along the nearby bypass, and both had been very kind to Mother and me after I moved back home and discovered that Mother had gone off her bipolar medication and had sold nearly all our antique Queen Anne furniture, some of which turned up for sale at one of their auc-tions. And the Kleins had helped us get back our heirlooms (to say more might take us into spoiler country where *Antiques Roadkill* is con-cerned).

After a brief sound check—Mother and I wore clip-on microphones and small transmitter packs, as did the auctioneers, while Steve's boom mic would pick up anything the audience might contribute—the auction officially started with Mother's pick: the bushel and peck wooden buckets.

Mother had scant competition from other bidders—whether out of respect to her or shy-ness because of the camera—and she easily won the items for two hundred dollars. That left me two hundred from our episode budget for my pick.

While their attire might have been corny, the Kleins displayed real showmanship, and I knew Mother had really added some spice to this episode with her idea.

As Loretta held up the tool, Gerald announced, "Next is a rare hand corn husker that'll take you right back to the golden age of Iowa farmin'. Let's pay our respects with an openin' bid of seventy-five dollars."

I held up my hand.

The auctioneer began his hypnotic spiel: "Seventy-five-dollar bid, now one hundred, now one hundred. Will you give me one hundred?"

A man seated in front of me gestured.

"One-hundred-dollar bid, now one-twenty-five, now one-twenty-five. Will you give me one-twenty-five?"

I signaled.

"One-twenty-five bid, now one-fifty, now one-fifty, will you give me one-fifty?"

My competition dropped out.

Gerald looked my way. "One-twenty-five going once, one-twenty-five going twice . . ."

"Five hundred dollars!"

I turned in my seat to see Camilla Cassato standing at the back. The tall, slender woman in her early fifties, with dark hair, an olive complexion, and deep-set eyes, wore a smirk that undercut her attractive features.

How could she know we were here?

Gerald's eyes returned to me. "Five-hundred bid, five-twenty-five, now five-twenty-five. Will you give me five hundred and twenty-five?"

Reluctantly, I shook my head.

"Five hundred going once, five hundred going twice . . ." The gavel came down with gun-crack finality. "Sold for five hundred dollars!"

Mother was out of her chair and striding back to Camilla with purpose.

Facing the woman, she demanded, "Must you persecute my daughter? You know that you grossly overpaid for that item just to embarrass us and demean her!"

Camilla tossed her head, and her dark hair did a gypsy dance. "I haven't the slightest idea what you mean, you unpleasant woman. As it happens, I've always wanted a hand corn husker."

"Fiddlesticks!" Mother blurted, making it sound like swearing. "You're just jealous!"

"Jealous of what? That scrawny daughter of yours?"

"My scrawny daughter has your husband's affections, and you do not! All you have is a corn husker you paid a small fortune for!"

I was at Mother's side now.

Camilla's sneer was dismissive and patronizing. "I *heard* you were a delusional madwoman, Mrs. Borne. I thought surely everyone was exaggerating. Thank you for showing me the error of my ways. You really *are* a lunatic!"

That was it. I can insult Mother all I want, but nobody else better!

And I gave Camilla a shove.

Just the tiniest little shove, really, but—as if I had really given her a push—she fell backward onto an empty folding chair, and they collapsed together with a metallic *wham*.

Of course, I immediately regretted my actions, particularly since if she wanted to press charges, the entire altercation had been videotaped by Phil himself.

And I couldn't be sure, but I thought our cameraman/director was smiling.

I guess he knew good footage when he caught it.

A Trash 'n' Treasures Tip

Before bidding, have a set amount you are willing to pay and don't go over it, even if it hurts to lose the item. Better to moan in disappointment once at a sale than every day, when you pass the item in the hall—like Mother's three-hundred-seventy-five-dollar butter churn.

Chapter Two

It Takes Two to Tangle

With the filming of *Antiques Sleuths: Season One* completed, Mother and I settled back into the routine of running our shop, which seemed to me (and Mother, too, I'm sure) painfully dull after the past few hectic months. Even Sushi acted a little bored due to the lack of action and screen time.

Truthfully, though, I didn't mind having the show "wrapped" for the season. I was not cut out to be a star, like Mother. And Sushi.

Phil Dean remained in Serenity—Jena, Steve, and Jamal having departed—the producer busy completing the final episode in a local editing suite, which was deemed more cost-effective than him returning to Los Angeles. This way, in case he needed retakes or extra footage, his "cast" was easily accessible.

Late Tuesday morning—just two days after the dustup between Camilla and yours truly—the little bell above the door tinkled and Tony walked in, bringing a chill wind with him. He was wearing his normal uniform of tan trench coat, blue shirt, navy-striped tie, gray slacks, and black Florsheim shoes, but his stern expression told me that this was not a routine friendly visit.

I was behind the counter, casually, even sloppily, dressed (now that I was blessedly not in front of a camera) in a gray sweatshirt and jeans and sipping a cup of hot coffee.

As Tony came toward me, Mother, in navy slacks and a navy sweater with sparkly white snowflakes, appeared from the living-room area, where she had been cleaning, a feather duster in hand.

Before I had a chance to speak to Tony, Mother chirped, "Well, hello, Chiefie dear. To what do we owe this honor?"

"Vivian," he said with a grudging nod, otherwise not answering her.

Sushi had trotted out from behind the counter to investigate the bell and, finding Tony, began to paw at his legs. He was her favorite man, too.

Tony bent to give Soosh a quick scratch on the head, then straightened, eyes returning to Mother. "Could I have a private moment with Brandy?"

A moment? Was that all I rated?

Mother gave Tony her best stage smile, the one with all the teeth that registered in the back row, and said, "But of course! I am never one to intrude or to wear out my welcome." Both highly inaccurate statements. Also, she didn't go anywhere, until my sharp look sent her retreating into the other room.

Tony really needn't have bothered asking her to leave. I knew darn well she was not only listening from around the corner but watching, as well. How so?

Well, having taken a page out of Nero Wolfe, Mother had arranged a framed picture on the adjacent living-room wall, where she could see through to the counter; but instead of Wolfe's painting of a waterfall, this was a Keane print of a sad, big-eyed boy. He may have been sad because he had a hole for one eye.

Of course, she'd done Nero Wolfe one better: on my side of the same wall was a similar Keane print—this one of a crying girl—also missing an eye, which not coincidentally lined up with the boy's, enabling Mother to observe the living room from the counter, as well. Took her all afternoon to line those two up.

Everyone clear? Two paintings, one in the living room, one facing the counter, shared hole between their missing eyes. And Mother's magnified peepers behind her large lenses made a perfect match for either print.

I said to Tony, "Why so serious?"

But I figured I knew: this had to be about my confrontation with his estranged missus.

He confirmed that. "I just spoke to Camilla."

"Oh," I said, too casual. "Really?"

"You may be relieved to hear that she won't be pressing assault charges against you."

I made a noise that I pretended was a laugh. "That's big of her—considering she *faked* that fall."

His frown was frustrated, not angry. "Brandy . . ."

"Phil showed you the playback, didn't he?"

"Yes. He did." His shrug was frustrated, too. "But it's not entirely clear she fell down on purpose."

I bristled, and it showed. "So you're taking *her* side?"

He let out a weight-of-the-world sigh. "I'm taking nobody's side. Well, really, *your* side."

"*My* side?"

"I convinced Camilla the tape was ambiguous and that she shouldn't bother going after you legally. Brandy, I'm just trying to keep you out of hot water."

I glanced at the crying girl Keane print; her great big left eye blinked.

I folded my arms. "Did you tell Camilla to stop harassing us? Because then you *really* would be on my side."

He gestured with both hands. "Brandy, Camilla hasn't done anything wrong. She's an antiques dealer, like you and your mother, and she's been outbidding you at auctions. Want to do something about that? Bring more money."

I fixed a stare.

"All right," he said, and he raised a single hand of surrender. "I'll admit she does seem to have a grudge against you."

"Thank you for recognizing the obvious."

He fixed a stare. "But my advice to you and Vivian is to go out of your way to avoid her . . .

and if you can't, just don't antagonize her. Follow me?"

With a shrug, I said, "I guess."

"No guess about it, Brandy." He shook a scolding finger. "If there's a repeat of what happened on Saturday, I won't be able to persuade her again."

"Okay."

My hand had been resting on the counter, and he put his over it, his eyes softening. "Do you think I like having to get in the middle of this?"

"Probably not."

"Do you know that I miss you?"

"I miss you, too."

"Maybe we could—"

The bell above the door sounded, and Tony quickly withdrew his hand.

"Maybe we could," he'd started to say. But apparently we couldn't, whatever he'd been about to suggest—not if he still felt the need to downplay our relationship.

Two middle-aged women in stylish coats entered, and Tony said stiffly, "Ah . . . thank you, Miss Borne, for your cooperation."

"You're very welcome, Chief Cassato," I returned curtly.

He turned away, nodding to the women as he left.

As the pair, one plump, the other trim, approached the counter, I said, "Welcome to Trash 'n' Treasures. Let me know if I can help you find anything."

(Sidebar rant: Why can't every salesperson acknowledge a customer that way? Why must they ask you the question "Can I help you?" Which makes us all go through the lame "I'm just looking. Thanks" routine.)

The plump woman burbled, "We wanted to tell you how much we love your show!"

And the trim woman cooed, "We think it's the very best reality show on basic cable."

Hearing such high words of praise, Mother scurried in from the living room, blinking the eye she'd been overusing.

"Why, *thank you*, ladies!" Mother said, adding, "Perhaps you'd be interested in one of our T-shirts? They come in all sizes, small to XXL!"

After making this not so subtle reference to the girth of the plump potential customer, Mother pointed to two red shirts hanging behind the counter. The front of one read I ♥ VIVIAN; the other, I ♥ BRANDY. We also carried a third shirt, I ♥ SUSHI, but it was sold out.

The women silently consulted each other.

"Free," I added.

Mother shot me a disapproving look, and I gave her a one-shoulder shrug. Even with the show's local popularity, we were having trouble getting rid of the swag. The non-Sushi variety, anyway.

"No thank you," the pair spoke in unison.

See what I mean?

Mother could barely hide her irritation. "Well, then, if there's some *particular* item you're looking for—"

"Oh, no," the trim one interrupted. "We just wanted a peek at what we've seen on TV. We have no real interest in antiques."

For a long moment, Mother and I just stared at them. Then I asked, "Then why do you watch our show?"

The plump lady replied, "Well, frankly . . . we're just waiting to see if you finally bop that interfering Camilla Cassato on the head the next time she outbids you."

Then, giggling like schoolgirls, offering up tiny childish waves, our noncustomers turned and left.

"Well," I muttered, "at least they won't be disappointed by the final episode."

"Should be a crowd-pleaser," Mother agreed.

Then she went back to her dusting, while I sulked at the counter.

Fifteen minutes dragged by, and Mother returned, a tad too cheerful.

"Dear," she began, "Christmas is coming, you know."

"It usually does."

"Well, don't you think it's about time we put out our Christmas merchandise? After all, we don't have much left over from last year."

I could sense an errand coming.

"Why don't you run over to Klein's and see what they have in the way of Yuletide goodies?"

I made a face. "I'm not really in a Christmassy mood."

"Thanksgiving's over, child. Most retailers were in a Christmassy mood weeks ago! Anyway, all this moping around of yours is a real bring-down."

Since a brought-down Mother was even worse

than a brought-down Brandy, I capitulated, sliding off my stool. "Anything in particular I should buy?"

She put a finger to her lips. "Let me see. . . . We do quite well with vintage tree lights, especially in their original boxes. Just make sure the cords aren't frayed."

We'd learned that the hard way when our own real tree at home caught fire from a bad vintage cord.

Mother was saying, "And anything with Sundblom's Coca-Cola Santa always sells—trays, ornaments, Christmas cards. But no repros! Oh, and get a nativity scene. The only one we have doesn't contain the baby Jesus."

Not my fault. She'd bought it without noticing the guest of honor was missing.

I asked, "What's my ceiling?"

"Don't go over a hundred . . . and try to worm more than our ten percent dealer's discount out of them. The Kleins are tough bargainers, though. Just do your best."

"Aye, aye, sir," I said with a salute that was nearly sarcasm free.

Sushi sensed that I was leaving and appeared at my feet, dancing for attention. Then when I reached for my black wool peacoat and bag, that confirmed her suspicions, and she began yapping to go along. So I plucked her up. She was good company.

Soon we were tooling along in the C-Max up Mulberry, a main artery leading from the downtown out to the treacherous bypass. I called the four-lane highway treacherous because it had only a handful of stoplights to accommodate the traffic heading across it to and from an ever-growing number of housing additions. At the intersections where there were no lights, numerous accidents had happened—some fatal—because the four-lane had no center island where a driver could hole up if he or she miscalculated his or her crossing.

But Mulberry did have a light, and Sushi and I zoomed safely across. I drove on about a quarter of a mile, then turned into a gravel driveway that led to a modern one-story warehouse with tan siding. A large red sign with black letters above the front door proclaimed KLEIN'S ANTIQUE STORE & AUCTION HOUSE, GERALD AND LORETTA KLEIN, PROPRIETORS.

Only a few other cars were in the lot, and I snagged a spot near the entrance, then got out, Sushi in hand, my bag slung over one shoulder.

I stepped into a vestibule designed to keep out the inclement weather and faced another door, which was covered with printed notices: SMALL CHILDREN MUST BE ACCOMPANIED BY AN ADULT; CHECK ANY LARGE BAGS; NO PHOTOS WITHOUT ASKING; NO ADMITTANCE FIFTEEN MINUTES BEFORE CLOSING; NO PERSONAL CHECKS; YOU BREAK IT, YOU BOUGHT IT. There were two new postings since I'd last been here: RESTROOMS FOR PATRONS ONLY and NO PETS.

Clearly, the antiques biz was starting to get to the Kleins.

Hmmm, I thought. If I made Sushi wait outside in a cold car, she'd only get back at me later. . . .

WAYS SUSHI HAS GOTTEN BACK AT ME LATER

(in order of vindictiveness)

1. Asked to be put outside in the middle of the night and then didn't do anything.
2. Hid my purse under the couch.
3. Chewed on an expensive leather belt.
4. Peed on my pillow.
5. Left a little "cigar" in one of my new shoes, which I didn't find until I put it on, and which gave "exploding cigar" a whole new meaning.

I unbuttoned my peacoat and tucked Sushi inside, with only the top of her head, eyes and nose, peeking out. Then I went through the door of a thousand notices and latched onto one of the store's red plastic baskets just inside, which I used to hide Sushi's cute face.

About twelve feet or so to my left, beyond a grouping of large stoneware crocks too heavy to be easily swiped on the way out, was a display case/checkout counter where a young man was tending to a customer. The young man I'd never seen before, but the customer was Mrs. Crumley, a gossip worse than Mother, which is saying something. Her purchase was a ceramic garden gnome that wasn't quite as ugly as the nasty news she loved to spread.

Of course, I noticed all of this in a nanosecond before making a right turn down a row of high glass cases, disappearing from view with my smuggled canine.

The Kleins' vast store wasn't that much different from your typical antiques mall; there were wide aisles (identified here by state names so you could remember where you saw something) and booths separated by Peg-Board walls. But because the Kleins owned all the merchandise, they had decided to group like items together— bedroom sets, dining-room tables and chairs, china, and so on—which made it easy if you were looking for something in particular. But I felt this format took the charm out of the surprise of discovery when you stepped into different dealers' booths containing a variety of merchandise.

Still, this arrangement meant I knew just where to go for Christmas decorations: a booth toward the back, near the vacant area where the auctions were held.

Into my red plastic basket I plunked a framed Christmas tree fashioned from gaudy buttons glued on green felt; a wreath made of real fruitcake that had been thankfully lacquered; and a tall green Styrofoam cone with dozens of old toothpicks, on which could be stuck little cooked weenies—the perfect centerpiece for a loopy holiday party. Sushi seemed to regard all these selections with understandable skepticism.

This should teach Mother not to send me out for Christmas items.

I was heading toward the front of the store when I spotted Camilla, of all people—wearing a camel coat over black slacks, a Burberry plaid bag slung over one shoulder, standing in the mouth of a booth devoted to antique picture frames. She was holding a large ornately carved one, examining it closely.

The frame had a "sold" tag taped on it, along with a separate price tag, and I watched in disgust as she casually removed both tags, stuck them on a similar but not as nice a frame . . . then put the price tag of the lesser frame on the one she wanted!

My initial thought was to rat Camilla out, but then I remembered Tony's warning to avoid contact with her, so I backed out of sight. How could Tony ever have been with such a wretched creature?

Trying to allow Camilla enough time to pay for the frame and take her leave, I wandered the back booths for a while. Only then I rounded an aisle and ran right into her.

She gave a startled "*Oh!*"

I murmured, "Camilla," and moved past her with my basket of kitschy treasures and Sushi.

"Brandy," she called to my back. "Could we speak for a moment? Please?"

Warily, I turned. "Yes?"

My nemesis came closer, the ornate frame hooked on one arm like an absurdly oversize bracelet.

Inside my coat, Sushi, sensing my apprehension—or perhaps noticing the increase of my heartbeat—emitted a soft growl.

Camilla said, "I'd like to apologize for my behavior of late."

"You would?"

She nodded. "I've been following you to auctions with the purpose of outbidding you, and it was petty and vindictive of me, and I'm really sorry."

I couldn't have been more surprised if she'd said she was ready to give Tony that divorce.

Camilla tilted her head. "Still . . . you shouldn't have pushed me down."

She wanted an apology, and in the name of peace and goodwill (Christmas *was* coming), I gave it to her.

"Didn't mean to hurt you," I said.

Pleased, Camilla said, "I'd like us to be . . . friendly, Brandy, if not quite friends. And to show you I'm sincere, as a peace offering, I'd like you to have that corn-husking tool I bid you out of. Strictly as a gift."

"Okay. That's generous."

Her smile seemed genuine; she was really very pretty, even though her eyes were rather close set. "Can you come by my shop later—say, four o'clock?"

"Well . . . sure. All right."

"Great!" Her eyes traveled to my basket. "What did you find?"

Embarrassed by the tacky Christmas items, I said, "Not much," then nodded to her picture frame. "That's a lovely find."

"Yes, isn't it! And a real steal at fifty dollars."

"Yes," I said, "a steal." I watched her face closely, but she gave nothing away. I raised the ante. "One might even think there was a mistake in the pricing."

Not a twitch.

Still smiling, she said, "Well, I better get back

to my shop. Since I'm the only one there, I have to close over the lunch hour. See you later, Brandy."

"See you later."

Watching her walk away, I pondered what her motive for being so civil to me might be. Simple human decency? Naw . . .

I browsed a little longer, then made my way to the checkout counter, where the young man sat at the cash register, reading *Wallpaper* magazine. In his early twenties, he had short spiky brown hair, black plastic Buddy Holly–style glasses, and two days' worth of stubble. He wore a vintage navy sports coat with shoulder pads over a gray-and-pink argyle sweater, and tight glen plaid slacks. I couldn't see his shoes, but I bet they were Converse high-tops.

Classic hipster dude.

HOW TO BE A HIPSTER

1. Be in your teens to thirties.
2. Wear a mixture of vintage and modern clothes, paying no attention to colors or patterns.
3. Eschew big-box stores in favor of the mom-and-pop retailer, even if it means paying a little bit more. (And bring your own reusable cloth checkout bag.)
4. Be well educated, preferably a college graduate, majoring in liberal arts, graphic arts, or the fields of math and science, and owe a ton of student loan debt.
5. Listen to alternative music, read offbeat magazines and books, and watch indie films.

6. Be savvy in all aspects of social media, adopting new trends (if deemed worthy) before the curve.

I set my basket on the counter and said, "Hi. Haven't seen you working here before."

He put down the magazine and smiled a little. "Yeah, just started last month." His eyes traveled to Sushi.

I shrugged. "Sorry. Didn't know about the new 'no pets' policy." I stuck out a hand. "Brandy Borne. My mother and I own the Trash 'n' Treasures shop." He shook it.

"I recognize you from TV." He tapped his chest. "Dexter Klein."

"You're related to Gerald and Loretta?"

He shrugged and pushed his glasses up. "Shirt-tail—but it helped get me a temporary job while I'm looking for one in my field."

"Which is?"

"Graphic art. I know, I know. . . . Good luck with that around here!"

As Dexter began removing my treasures from the basket, he deadpanned, "Well, now. I can see you're a woman of good taste and refinement."

"Doesn't *everyone* need a weenie tree?"

That got a small smile out of him. "Apparently not, considering that that one's been gathering dust here for, oh . . ." He checked the back of the price tag. "Three years."

"Shouldn't that qualify me for more than my ten percent dealer's discount?"

Still smiling, he shook his head. "Sorry. I

can't make that call . . . and the Kleins'll be out till mid-afternoon. Still want this gem?"

I shrugged. "Where else would I find another one, at any price? Ring it up."

While Dexter tallied up my total, I contemplated mentioning Camilla the Tag Switcher but decided against it. Not a good way to start our new "friendly" relationship. And, anyway, wasn't I Brandy the Dog Sneak?

I paid for my items with cash, risked hipster wrath by asking for a plastic bag, then headed out.

On my return to the shop, I found Mother cleaning the six-by-four-foot glass curio case just inside the front door. This was always reserved for seasonal items, and she was preparing for the bounty that I was bringing back.

I almost felt bad over my tongue-in-cheek haul.

I set Sushi down and put the plastic bag on the counter, along with my coat.

"Well, let's see what you came up with!" Mother said excitedly, coming over with a slightly demented smile.

From the sack she removed the gaudy button Christmas tree glued on felt, the lacquered fruitcake wreath, and, of course, my Styrofoam weenie tree.

I waited for my rebuke.

Instead, Mother squealed with delight, clapping her hands, a little girl on Christmas Day who'd gotten every single thing she wanted. "Dear, your idea of getting such outré holiday items is simply *brilliant*! We'll put them in the curio, along with a sign reading MERRY KITSCH-MAS!"

"Ah, yeah, wasn't that a stroke of genius on my part? But we'll need more such treasures to fill up the case."

Mother raised a finger skyward—or, anyway, ceiling-ward. "Au contraire! There are many similar such items in storage at home."

She meant our garage, a stand-alone filled to the brim with her questionable yard-sale purchases. The garage hadn't seen a car for years. It wouldn't know what to do with a car.

"Such as?" I asked.

Her eyes gleaming, like those of an old prospector spotting gold flecks in his pan, she said, "Oh, how about a knitted Santa toilet-roll cover? And a hat covered with Christmas-tree balls, and an elf-arrayed poncho made out of a nineteen-fifties plastic tablecloth, and a—"

"You made your point," I said. "Stop right there, or I'll be dreaming about *Pee-wee's Play-house* all night." I retreated to the stool behind the counter. "You'll have to retrieve that stuff from the garage yourself. I'm not current on a tetanus shot."

Mother studied me for a moment. "Dear, is something troubling you?"

"You mean, other than having a mother who actually bought a Santa toilet-roll cover, a hat of Christmas-tree balls, and a poncho made of a plastic elf tablecloth?"

"It must be more than just that."

I sighed and told her in detail about seeing

Camilla at Klein's, from her offer of friendship to switching tags on a frame she bought.

"No nasty thing she might do would surprise me," Mother sniffed. "She has such close-set, beady eyes."

Actually, she sort of did.

Then I told her about Camilla's offer to give me the corn husker, gratis.

Mother frowned in thought. "Could she really want to bury the hatchet? Figuratively, not literally?"

"Is that what you really think?"

"Of course not. The creature is up to something. Why, she paid a small fortune for that item! But take her up on it, dear, and snag that corn husker. It should have been yours!"

I pursed my lips and glanced at my watch. "If she *is* 'up to something,' I guess I'll find out at four o'clock."

"Take Sushi along for protection, dear."

I shook my head. "Better not. If things turn ugly, Soosh might bite her. And we all know what happened to Toto."

Since I had several hours before leaving for my meeting with Camilla, I busied myself working at balancing our books for a while. Then at five minutes to four, I got my coat and purse, bid Mother and Sushi good-bye, and went out.

Camilla's antique store, Yesteryears, was only a block away, and I'm sure her choice of location in proximity to ours was intentionally meant to annoy us. The Victorian structure where she occupied the first floor (apartments above) was typical of others in the downtown area: red brick, four stories, narrow interior, the building extending from the street in front to the back alley.

Before Camilla moved in, the first floor had been rented to a computer repair shop (they hadn't been able to revive my ancient laptop) that had divided the area into two rooms (customer service and repair shop). I was curious to see if Camilla had removed the partition to maximize the floor space.

As I entered, with no bell announcing my arrival, I saw that she indeed hadn't remodeled, her merchandise occupying only the first room, a store-bought sign on the door to the second one reading NO ADMITTANCE BEYOND THIS POINT. Behind the door, I could hear a male voice informing Camilla of some specific antiques he was looking for.

With Camilla occupied, I took the opportunity to check out her admittedly impressive array of antiques and collectibles. While the merchandise was limited, it was all first rate—from the magnificent Queen Anne needlepoint couch and matching chair to a pristine blond Heywood-Wakefield dining-room set, and from the original Fiestaware dishes to the highly collectible Radko blown glass ornaments. No smiley-face clock here, like in our shop, and certainly nothing remotely like a weenie tree. This was a kitsch-free environment.

But a price-tag check showed that the stock was overpriced—way the heck over. How did she ever sell anything?

And there was something else odd about the

antiques and collectibles on hand. While everything was nicely displayed, something seemed staged about it. I was reminded of when Mother and I went to the store in the show *American Pickers*, where everything was also unique, but so overpriced that it discouraged the tourists from disturbing the "set." As a reality show veteran myself now, I understood. But nobody was shooting anything at Camilla's, right?

All was now quiet behind the door to the second room, so I knocked on it, calling, "Camilla? It's Brandy."

After a moment I opened the door and entered, noticed the blinking answering machine on a nearby desk, and realized I hadn't overheard a conversation. Rather a man had merely been leaving a message for Camilla.

Which she hadn't heard.

She wasn't hearing anything lying on the floor on her back, blood pooled beneath her head, a certain blunt object nearby.

A cast-iron corn husker.

A Trash 'n' Treasures Tip

Hiring an appraiser can be expensive, especially if you have a large collection. Shop around, as rates can vary widely. Mother used a barter system: a local dealer appraised her collection of creepy vintage Annalee dolls in exchange for a part in one of Mother's community theater plays, *The Bad Seed*.

Chapter Three

Arrested Development

I didn't check for a pulse on Camilla's wrist; after all, I can never find my own. Anyway, she was dead. That seemed evident enough.

Nine-one-one got the first call on my cell; Mother the second. While I'd kept my composure while talking to the dispatcher, now my voice cracked like that of an adolescent boy who was becoming a man. But I was a mouse, as I said, "Mother, you're not going to believe this, but Camilla . . . Camilla's been *murdered*."

Mother sucked in a breath, but in fact she had no trouble believing it and immediately shifted into amateur sleuth mode. "How, dear?"

"Hit on the head, really hard. Terrible blow. So much blood."

"Was the weapon around?"

"Yes. It was that . . . that stupid corn husker."

"Interesting choice. You haven't by any chance notified the police, have you, dear?"

"Before I called you, I did."

"That's unfortunate. I would have thought you'd know better by now."

"Mother, really!"

"I would have liked to have examined the crime scene first. The authorities always make such a mess of things. Oh, well. Just take plenty of pictures with your phone before they come."

I goggled at the cell. "Couldn't you be at least a *little* more sensitive? I know we didn't like Camilla, but we did . . . *know* her."

"Sensitivity won't help that poor woman now, dear, much less find her killer."

"You make it sound like finding her killer is our job."

She said nothing, but there was a sound from her end. . . . Was that a chuckle?

Then came the approaching scream of a siren. "I have to go."

"Take those pictures, dear!"

But it was way too late for that. And, anyway, I was too creeped out to follow Mother's instructions. I moved immediately into the outer room so I could open the door for the first responders, who showed in seconds—two paramedics, one male, one female—and told them where they could find Camilla.

Already on the move, the male glanced back at me and asked, "Any signs of life?"

"Not really."

Next to arrive was Officer Mia Cordona, a
dark-haired beauty in her thirties, whose jacket
and uniform did a poor job of concealing a
voluptuous figure.

Mia and I used to be friends, a long time ago.
But these days, when she saw me at a crime scene,
Mia's usual expression was a scowl. This time, for
once, she wore a look of alarm and concern.

Then she threw an inner switch and became
coldly businesslike. "Stay put, Brandy. I'll want
to question you later."

I asked, "Does Tony know about this?"

She nodded, then hurried into the back
room.

I dreaded his arrival. The deceased was his
wife, estranged or not, and was the mother of
their daughter; obviously, he'd loved her once.
Why did I, of all people, have to be the one to
find her?

I backed into a corner of the shop, well aware
that the impulse was symbolic. And did the clown
painting on the wall next to me signify anything,
as well?

Tony burst through the front door, like a cop
on a raid. Only there was nothing for a man of
action to do here. Confused eyes found me, and
all I could so was lower my head.

Had there been something accusatory in that
look—however brief? Could some part of him
think I was capable of having done this? A heart-
sick feeling took over every bit of my being.

He came forward and stood before me. His
voice was nearly kind. "Are you all right?"

I nodded numbly. "I don't know what to say. Just that I'm . . . I'm sorry for your loss."

Tony drew in a breath, touched my shoulder briefly, then went deeper into the shop to join Mia and the paramedics. Meanwhile, I moved to the Queen Anne couch near the front windows and sat.

Two forensic techs came next—a man I didn't recognize and Mother's friend Heather—toting their gear, barely giving me a glance as they moved into the back room.

Another police car drew up in front, double-parked, rooftop lights going, and Officer Munson disembarked; the tall, gangly man with a long face immediately took a position on the sidewalk to deal with the curiosity seekers who had started to gather. A lot of people lived in apartments downtown.

I left the couch and moved to a front window, where I saw Mother push her way through the bystanders, then confront Munson, who was guarding the door. I was at once horrified and relieved by her presence, and not at all surprised.

I heard her cry in theatrical indignation, "My *daughter's* in there!"

The officer, his back to me, responded to her by raising a hand in a "halt" manner.

Mother wailed, "But my child might *need* me!"

As if she were concerned about me. Her contrived hysteria just meant she wanted access to the crime scene.

Munson told her, "No one goes in," then

raised his voice to the crowd. "Everyone disperse! There's nothing to see here."

A few conscientious citizens obeyed his order, but the rest merely dropped back a few feet.

Mother, noticing me behind the window, put a hand up to her face in cell-phone manner and mouthed, "Call me."

I shook my head.

She wiggled her thumbs, as if to say, "Text me."

I shook my head again and returned to the couch.

After ten, maybe fifteen minutes, Tony and Mia appeared from the back room.

Tony, his eyes hooded and red, planted himself in front of the couch and looked down at me. "Brandy, I'll need to ask you some—"

Mia, slightly behind him, touched his arm gently. "Chief, I have to remind you what policy demands in a situation like this. I think you know that you need to recuse yourself from this case."

He sighed deep, then nodded and stepped aside.

Mia sat in a Queen Anne armchair next to the couch, then plucked a small voice recorder from her utility belt.

"I'll be taping our conversation," she told me, "unless you object."

"Of course I don't object."

"Interview with Brandy Borne," my old childhood friend began. She added the time, date, location, then asked, "Why were you here?"

"Camilla invited me," I said. "I saw her this

afternoon at Klein's Auction House, and she asked me to come by at four."

"And why would she do that?" Mia asked. "My understanding is that you two didn't get along."

I shifted uncomfortably on the couch, avoiding Tony's gaze. "That's true. But Camilla indicated today that she wanted us to be friends, or at least not enemies. The boy working the front counter, Dexter Klein, should be able to corroborate that our conversation was friendly. Possibly there's a surveillance tape of the two of us talking in a civilized way."

Mia asked sharply, "If you'd already had a *friendly* conversation, coming to terms, so to speak, why did Mrs. Cassato want to see you again?"

I hesitated, knowing things were about to get sticky.

"She, uh, wanted to give me something," I said.

"What?"

"A corn husker that she'd outbid me on at an auction recently. It was a sort of peace offering."

Mia's eyes flashed. "You mean the murder weapon? The tool found beside her body? That was a 'peace offering'?"

I felt my cheeks growing hot. "Yes, but I didn't touch it! Camilla was already . . . like that . . . when I got here. Don't you need to read me my rights or something?"

Mia ignored that, asking, "What time did you arrive?"

"Four o'clock. Maybe a few minutes after."

"Are you *sure* about that? Did you check your watch or otherwise establish the time?"

I didn't like the way she asked that, so I snapped, "As I told you before, I left our store a few minutes before four. We're only a block away, you know."

"Then what happened?"

In detail, I told her and her recorder.

When I'd finished, Mia said, "So when you arrived, you thought a man was talking to Camilla in the back, but it was really just the answering machine."

"Yes."

"How would you know that unless you were there in the back room yourself?"

I said testily, "You *could* check the machine for a four o'clock time stamp and a long message from a man. . . . Or is that too much trouble? I think we're done here."

Mia glared at me. She apparently wasn't over Mother and me bungling into a sting operation she'd been working on for months not so long ago.

"All right," Mia said, rather sourly I thought. "You can go."

She rose and walked back to the crime scene, leaving me alone with Tony.

I got up from the couch and faced him.

"That was everything," I said. "I didn't hold anything back."

"I believe you," he said with a curt nod.

I wished he'd said that with a little more conviction.

"I'm really sorry about Camilla," I said.

And he probably wished I'd said that with a little more conviction.

"Well," he said, with a tight smile, "I'd better rejoin Mia. This isn't my case, but I do have . . . a vested interest."

He left.

And I left.

Back at our store, Mother—who had returned after failing to access the crime scene—rushed me as soon as I'd stepped in the door, demanding chapter and verse. But I told her I wasn't up to it right now and wanted to go home.

Her face fell, but she could see I was hurting, and found the decency to reply, "Of course, dear. You round up Sushi and go on out to the car. . . . I'll lock up."

I drove in silence, Mother respecting my wish not to talk, but I could almost hear her thinking. If those wheels of hers had been turning any faster, they'd have clanked.

We live on a street lined with old oaks, in a white three-story house with a wraparound front porch and that stand-alone garage that had become our personal storage unit (at least it was free).

The inside of the home was a study in decors from different eras: the living room was 1900s Victorian; the dining room, Neoclassical; the kitchen, 1950s Retro; my bedroom, 1930s Art Deco; Mother's bedroom, 1920s Art Moderne; and the spare bedroom, 1970s Psychedelic (which encouraged guests not to stay too long). The only room that didn't have a special design period was the music room/library/den, which opened with French doors off of the living room. This room consisted of a wall-screen TV, various books on shelf-lined walls, an ancient upright piano that needed tuning, and an assortment of old instruments Mother had collected but that she mostly couldn't play. (Sometimes she would pick up a smelly, dented cornet and blat out "Boogie Woogie Bugle Boy," which, when I was a child, would send me fleeing outside. Also as an adult.)

I had barely set Sushi down and taken off my coat when Mother called to me from that room.

With Sushi trotting behind me, I went in to find Mother rolling out her "suspect board"—a large antique schoolroom blackboard on wheels—from behind the stand-up piano.

She was saying nonchalantly, "Of course, we must return to Camilla's shop after the police have gone. That much is obvious."

I wasn't sure I'd heard Mother correctly. "You want to break into the *crime* scene?"

"Unless you were thoughtful enough to have acquired a key before the authorities arrived."

"No, I didn't think to 'acquire' a key!" An edge came into my voice. "Have you been taking your Prolixin?"

She fired back, "Have *you* been taking your Prozac?"

Every so often we were reduced to this. Rarely more than once a month, or twice a murder case.

Mother calmly sat on the piano bench, then patted the space next to her. "Let's not treat each other like the enemy, dear."

With a sigh, I joined her.

She took my hand. Patted it. "My darling

child, have you no sense of the gravity of the situation you, and fate, have put yourself in?"

"I don't follow you, Mother."

"Well, do you recall picking up that corn husker at the auction and examining it? Because I certainly remember your doing so."

It dropped on me like a box of corn huskers. "Oh no. My prints could be on the murder weapon!"

"Probably *are* on the murder weapon."

Those prints were also on file with the local police, following my spending a month in the county jail, along with Mother, for overstepping the law while solving a case.

"Yes, dear," Mother said, nodding fatalistically. "That's why we have to act quickly to discover whatever we can before . . . well . . ."

"Before I'm . . . arrested?"

"Prints on the murder weapon, a public display of violence against the victim, who is your current flame's wife? I should think getting arrested is a distinct possibility."

I sat there, stunned.

Finally, I said, "If you saw me pick up the corn husker, someone else might have noticed that, too."

But Mother was shaking her head. "I don't believe anyone else was looking at those tools at the time we were, dear."

"Other prints will likely be on that corn husker," I pointed out, somewhat desperately. "Mrs. Klein's and Camilla's . . ."

"True. As to the former, Loretta did hold the tool when it was auctioned, which explains *her* prints. As to the latter, well, the late Mrs. Cassato hardly killed *herself.*"

"*Must* you call her that?"

"Would you prefer dead-and-gone Camilla? No, we must shake a leg, dear. It's nearly dark already." She released my hand and stood tall before me. "But perhaps some nourishment might be prudent prior to our excursion. Detecting on an empty stomach is always ill advised."

"Detecting! Breaking and entering, you mean. No thanks. Somehow I don't have much of an appetite."

"Well, I do! A good murder case always makes me peckish. I'm going to heat up some of that wonderful potato soup!"

And off she strode to the kitchen.

The recipe had been passed down to Mother from her Danish grandmother.

Kartoffelsuppe
(Potato Soup)

1 meaty ham bone
2 cups chopped cabbage
2 medium potatoes, peeled and diced
3 celery stalks, chopped
2 medium carrots, peeled and diced
6 green onions, stems removed and diced
¼ cup minced fresh parsley
4 tablespoons all-purpose flour
¼ cup cold water
1½ cups half-and-half
Ground nutmeg, to taste

In a large pot, simmer the ham bone in 2 quarts of water for 1 hour, or until the meat pulls away from the bone. Remove the ham bone to a large plate or a cutting board, and retain the water in the pot. When the ham bone has cooled, remove and discard the bone, trim away any fat from the meat, and dice the meat.

Return the meat to the pot, and add the cabbage, potatoes, celery, carrots, green onions, and parsley. Cover and cook over medium heat for 40 minutes.

Combine the flour and the ¼ cup cold water in a small bowl and blend until smooth. Slowly pour the flour mixture into the soup, stirring constantly.

Bring the soup to a boil and cook for 2 minutes. Reduce the heat and then stir in the half-and-half. Remove the soup from the heat. Sprinkle the top with nutmeg and serve.

Yield: *6 servings*

Okay, so despite my depressed state, I did join Mother in the dining room, at the Duncan Phyfe table. If we got caught breaking into Camilla's shop, having a serving or two of hearty, delicious soup in my stomach might mean I could skip tonight's jailhouse slop, should we be apprehended.

Afterward, Mother disappeared upstairs, while I cleared the table, then washed the few dishes. The normalcy of that was somehow comforting, like the soup. I was putting things away when she rejoined me.

Dressed all in black—sweater, slacks, shoes—Mother looked like a geriatric ninja. She took her role as a burglar very seriously. Of course, she took every role seriously, from the lead in *Everybody Loves Opal* to confronting a probable murderer.

My gray sweatshirt and jeans would simply have to do for the role of Secondary Burglar.

Indicating her black fanny pack, I asked, "What's in there?"

"My lock-picking instruments."

Mother had gotten the two small tools—an L-shaped tension wrench and a pick with a hooked end—at her favorite Internet spyware site and had been practicing on various locks around the house for weeks. She was getting good.

I pointed to the little black gizmo that was attached to the bridge of her large glasses: the combination camera and sound recorder looked like a third eye. "Think that's wise?"

"We *should* have a record of what happens."

"You mean, a record of our breaking and entering into a crime scene."

"No one will see the playback but us, dear."

"Tell it to Nixon. Let's not make a record of our crime, okay?"

Mother sighed. "Very well. I'll leave it behind." She detached the gizmo from her glasses and rested it on the counter.

We moved into the living room, where Sushi was curled up on a blanket on the Victorian couch—even a dog needed some cushioning to get comfortable on that thing—and for a change, she didn't ask to go with us.

In the foyer, we put on coats and gloves, then headed out into a chilly night air, toward the driveway and our car.

Once downtown, I parked the C-Max on a side street around the corner from Camilla's shop, and soon we were making our way down the dark alley behind the row of Victorian brick buildings, stopping at a steel door.

The door didn't have yellow police crime-scene tape across it, but that didn't surprise me, as forensics had no doubt gotten what they wanted here. And besides, such tape often drew unwanted attention to a vacant site, drawing burglars.

Like us.

As Mother removed the lock-picking tools from her fanny pack, I looked across the alley at a rambling two-story apartment house, doing my best to make sure we weren't being seen. Lights were on in a few rooms, but the shades were drawn.

After giving Mother a "Go ahead" nod, I watched as she inserted the shorter end of the L-shaped wrench into the circular lock, then turned it to the left. Next, she put in the pick, hooked end first, and pulled it slowly back out, dragging the hook across the inner tumblers, which unlocked the door.

We slipped into the back room and were engulfed in pitch black. My car key chain had a small attachment light, which I was about to turn on when a quick rustle of clothing preceded somebody pushing Mother into me hard, and we both hit the floor, the car keys tumbling from my hand in a little metal jingle, as the blurred figure flew out the door into the alley.

The attack was so sudden and unexpected that we lay, stunned, in a tangle of limbs, and by the time I'd extricated myself from her, gotten up, and reached the door, our assailant was nowhere to be seen.

After closing the door, I turned on a nearby wall switch and squinted from the brightness of the overhead light. Mother was trying to get to her feet, and I went over to help.

"You all right?" I asked her.

She patted herself. "Double hip replacements seem to be intact. And you?"

"In one piece. But we'll both have bruises tomorrow."

Mother pursed her lips. "That door was locked, so our fellow intruder must have had a key."

"Or picks," I replied.

She grunted, then looked around. "Dear, was the desk like that when you found Camilla?"

Mother was referring to open drawers whose contents had been scattered on the floor.

"No," I said. "And I doubt Mia would have left that mess. Everything would have been bagged as evidence."

"Then the third member of our little party must have been looking for something. The question is, did he find whatever he was looking for?" Mother pointed to the items on the floor. "See if there's anything of interest, dear."

I got down on my haunches to examine some store stationery, an assortment of office supplies and file folders, though oddly no billings for rent and utilities.

"What's that?" Mother asked, pointing to a small tan book.

I reached for it and had a look. "A sales receipt pad."

Mother harrumphed. "Wasn't she using a computer for that?"

"Apparently not. The only thing I remember seeing on that desk was the answering machine—which the police seem to have taken."

Mother pointed again. "And that . . . Is that a bank deposit receipt?"

I picked up the little white paper. "Yes. From the First National Bank, for five thousand dollars."

"Dated when, dear?"

"Last week." I thumbed back through the sales receipt book. "According to this, Camilla barely sold anything all month—and certainly nothing that added up to five thousand."

"So, then . . . where did she get the five Gs?"

On a case, Mother sometimes got a little carried away with the detective-speak.

"I have no idea where she got the 'five Gs.' But it would be really nice to know."

A car horn honked in the alley, spooking me.

"We better go," I said, replacing the sales book on the floor.

I stood, and we moved to the back door, where I clicked off the light. After checking the alley, we slipped out, making sure the door was locked behind us.

On the way home, something occurred to

me. "Mother, I don't remember seeing that frame Camilla bought. The one she switched price tags on? It wasn't in the front shop when I went earlier, and it wasn't in the back room to-night."

"Might that be important, dear?"

"I don't know. Might it?"

Mother was stroking her chin thoughtfully. "It's possible Camilla could have sold the frame before you arrived."

"Then it should have been annotated in the sales receipt book," I countered. "*Mother!*"

I hit the brakes.

A police car was parked in our driveway!

Mother reached for my knee. "Follow-up questions, dear. Not to worry."

As I pulled the C-Max up to the squad car, Mia exited on the driver's side. Really moving.

I shut off the engine. Mother and I got out, and Mia was already on top of us.

"Hello, Officer Cordona," Mother said cheer-fully. "Would you prefer to conduct your ques-tions inside, where it's nice and warm?"

Mia replied, "That won't be necessary, Mrs. Borne." Her eyes flew to me. "Brandy, you're under arrest for suspicion of the murder of Camilla Cassato. You wanted me to read you your rights. Well, here goes. You have the right to remain silent. . . ."

I grabbed Mother's arm.

"Courage, dear," she said. "Mother will get you out. Now, aren't you glad you had a decent meal earlier?"

A Trash 'n' Treasures Tip

Collections should be inventoried and numbered, especially if you intend to leave them to heirs in your will. Mother—whose will has more codicils than an old tugboat has barnacles—has bequeathed me her collection of glass telephone-pole insulators. Whoopee.

Chapter Four

Suitable for Framing

After Mia ushered a hands-cuffed-behind-me me into the back of the police car, she slid behind the wheel and backed out of the drive. As we drove away, I twisted to see Mother from the rear window, who was waving to me as if I were about to embark on a long journey, which, I guess, maybe I was. I watched forlornly until she was swallowed up by the night.

At the police station downtown, a large modern redbrick building attached to the fire station, I was taken in through the back, where a male officer on night duty recorded my personal information on his computer. The uncomfortable cuffs were unlocked so he could take my fingerprints; then I was walked into a cement-block cubicle, where somebody snapped a photo that would make the DMV's latest shot of me look glamorous. The two possessions I had were removed from my person and inventoried: my cell phone and a new Fitbit watch/Wi-Fi/GPS/ calorie counter/step tracker/heartbeat monitor, which I had had for three months and didn't begin to know how to use properly.

Then I was escorted to a holding cell (really just another cubicle) and dumped.

Disheartened, I sat on the bed, which was more like a padded bench, and stared at the only other fixture in the cramped room: a combination toilet/wash basin/fake mirror made of stainless steel. Turns out stainless steel does stain, and there were more amenities in the john of a 747.

I was giving bawling some serious consideration when Tony's face appeared in the Plexiglas window of the door. The lock clicked open, and in he came, carrying some of my clothes from home.

"How are you doing?" he asked gently, looking down on me.

"All right," I lied. "And you?"

"All right," he echoed.

But he didn't look all right: eyes puffy, face drawn, his usual ramrod posture defeated by slumped shoulders.

Tony said, "Vivian gave me a few things for you, and I had them cleared—pajamas and something to wear to the arraignment tomorrow."

Arraignment tomorrow. That sounded ominous.

As he handed me the clothes, I asked, "What about my meds?"

"Your Prozac? The doctor who tends to the prisoners will dispense it. I've already put that in motion."

"Thank you."

Tony sat on the bench/bed, next to me.

"Brandy," he began, "I know this is a bad time to leave you on your own, but . . . I simply have to take Camilla back home. Back east. That's where her family's burial . . ."

He let that trail, and I craned toward him. "Do you know how long you'll be gone?"

"No idea, really. There's the funeral to plan, and, of course, I'll want to spend some time with my daughter."

She was in a private school somewhere. Other than that I knew little about her.

"I understand," I said, making it sound supportive. Still, I couldn't help feeling abandoned.

Tony took my hand. "I'll be checking in on the investigation at least twice a day—making sure it's being handled right."

I nodded, grateful for that. "All I've been told is I'm being held on suspicion of murder."

He drew in a breath, then let it out slow. "I'm afraid you're going to be charged, Brandy."

"What evidence do they have?"

When he hesitated, I said, "I have a right to know, don't I?"

He sighed. "Your fingerprints were on that corn husker, which has been confirmed as the murder weapon."

Score one for Mother.

He went on, "Vivian told me that, quite innocently, you touched the tool at the auction, but—"

"But she's my mother, and her word won't mean much."

And there was the small matter of her mental health status, not to mention her popularity with the local court system.

I asked, "Couldn't I take a lie detector test to prove I picked that tool up?"

"That's not admissible, Brandy. You know that."

I said softly, "But at least it would prove it to *you*."

He took my hand. "Brandy, you don't have to worry about that. I believe you. You'd never do anything like this. In the meantime, as soon as I can get back, I'm going to do everything I can to find whoever killed Camilla."

We fell silent. He seemed about ready to go, so to keep him around a little longer, I asked, "What about Rocky? Where's he staying while you're gone?"

Rocky was Tony's dog, a black-and-white mixed breed with a black circle around one eye, a retired narcotics sniffer-outer that Tony had brought with him from New Jersey, a smart animal who could climb a ladder, fetch Tony's gun, and respond to dozens of commands.

Tony was saying, "Vivian offered to take him in, so I dropped him off when I got your clothes."

I managed something that was almost a laugh. "Sushi won't even know I'm not around, with

Rocky for company." The little devil was nuts about Rocky, and he good-naturedly put up with her crawling all over him.

Tony patted his thighs, sighed, and stood. "I should go."

I nodded. "Thank you for this. Listen, uh . . . safe trip."

What I said to myself was, *Short trip.*

He kissed me on the forehead, which was better than nothing, and slipped out, flashing me the saddest smile I ever saw. After he'd gone, I lay down on the bench/bed, facing the wall, and toughened myself for what lay ahead.

Not really. What I did was bawl my eyes out.

The next morning, I was given breakfast in my cell, a feast consisting of rubbery scrambled eggs, limp toast, watered-down orange juice, and weak coffee. I washed up at the basin as best I could, then put on the outfit Mother had picked out from my wardrobe for me to appear before the judge: a sexy black dress with a low neckline and a short hem.

What had she been thinking?

That I'd wow some male magistrate into releasing me? Arraignments were cut and dry. I could be wearing a plastic garbage bag and it wouldn't make one bit of difference. I got back into the gray sweatshirt and jeans, the break-in wardrobe of the night before.

At 8:45 a.m. my cell door opened, and a blue-uniformed Mia stepped in.

"I'm to take you to the courthouse," she said,

businesslike. Her dark eyes appraised me and my rumpled clothes. "That's what you're wearing for the appearance? I thought your mother sent you clothes last night."

"She did," I said and gestured to the sexy little black dress draped on the bench/bed. Next to it was my other option—pajamas with leaping lambs.

Mia's eyebrows were up. "Your mother really doesn't do you any favors, does she?" That was almost sympathetic. "We need to go now to get to the courthouse on schedule. . . . There's a mob outside."

I frowned. "Mob?" Had the townsfolk rallied to protest my incarceration? Or were the villagers carrying torches to the castle?

"Reporters," Mia replied, making a face like the word tasted rancid. "And not just from around here."

News of the arrest of a reality TV show personality (sort of) must have gone viral. And now I understood Mother's choice of a sexy little black dress, more appropriate for a premiere: she never missed an opportunity for publicity.

But I stayed in the sweatshirt and jeans.

Although the courthouse—a turn-of-the-last-century rococo wedding cake of a structure—was merely across the street (albeit kitty-corner), I was to be transported via a squad car that had been pulled up to the rear door of the police station.

Amid the flashing of cameras, the hungry eyes of video cams, and the shouting of reporters, Mia again hustled a hands-cuffed-behind-me me, got behind the wheel, then drove the short distance to the courthouse as the pack of media ran after us.

She pulled the car up to a special entrance for prisoners, and within moments we were inside, being greeted glumly by Officer Munson. As we three climbed a back staircase, a few wily reporters ambushed us on a landing, shouting overlapping questions that I couldn't even make out, and Officer Munson fended them off while Mia and I continued on.

On the second level Mia hurried me into a small conference room, then shut the door and barricaded it with her back in case anyone else from the Fourth Estate might try to enter.

"Good Lord," Mia huffed. "Is your show really that popular? Or did Vivian call every news agency in the country?"

"I'm going to say the latter," I managed, out of breath. The old girl had probably been up all night.

We weren't alone in the room. There was someone else—a small, frail elderly man with thinning white hair, swimming in a navy pinstriped suit. He was asleep at the conference table, head cradled on his arms, like a kid in class who'd nodded off at his desk.

Wayne Ekhardt was Mother's longtime attorney and, consequently, mine, as well. Now pushing ninety, the trial lawyer had rocketed to fame in the 1950s, when he got a woman acquitted for murder after she (in self-defense, of course) shot her abusive husband five times in the back.

These days, Ekhardt still kept an office downtown, maintaining a limited practice, which included us, but recently his health appeared to be in decline.

Mia asked me, "The counselor would seem to be a little out of it. Want to call someone else?"

"No. I'm sure he'll be fine."

Pretty sure.

Almost sure.

Not sure at all . . .

"Up to you," Mia said, hiking a skeptical eyebrow.

The policewoman stepped out, and I crossed to the table and sat next to the slumbering lawyer, my hands still uncomfortably cuffed behind me.

"Mr. Ekhardt?" I said. Then louder, "Wake up, Mr. Ekhardt!"

His eyes opened, and he straightened, turned to me, frowned, then asked, "Where am I?"

"The courthouse."

"Of course I am. Who are you again?"

"Brandy Borne. Vivian's daughter? You're representing me at my arraignment in a few minutes."

"Is that right?"

"Didn't my mother call you last night?"

"I believe she did. What is her name again?"

I was starting to sweat. "Vivian Borne."

He frowned. Then he brightened and said, "Ah! Now I remember. She got me out of bed, the vixen. Killed someone, did you?"

"No! I'm innocent."

"No matter. Just say you're not guilty when the judge asks."

"Don't you have some questions to ask me?"

"Later. This is just a formality, don't you know. Come. Let's get this over with so I can get home. I didn't get my eight hours. You'll want me to have had my eight hours when I represent you at the trial."

I helped him to his feet. It was like picking up a bundle of kindling.

My arraignment was held down the hall, in a secondary courtroom used mostly for traffic violations, where herds of ensnared citizens were processed in a quick, noisy cattle call to vehicular justice. I'd been in there many times for Mother's various vehicular infractions, and the antiquated room was always stifling. In the summer there was no air-conditioning, and the high ceiling fans did little but move the hot air around; and in the winter the old radiators put out too much heat. Discomfort was always the verdict here.

At precisely 9:30 a.m., a male bailiff in a tan uniform escorted me into the courtroom via a side door next to the judge's bench, walked me to the table where Ekhardt sat with his eyes closed, placed me in the chair next to the lawyer, then took his rigid position next to a flag of the USA on a pole nearly as straight as he was.

The only other people in the room were the judge, the county attorney, and Mother. (The court reporter had been replaced recently by a computer system called DART, which made Mother furious because one of her favorite moments in a *Perry Mason* episode was when the judge asked the court reporter—usually played by the same milquetoast actor—to read back part of the transcript.)

His Honor, black robed, about sixty, with silver hair and heavy bags beneath his eyes, banged the gavel.

"The State versus Brandy Borne," he said in a properly booming voice. "Does the defendant have representation?"

All eyes went to Ekhardt, who was quite asleep, eyes closed, head bowed, softly snoring. At least his head wasn't on the table.

I twisted to look with alarm at Mother, who was seated directly behind the lawyer; she leaned forward and tapped him on his shoulder. It took several taps.

"Wayne," she whispered. "Wakey-poo!"

Slightly put out, the judge repeated, "Does the defendant have representation?"

Ekhardt, who didn't stand or open his eyes, said, "Yes, Your Honor."

"For the record," the judge noted, "Wayne Ekhardt is representing the defendant. And, for the record, representing the State is the county attorney, Jason Nesbit."

Nesbit was young, slender, with dark hair overly styled with product, glasses with invisible wire frames, and a fashionable two-day stubble on his narrowly handsome face. He was going places. I hoped his next stop wouldn't be putting a minor celebrity in prison for something she didn't do.

The judge continued, "Ms. Borne, do you understand the process of this arraignment?"

I stood. "Yes, sir." My voice sounded small, particularly next to His Honor's rafter-rattling boom.

"You have been charged with felony murder. How do you plead?"

Behind me, Mother whispered, "Nolo contendere, dear," which had always been her obstinate response at arraignments. But I didn't feel like being obstinate. I didn't feel anything but scared witless.

"Not guilty, Your Honor," I said.

And he said, "A trial date will be set. Until then you will be remanded to the county jail and held without bond."

I looked at Ekhardt, who didn't protest the no bond ruling, perhaps due to the murder charge, but I was disappointed that the old boy didn't even try.

The judge banged his gavel.

As the bailiff moved toward me, I turned to Mother, who said cheerfully, "Say hello to the girls in stir for me, dear!"

Not exactly the words of encouragement I had hoped to hear from her, though I wasn't really all that surprised. She had been a guest at the county jail a number of times and had made more than her share of friends.

Then I was led away.

The county jail was relatively new, a state-of-the-art facility with no barbed-wire fence or guard tower or bars on the windows, either— nothing to give any impression that the three-story, octagonal structure was a place to store prisoners. It might have been a large office complex or clinic.

But it wasn't.

My new home was located conveniently across the street from the courthouse and directly behind the police station, an arrangement that made the wheels of justice in Serenity turn most efficiently.

As I've mentioned, I was not new to the county jail, even if I couldn't rival Mother in number of visits. But this time around I knew to ask for a well-laundered faded-orange jumpsuit, instead of a bright newer one, which could be scratchy. Also, I requested that my matching slip-on tennies be a size larger so they wouldn't rub the backs of my heels raw.

Live and learn.

I was turned over to a guard named Patty, with whom I had some history. Patty—a woman in her forties, rather plain faced, with short dishwater-blond hair and no real enthusiasm for her job—took me through a series of locked doors to the area where female prisoners were kept on the first floor. (The men were on the second and third.) The women's section had a central area where they watched basic cable TV on an old tube number, played board games lacking assorted pieces, and ate starchy, lousy meals. This shared area was encircled by about a dozen single-person cells.

At the moment, the doors on those cells were closed for the usual enforced morning lockdown, during which the women were supposed to take a rest break. A break from what? I couldn't tell you, since there was no work for them to do. A rest from each other, probably. Anyway, I was thankful for the lockdown, as I didn't feel much like meeting "the girls" right now.

Patty escorted me to my cell, which was only slightly larger than my previous accommodations at the police station. But here I had a regular bed (single size), a toilet and sink (separate), a built-in closet (no door), and a high window (that perhaps a toddler might squeeze through).

Truth is, the cell was larger and, well, better than many college dorm rooms, and at least in this case I didn't have a drunken roommate.

Patty said, in her bored, businesslike way, "Lunch in one hour." Then, a little snotty, she added, "But you know that, don't you?"

She left, and the door locked.

Bone tired, I curled up on the bed in a fetal position, facing the wall, and was about to drop off when I noticed something written on the wall that was partially hidden by the bed. After propping myself up on one elbow, I pushed down on the mattress to read the missive in block letters.

"Vivian was here. Have a nice day!"

And a smiley face, of course.

I was shaken awake, if gently, and sat up to see leaning over me, with a smile, a pretty, rail-thin young woman with long, straight blond hair. I knew her, as well as the older woman standing behind her, a husky inmate sporting a crew cut.

The thin one was Jennifer; the stocky one, Carol. They were the two prisoners who, back when Mother was in residence, had tried to escape while performing her play at the Fort Dodge penitentiary (*Antiques Knock-off*).

Now back in captivity, the pair had had another sentence added to their original ones, for drug use (Jennifer) and assault (Carol).

"Time for lunch," Jennifer said.

"What's on the menu?" I asked.

Carol made a face. "Cold turkey sandwiches, stale potato chips, and canned fruit."

Actually, that didn't sound too bad; I was hungry enough to eat gruel. Maybe that would be for supper.

Jennifer backed away as I stood, but they remained planted before me and seemed to want something.

"You know," Carol said, "your mother got us better food when she was in here. Maybe you could do the same?"

Since her question sounded more like a demand, I just smiled. "Well, I can certainly try. But I can't compete with my mother."

The stocky woman nodded. "Y'know, Viv was really good to us when she was top dog here."

"Oh yeah," Jennifer chimed in. "If it wasn't for her puttin' us in that play, we wouldn't've almost got away."

"How *did* you get caught?" I asked. Mother had never shared that.

"Oh," Jennifer said, "'cause we were clowns."

"Well," I said, "don't be too hard on your-selves."

Carol said, "She means we were *dressed* as clowns in the play and should've figured a way to change our clothes."

Or their ways.

"Anyway," the stocky woman went on, "Jennifer and me would like to pay Viv back for all that."

"Oh?"

Carol nodded. "We wanna do something for you."

"Well, uh, that's really sweet of you," I said, eyeing them warily, hoping that "something" didn't include embroiling me in another half-baked escape. "What d'you have in mind, ladies?"

"We're gonna have your back," Carol replied. "Really look out for you. Of course, there's only three other women in here right now—but, kid, are they *tough*."

"Really mean," Jennifer added with a shiver.

Carol jerked a thumb at herself. "But they'll steer clear of you when they see we got you covered."

"I appreciate that," I told them.

We left my cell together for the common area, where food waited on a cart. As usual, the noon-time meal was a cold box lunch, while the evening meal would be hot (gruel?), eaten on plates with plastic sporks. Whoever came up with that term ought to do some time him- or herself.

In the center of the room was a picnic-style

table, where two other inmates were already eating, seated next to each other. Carol, Jennifer, and I got our box lunch (which included milk) and then sat opposite them.

I said, "Hi. I'm Brandy."

The pair stopped eating.

"Lupe," said one. She was curvy, with long dark hair streaked with red, and an attractive if hard-looking face. I guessed her to be about thirty-five.

"Tamicka," said the other, a little younger. She was muscular, with angular features and black hair worn in a ponytail.

Lupe said, "I hear you're in for murder."

I nodded. Not the time or place to plead innocent. "How about you girls?"

Lupe sneered over her sandwich. "Violating my probation."

"For . . . ?"

"Credit card fraud." She seemed almost proud of it.

I turned to Tamicka.

"Manslaughter," she said, then shrugged. "Involuntary."

I said to Carol, who was sitting next to me, "You said three other prisoners. Isn't there another?"

Behind me a voice said, "That would be me."

Coming around the table was a woman in her forties, with mousy brown hair and cow eyes. She tossed her box lunch on the tabletop, then plopped down across from me. "Fancy meeting you here, Brandy. Small world. Small county."

Although a submarine dive alarm was going off

in my head—*ah-oo-gah*! *ah-oo-gah*!—I responded casually, "Well, hello, Frieda."

I can't use the woman's real name without spoiling one of our cases for those who have not read it; therefore, she will be referred to herein as Three-Fingered Frieda, or TFF, for short. Her first name is not Frieda, but she does have only three fingers on one hand, and readers who have kept up with our accounts will know who she is. What those of you who haven't read *Antiques Fate* need to know is (a) Frieda was in "stir" because of Mother and me, and (b) she very likely blamed the loss of those three fingers on us, as well.

Tamicka looked from TFF to me. "You girls know each other?"

TFF smirked, "Indeed we do, don't we, Brandy? You see, she and that crazy mother of hers put me in here."

"Wow." Lupe laughed at me. "You just got here, and already you pissed off the top dog."

TFF was top dog? I wasn't sure Carol and Jennifer *could* protect me.

But my fears receded somewhat when Carol told TFF, "Look, there's gonna be no payback around here, understand? We're all stuck under this roof for this and that. No more fusses or rough stuff. We've lost too many privileges already."

"Yeah, and we just got back TV," Jennifer said. "And anybody who makes me miss any more episodes of Caitlyn Jenner is gonna have to deal with *her*." She nodded to Carol.

Three-Fingered Frieda spread both hands.

"Hey, I'm not lookin' to cause any trouble. I say let bygones be bygones."

"Really?" I asked dubiously.

"Sure. It's all fingers under the dam." She cocked her head. "Besides, from what I hear, you're in just as deep as I am."

Not exactly. TFF had been charged with three counts of murder; me, merely one.

Guard Patty came over. "Brandy . . . visitor."

I was so glad for an excuse to get away from TFF that I didn't bother asking who it was. Of course, there were only two possibilities: Ekhardt or Mother.

Patty took me through a security door, down a short hallway, then through another locked door, and finally to a small cubbyhole room much like those provided by banks for customers to look over the loot in their safe-deposit boxes. While Patty waited outside—there really wasn't room for more than the two of us, without the guard taking part in the conversation—I sat in the only chair in front of a Plexiglas window.

Opposite was Mother, looking well rested, wearing a cheerful holiday sweater of dancing reindeer who were doing a Rockettes high kick.

Instead of phones, a little microphone was embedded in the Plexiglas, and we leaned forward a little to speak.

"How are you doing, dear?" Mother asked.

Before I could answer, she raced on. "Are any of my special girls in there with you? You remember, dear . . . Sarah the bank embezzler, Angela the drunk driver, Rhonda the burglar. . . . I know Carol the assaulter and Jennifer the drug dealer are there! Naughty girls. They really put an end to my play's prison tour! Oh, how I envy you. What I could do in your place, organizing a new play! There's a new one Off-Off-Broadway called *The Penis Papers*, which would make a great companion piece to *The Vagina Monologues*. Of course, the girls would have to play men in this one, but Carol would be *terrific* as the cabdriver."

She finally stopped for air, while I just sat there, staring.

"What's wrong, dear?" Mother asked. "You look a fright."

"Maybe I should be wearing that little black dress you so thoughtfully provided me," I said.

She shook her head. "Probably not appropriate inside."

Staring her down, I said, "Mother, guess who's in here with me? An old pal of ours."

She lit up. "Who, dear?"

"Three-Fingered Frieda."

Mother's eyes, already magnified behind her large lenses, grew to enormous size. "Good Lord! She *would* be, wouldn't she? Why, I had forgotten all about her."

"Well, she doesn't seem to have forgotten about us."

Mother shifted uncomfortably in her chair. "Good heavens. We've simply *got* to get you moved—or get Three-Fingered Frieda moved! I'll talk to Sheriff Rudder right away. Now, don't you worry, dear. Mother's on it!"

"Actually I'm not all that worried," I said and

told her that Carol and Jennifer were looking out for me.

"Splendid, dear," she said. "Those two can be trusted. Except not to try to escape."

"I think I can count on them. Mother? Who's watching the store? Joe?"

"Yes, dear. I've told him we need his services until I can get you cleared."

I wondered if that was going to take a while. "Have you heard from Jake?"

Jake was my fourteen year-old son, living with my ex in Chicago.

"Yes, dear. He wants to come and support you in this, but I told him that this felonious charge against you would soon be dropped."

"Do you believe that?"

"Whether I believe it is not as important as Jake believing it."

"Do you think he does?"

Mother's eyebrows went up. "Of course. Do you know a more accomplished actress?"

I let that pass, then asked, "What about Peggy Sue? What does she know about this?"

Peggy Sue was my birth mother, who I'd long thought was my much-older sister; Peggy Sue was in D.C. with her husband, Senator Edward Clark, the father I never knew about . . . until a few years ago.

Mother shifted in her chair. "Naturally, Peg's very concerned."

I grunted something like a laugh. "About how my arrest may affect the senator's reelection, you mean?"

"Well . . ."

"Never mind."

She frowned. "Dear, I need to cut our visit a little short so I can see Sheriff Rudder about getting you protected." She pushed back her chair and stood. "Give my love to Carol and Jennifer."

And then she was gone.

Back in the common area, lunch was over. I hadn't had a chance for one bite of mine before Mother's visit. Tamicka, Lupe, and TFF were watching television; Carol and Jennifer were playing cards at the picnic table, and I went over to join my bodyguards.

"Was that your lawyer?" Carol asked, taking her eyes off her cards.

"No," I said. "Mother. She says hello."

"She have anything else to say?" Jennifer asked eagerly, as if craving more news.

I certainly wasn't going to mention *The Penis Papers*, so I said, "Only that she's concerned about Three-Fingered Frieda maybe wanting to get even."

Carol put her cards on the table, facedown. "You told her we'd look out for you, right?"

I nodded.

She shrugged. "Well, then, no worries. Hey, want to join us in a game of poker?"

"Texas Hold 'Em, Seven-Card Stud, Omaha Hi-Lo, or Crazy Pineapple?" I asked. At community college, it's just possible I spent more time in the student lounge, playing cards, than attending class.

Jennifer's eyes widened, and she looked at her partner. "Maybe Brandy shouldn't join us. She may be a ringer."

"Don't worry," I said, sitting down next to Carol. "I'm lousy at all of them."

Tamicka and Lupe also wanted in—TFF remained in front of the TV—and the next hour passed quickly. True to my word, I was the worst player and was glad we weren't playing for money.

After Tamicka came out on top, the game broke up, and Tamicka and Lupe rejoined TFF in front of a soap opera, which left Carol and Jennifer and me at the table.

After a moment, the younger woman asked, "Brandy, would you do something for Carol and me?"

"What?"

The two exchanged looks, and then Jennifer said, "Well, we done a story about our almost escape, and since you wrote some books, would you maybe take a look at it?"

"Sure. Where is it?"

"In my room."

We left the table and went to Jennifer's cell, which was two doors down from mine.

While Carol stood in the doorway, I followed Jennifer to the bed, where she lifted the mattress, then pulled out some sheets of paper. She handed me the pages, and I leafed through them.

They were blank.

Puzzled, I look up from the pages to find that

Jennifer had moved next to Carol by the door; then Three-Fingered Frieda strode in, and they stepped aside.

Carol shrugged. "Sorry, Brandy, but Frieda's top dog, and we gotta do what she says."

"Yeah, sorry, kid," Jennifer said, clearly ashamed, gazing down at her orange tennies.

Then my so-called bodyguards left, closing the door.

"Well, Brandy," TFF said, smirking, coming toward me. "I thought it was time we had a little chat. . . ."

A Trash 'n' Treasures Tip

The inventory record of your antiques should be updated as new items are added or others are sold. Keep a copy in a different place than the original, like in a bank safe-deposit box. Mother, in honor of the Great Depression, has her copy buried in the backyard, in a plastic Baggie. *Maybe* she remembers where she buried it.

Chapter Five

Unlucky Streak

Dearest ones! This is Vivian, aka Mother, seizing the narrative baton from my darling jailbird daughter, Brandy.

But before I continue with our exciting story, I'd like to give a shout-out to Ms. Blanca Contreras of Cape Coral, Florida, for sending a letter to our editor at Kensington, requesting that more chapters be written by *yo*. As a result, our esteemed editor has promised to bring the notion up in her next staff meeting. While said editor's response was not everything I had hoped for—nothing quite beats a resounding affirmation!—it does represent a tentative first step, a bold editorial toe in the water. So keep up the campaign, boys and girls and ladies and men!

Plus, I'm happy to report that my five-thousand-word limit per chapter has once again been lifted (after having been lifted, then reinstated, and lifted, then reinstated). Bless all of you who have contributed to that latest effort via snail mail, e-mail, tweets, and blogs. Protest demonstrations outside Kensington's office have not yet been necessary. But we keep our options open!

I'd also like to take the time—now that the unfairly restrictive word-count limit has been lifted—to respond to Mrs. Agatha Bertwistle, who wrote to me from Middleton-in-Teesdale, Durham, England, asking if I have ever had a face-lift. While I consider this an impertinent question, I appreciate the interest, nonetheless, and will answer: No, I have not. I have been blessed with resilient Danish genes—except for those that gave me a bipolar disorder, depression being a recurring problem for a populace forced to sit staring at fjords—and the paltry wrinkles that I do have, I wear with pride, as each one tells a story (granted, some of the stories are not worth telling). Lines of character on a mature face are well earned and to be expected!

Moles, on the other hand, are not, and when I find one of those, I beat a path to my dermatologist's door so he can get rid of the offensive thing by freezing it with liquid nitrogen. (He also killed the spider veins on my legs by injecting them with a saline solution through a tiny needle. FYI: After about fifteen minutes of the procedure, you'll want to scream—but hang in there. It's worth the pain to once again wear shorts in summer with confidence!)

Returning to Mrs. Bertwistle's question, I *will* admit to borrowing a trick used by the aging Bette Davis, which is to pull sagging facial skin back behind the hairline using tape and rubber bands (kits available on the Internet). The process is quite uncomfortable, so I resort to it only for special occasions, like class reunions or having my driver's license photo taken.

Which in the latter instance, incidentally, was a disaster due to the tape on one side coming unglued and rubber bands going flying just as the picture was snapped, and now I'm stuck with a photo of a half-young-looking, half-older-looking face, as well as some blurred unidentified objects by way of those rubber bands. I believe the disaster occurred when I was instructed to remove my glasses for the picture, a ridiculous dictum considering my license, back when I had one, was restricted to use of eyeglasses. And I'd forgotten that some of the rubber bands were secured to my frames. Shouldn't a taxpayer be granted a take two in the case of catastrophe? Anyway, since most people hate their driver's license photos, the state could get some extra income out of charging for such retakes. Fortunately, I don't have to show my license too often, particularly now that it's been marked invalid.

(Note to Vivian from Editor: *You are dangerously close to having your word count reinstated and your artistic license revoked, photo or no photo. Now please get back to the story at hand.*)

(Note to Editor from Vivian: *Yes, ma'am.*)

During my jailhouse visitation with Brandy, I tried not to show the child how very concerned I was about her being incarcerated with Three-Fingered Frieda. By the way, I could have come up with a better pseudonym for that vile woman, but out of respect to Brandy, I will go along to get along. (Digit-Challenged Dotty, perhaps? Seven-Fingered Sally?)

Where was I?

Oh yes. I'm sure Brandy, due to my thespian abilities, wasn't aware of my unease. And I *was* comforted somewhat by the fact that she was in a state-of-the art facility, which, by the way, I played a substantial role in getting erected after my first stint in the old crumbling, bug-infested jail. After all, a woman's first time is special, no matter how disappointing!

Anyway, I left Brandy, determined to do something about the dangerous situation she found herself in.

After being escorted out of the visitation area by a young male deputy, I collected my purse from the locker in the main lobby before making a beeline over to a Plexiglas window behind which sat a middle-aged female dispatcher with permed brown hair and a bank of computer screens.

"Vivian Borne to see Sheriff Rudder," I said, "and do shake a tail feather, if you would, my dear."

She took her eyes off the monitors, stared at me as if I might be an apparition, then spoke joylessly through a microphone embedded in the window. "I'm afraid he's busy right now, Mrs. Borne."

"Is that what he told you to tell me?"

The dispatcher said nothing.

"He *does* know my daughter is a guest of his facility, does he not?"

The dispatcher shrugged.

So I said, "Remind the sheriff, if you would, of the time he lost his gun and I happened to find it and returned it to him, with no one the wiser—except, of course, you now."

She swiveled to a multiline phone, spoke low into the receiver, then swiveled back.

"The sheriff will be out in a minute."

"Thank you, dear."

You just have to know how to handle people.

I walked over to a row of plastic chairs hooked together next to a couple of vending machines and sat, the sole soul in the waiting area.

Knowing Rudder would most likely keep me waiting—a "minute" being a relative term to a ranking civil servant—and never one to sit twiddling my thumbs, I retrieved my cell from my purse to pass the time by playing *Candy Crush*.

The object of the game is to match different candies to earn points and advance to another level. The only problem I had with it was that afterward I always got a terrific hankering for something sweet. Imagine how the easily impressionable might react! I wondered if the candy cartel was behind it all.

I had been playing the game for about five minutes, craving Life Savers, when the locked steel door to the sheriff's inner sanctum opened and the big man strode out. He was tall and carried his weight with confidence. If I squinted, I could see in Rudder something of the older John Wayne; he even walked a little sideways like the Duke. Was that on purpose? Of course, corns or hemorrhoids might be responsible.

I stood as the sheriff approached.

"What is it, Vivian?" he asked, not bothering to hide his irritation. How very ungracious.

"Were you aware that Brandy is inside with Three-Fingered Frieda?" I demanded, knowing full well he had to be.

Rudder, rather blandly, asked, "Why? Has Brandy complained about being threatened?"

"Not directly," I admitted, then added quickly, "But her position is obviously perilous. And I must insist that you do something about it!"

The sheriff rocked back on his heels. "And what would you suggest?" His tone seemed unnecessarily patronizing.

"Oh, I don't know. . . . How about *moving Three-Fingered Frieda to another facility!*"

He shook his head. "Not possible. She's been remanded to the county jail by judge's orders. But I could put Brandy into solitary confinement, if that would make you—and her—feel better."

"It would not!" I snapped. "Why should Brandy suffer? Isn't this a little ungracious of you, considering that my daughter and I handed you that murderous woman on a silver platter? Why don't you put *her* into solitary?"

"I could, and will, should she threaten Brandy.

Until then"—he shrugged—"things stay as they are."

I whipped up a few tears. The actress calls upon sense memory for such things. "That could be closing the barn door after the cow escapes!"

"You mean horse." The sheriff's expression softened, and he placed a hand on my shoulder. "Vivian, nothing is going to happen. I have full confidence in our guards."

I certainly didn't, particularly that lackadaisical louse Patty.

Rudder was saying, "Now, you go on home, Vivian, and stop worrying, and leave this to us."

"All right," I sniffled. "Perhaps I *am* overreacting."

Apparently satisfied with my reaction, the sheriff turned and sideways walked back to the locked steel door, Pilgrim. *True Grit*, my bunions! It was clear I would get no satisfaction here.

There seemed to be only one way to protect Brandy, only one way I could make sure she was safe inside. . . .

And that was if I was inside, too.

Which could mean only one thing: I had to get myself arrested.

But first, I needed a sugar boost. I walked over to a vending machine. Outside, I stood on the sidewalk, snarfing Skittles, considering options. Whatever I came up with couldn't be too drastic—like robbing a bank or setting a building on fire—because I wanted to be incarcerated only long enough to make sure Brandy would be all right. And, anyway, setting a building on fire would be wrong.

By the time I finished the Skittles, I had my plan.

Since Brandy's arrest late Tuesday night, I had been surreptitiously driving the C-Max around town, rather than utilizing forms of legal, but inconvenient, transportation.

So far, I'd gotten away with my deception by disguising myself to look like Brandy while in transit. I would snug on a blond wig that was similar to the dear girl's hairstyle and don one of her youthful-looking coats. The only snag in my resemblance is that I wear glasses and she doesn't. But I've solved that little problem by not putting on the specs till I've gotten where I'm going.

(Granted, I'd made a few minor flubs. This morning, on my way to see Brandy, I mistook someone's driveway for a street, plowed into their yard, hit a plastic garden gnome, launching it into outer space. A few blocks later, I found myself on the wrong side of the road, with a Toyota coming toward me. What was that reckless driver's idea, going so fast? I managed to swerve back into my own lane in the nick of time, but as our cars passed, the other driver, male, shouted something that wasn't fit for mixed company, so I yelled back, "Cheerio!" in my finest British accent, which would provide an implied explanation of my blunder.)

Right now the C-Max was parked in a residential area not far from the center of justice, and soon I was behind the wheel . . . but this time as myself. Then I drove the short distance to the police station and parked across the street, just a little ways down so that I could watch the comings and goings of the boys (and girls) in blue.

After a few minutes, Officer Munson—what luck!—came ambling out a side door and headed to a row of police cars in the adjacent lot. He was well aware that my license had been suspended! As he got behind the wheel, I turned on the C-Max and gunned the motor, or at least as much as a hybrid motor can be gunned. When he eased his vehicle to the mouth of the lot and paused to check for traffic, I shot away from the curb, tires squealing.

Zooming past him like Mr. Toad on his wild ride, I yelled out my open window, "Lovely day for a drive, isn't it, Officer?"

I picked up speed—going well over the twenty-five-mile-an-hour limit—and, after two blocks, eased over to the curb and shut off the motor to await my imminent arrest.

A check in my rearview mirror corroborated that Munson was in pursuit, squad car lights flashing, siren screaming. *Goodie!*

I rehearsed my lines: "Sorry, Officer, but I can't show you my driver's license. . . . Seems I don't have one! In fact, it's been suspended five times. So book me, Danno!" (This would make a nice little nod to *Hawaii Five-O*—the original seventies series, not the remake!)

So you can imagine my astonishment when Officer Munson did not pull in behind me but sped on by, obviously responding to something more urgent than arresting little ole me! Maybe someone had robbed a bank or burned down a building.

That meant I had to concoct another scheme to gain entry to the hoosegow, and one came to me when my stomach—apparently not satisfied with mere Skittles—growled.

A few blocks away on Main Street was George's Bakery, a speciality doughnut shop, where those who serve and protect liked to stop for a mid-afternoon coffee break. With any luck, I'd find a few officers there. Clichés become clichés for a reason, you know.

So I was elated when I walked in and spotted two patrolmen seated at a table, their backs mostly to me, cups of java before them. They were a Mutt and Jeff team, known to me from past encounters on the Amateur Sleuth Trail. The tall, thin one was Officer Kelly; the short, stocky sort, Officer Schultz.

Schultz was saying sotto voce to his partner, "Chief's not gonna be happy till he finds out how those drugs are comin' in."

"Why, hello, Officer Kelly . . . Officer Schultz," I said, greeting the pair cheerfully.

"Good afternoon, Mrs. Borne," Kelly replied for the two of them.

I proceeded on to the glass display case, where an assortment of delightful baked goods were arranged on shelves, on white paper doilies.

Ringing the little bell for service, I summoned George from the back. He was a paunchy man, a little too fond of his own wares, but he had all his hair and a full set of teeth, despite all that sugar.

He was wearing a white apron spattered with various colors, a Pollock painting in dried frosting.

George did all the baking himself now. His ex-wife had previously done most of it, along with a young male apprentice, and apparently, while George had been waiting on customers out front, the two had been in back, where more than just the yeast had been rising.

"Vivian," George said coolly.

He was still at least mildly miffed at me for spurning his attempts at wooing *moi* after his divorce had become final. (I had no desire to toil away in a bakery, possibly the aftermath of portraying Mrs. Lovett in *Sweeney Todd* at the Serenity Playhouse.)

"George," I returned pleasantly.

"What can I do you for?"

"A dozen doughnuts, please."

He turned, got a large box, placed it on the countertop. "Anything special in mind?"

"Certainly. One each of the following. Bear claw, Brown Bobby, cream horn, cream-filled Long John, Cronut, cruller, elephant ear, fasnacht, fritter, old-fashioned, and a yum yum."

He filled the box—giving me two Cronuts, instead of a cruller, not that it really mattered—then rang up the bill on a cash register.

"That'll be twenty-five dollars and sixty-eight cents, Vivian," he said.

"Oh!" I said. "I almost forgot that I wanted a cream horn for myself in a separate sack, but please make me a fresh one."

"The ones in the case *are* fresh," he said defensively.

I smiled sweetly. "They may have been this morning, Georgie dear, but it's mid-afternoon now."

The baker sighed. "If you insist, Vivian."

"I do. And thank you ever so."

Grumbling, he disappeared in the back.

I lifted the box off the glass counter and walked over to Kelly and Schultz, who were lingering over their coffee.

Setting the doughnuts on the table, I announced, "These are for you, boys, a gift from me to you for all the splendid work you do for the citizens of this fair city." (A tad corny perhaps, but I think my acting skills overcame the script.)

"Gee, Vivian," Schultz said, "that's swell of you, but I'm laying off the doughnuts for a while." He patted his protruding stomach.

Kelly said, "And I've already had two."

I tsk-tsked. "Boys, as hard as you work, you know you'll burn off those calories." If sitting in a patrol car all day burns calories.

Removing the lid on the box, I said, "Officer Schultz, I happen to know you love bear claws, and, Officer Kelly, you have a fondness for cream-filled Long Johns. . . ."

They stared at the pastries.

"Well," Schultz replied, drawing the word out. "I can always be good tomorrow."

"And my wife says I could stand to put on a few pounds," rationalized Kelly.

I watched them pick out their favorites.

Behind me George called out, "Got your cream horn here, Vivian!"

I replaced the lid on the doughnuts, picked up the box, then returned to the counter.

"That'll be twenty-eight dollars and thirty-six cents," he said, handing me a little white sack.

"All well and good, but I'm not going to pay it."

George frowned. "Excuse me?"

"I'm leaving with these doughnuts without paying for them. Do you follow? Do you understand?"

"You can't *do* that!"

"Watch and learn." And I headed toward the door.

"*Officers!*" George called out. "Stop her!"

Schultz stood, blocking my way, and I halted. "You'll have to tase me," I told him, "because I intend to go through that door with these purloined pastries!"

Officer Kelly, still seated, said, "I'll pay for the doughnuts."

I turned to him. "I don't *want* you to pay! What I want is for you to arrest me for petty larceny, which is what I deserve!"

The two officers exchanged puzzled looks.

Frustrated, I said, "According to Penal Law Section one-fifty-five-point-five, larceny occurs when, with intent to deprive an owner of personal property, an individual appropriates or unlawfully withholds that property. So take me in, boys."

Schultz shook his head. "We're not going to do that, Vivian."

"Then how about arresting me for bribing you and Officer Kelly?"

"When did you do that?" Kelly asked.

"Just a minute ago!" I said, exasperated. "I gave you each a pastry, which you accepted. Remember?"

Schultz asked, "Viv, what gives?"

When I said nothing, Kelly whispered to his partner, "She's probably come unglued about her daughter killing the chief's wife."

"That's not the reason!" I retorted. "And for your information, Brandy *didn't* kill Camilla. She has been unfairly arraigned and detained!"

I tossed the box of doughnuts on the table and left. But I kept the sack with the cream horn.

Out on the sidewalk I stuck my hand in the little bag and pulled out the confection, then walked along, chewing angrily. But I couldn't keep from smiling. It was so fresh!

When the cream horn was gone, my frustration returned. What was going on here? Usually, I had no trouble getting arrested. Now I needed a third idea for landing myself in the clink nonfeloniously.

Approaching the Riverview Restaurant, I recalled that the Romeos (Retired Old Men Eating Out) would most likely be lingering over a long lunch. As they had often said, it was a preferable way to pass an early afternoon than going home to an empty house or a nagging wife. The latter was certainly a sexist attitude, although, truth be told, there *were* some harpies in the mix.

I entered the riverboat-themed diner and easily spotted the group of old cronies at their usual round table toward the back. There were only four on hand today, the Romeos having dwindled due to new illnesses and the old grim reaper: Harold, ex-army sergeant; Vern, retired chiropractor; Randall, former hog farmer; and Wendell, onetime riverboat captain.

The Romeos were invaluable to me in any investigation, because these old gents knew more gossip than anyone in town, including me, which is something of a mind boggler.

I at one time had joined their counterpart group, the Juliets (Just Us Ladies into Eating Together), but had dropped out in disappointment after a single lunch: all those girls did was brag about themselves and their grandchildren, complete with utterly interchangeable pictures (from those who could figure out how to bring the pics up on their cell phones).

"Hello, boys," I greeted the men in my usual Mae West manner. "Mind if I join you?"

They had finished with their meals—which was fine by me, as I sometimes found it difficult to watch them eat, particularly hog farmer Randall—and the dirty plates had been cleared, save for coffee cups and water glasses.

After receiving smiling nods all around, I slid into an empty chair. Normally, women were not allowed at the Romeos' table, but I was an exception, much as Shirley MacLaine and Angie Dickinson had been welcomed by the Rat Pack.

Harold, on my right, asked, "How are you holding up, Viv, considering Brandy's situation?"

The ex-army sergeant looked a little like the

older Bob Hope with ski-lift nose, jutting chin, and thinning hair. Years ago, after both our spouses had passed, he asked me to marry him. That same night I had a dream I was in an army kitchen, peeling a mound of potatoes while Sergeant Bilko stood over me, barking, "*Hey yo hup!*" I chose to view this as a harbinger of things to come and politely declined Harold's proposal.

To garner sympathy from the men, I answered, "I'm doing as well as can be expected, with my daughter in jail, charged with murder."

A waitress noticed my addition to the group and asked if I wanted anything; I told her, "Black coffee," and off she went.

Randall, on my left, said, "We're all so sorry."

The former hog farmer might be best described as a less sophisticated Sydney Greenstreet. In the past, I would have been careful about sitting next to him, downwind, anyway; but he'd been out of the pig game long enough to lose his bouquet, even though he did retain his farm.

"Yes," added Vern, across from me. "We were just discussing this sad state of affairs. We don't any of us believe Brandy could do such a thing."

The retired chiropractor looked a little bit like Zachary Scott without my glasses. Wasn't he wonderful in *Mildred Pierce* (the version with Joan Crawford, not Kate Winslet)? And I mean if *I* weren't wearing my glasses, not if Vern were wearing them.

"That's right," replied Wendell, who sat next

to Vern. The onetime riverboat captain was a dead ringer for Leo Gorcey, of the once-famed Bowery Boys(that's what Wikipedia's for). Wendell had had his career cut short when he was piloting the *Delta Queen*, fell asleep at the wheel, and T-boned a barge.

"Thank you, boys," I replied, making my eyes moist. Sense memory! "Your kind words mean the world to me. Really they do," I said, putting just the right amount of Tallulah Bankhead spin on it.

The waitress was just setting my coffee down in front of me, after which (an eyebrow raised, for some reason) she moved on.

Vern leaned forward to ask quietly, "But, Viv, how *did* Brandy's fingerprints get on the murder weapon?"

These old goats sure had their oversize, somewhat hairy ears to the ground.

I took a dainty sip from my cup, then rested it on its saucer. "There *is* an explanation . . . but I must reserve that for the trial. I hope you understand."

Murmurs of "Of course," and "We do" belied their disappointed expressions.

After all, I wasn't here to *provide* information, but to *receive* it.

Randall said abruptly, "You know, Viv, funny thing . . . That antique corn husker was mine."

All eyes went to the former pig farmer.

"*Yours*?" I blurted.

"That's right," he said with a nod. "Tom O'Grady borrowed it to show to that dang tool club he be-

longed to, and shortly after that, he passed. Later, I asked Alma for it back, but she refused, claiming it was Tom's."

I said, "She was likely confused. I've always found Alma to be a very sweet woman. She's quite active in her church and gives a lot of her time to charitable causes."

Randall gestured with a hand whose fingers were plump sausages. "That's all an act! She's as mean as a doggone snake! And don't let her small size fool you. She can chop wood like a lumberjack." He snorted like a pig; well, he did. "And you should see the traffic that comes and goes from her place. What a load of riffraff!"

Randall's farm was adjacent to the O'Grady's.

"Any *particular* riffraff?" I asked.

Randall shook his head. "My eyes aren't strong enough to tell." He meant his binoculars weren't. "But judging by the beat-up cars and broken-down trucks that turn up her lane? Well, that tells the story. She's keeping company with some questionable folks!"

When the others had nothing to add about "mean as a snake" Alma, I threw out a question. "What can any of you tell me about Camilla Cassato?"

The men exchanged glances. Then Wendell spoke. "Well, she didn't really know much about antiques—at least not a good bargain when she saw one."

"Elaborate," I said.

The former riverboat captain leaned forward, putting his elbows on the table. "One day last month? I went into her shop?"

Good Lord! Uptalking had infiltrated the Greatest Generation!

He was saying, "I wanted to sell her some of my nautical antiques and memorabilia. She barely looked at the items, even after I gave her a darn good price."

I shrugged. "Maybe nautical items didn't fit her customers."

Wendell shook his head. "No matter. A savvy dealer doesn't turn his or her nose up over turning an easy dollar. All I could think was . . . maybe she didn't need the money."

"Perhaps she didn't," replied Vern coyly.

My ears perked up like Sushi's when she hears the rustle of a potato chip bag.

"Okay, Vern," I said, fixing my eyes on him. "Spill."

The former chiropractor's face reddened a bit. "Maybe I shouldn't say. . . . Really, it's confidential, and I don't want to get Holly in trouble."

Holly was Vern's niece, a teller at the First National Bank.

We all just stared at Vern, waiting for him to continue, no one buying his sudden pang of conscience. The Romeos didn't come to this table to be discreet, after all.

The former bone cruncher lowered his voice. "Well, here's the thing. . . . Viv, Holly often waited on that TV producer of yours. . . ." His eyes were locked with mine.

"Phil Dean," I prompted.

"Yeah, him. This Dean character would come

in once a week to cash a wire transfer that came to the bank."

I nodded. "From his production company in Los Angeles, most likely, to cover expenses for the show. Go on."

"Anyway, Dean always wanted the money in hundred-dollar bills, and this one time Holly is counting the hundreds out to him when she notices that on one of the bills, someone doodled a mustache on ole Ben Franklin. With a pen?"

While I cringed at the uptalking, Vern shifted in his chair.

"Now," he continued, "Holly knows darn well she's supposed to pull a bill like that out of circulation, 'cause it's damaged? Mutilated, she calls it . . . but Dean's in a big hurry, so she doesn't."

"A fascinating inside look at the banking industry," I said somewhat impatiently. "But what does this have to do with Camilla?"

"Only this," Vern said, leaning forward. "About an hour later, guess who comes in and makes a business deposit with Holly? Camilla! And there among the bills in Camilla's deposit is that same hundred-dollar bill with the Ben Franklin mustache!"

I frowned. "Could be other bills floating around like that, if somebody made a habit of doodling that way. And if it was the same hundred, Phil might've bought an antique from Camilla for our show."

Vern leaned forward, voice still lowered. "Maybe so. But Holly thinks it's odd that Mrs. Cassato never deposited any checks, only cash. And the same amount every week—*five thousand.*"

An amount that corresponded with the deposit slip Brandy had found on the floor of the woman's shop.

The waitress came over and refilled coffee cups. Everybody was absorbing Vern's information, particularly me. But the subject seemed exhausted.

After a few moments, Harold said brightly, "Say, I have it on good authority that Sheriff Rudder isn't running again."

My coffee cup, on its way to my lips, nearly slipped from my hand! "What's that you say?"

The ex-sergeant smiled slyly. "I'm just passing along what my barber told me. He heard it from his wife, who heard it from a neighbor, who heard it from Rudder's wife."

Impressive. Perhaps I'd been too quick to discount the man's marital offer. . . .

A waitress flew by with a plate of boiled potatoes.

No.

"Who's your barber?" I asked, always eager to locate a new snitch.

Wendell was smirking. "Hey, Viv, why don't *you* run for sheriff?"

The other Romeos laughed at the notion, which got my dander up. Or, as little Brandy used to say, *got my dandruff up.*

"I don't see what's so amusing about the notion of my becoming sheriff," I huffed. "After all, for several years now, I've solved every single one of the county's murder cases."

Wendell made a "Calm down" gesture with

both hands. "Now, Viv, we're just having a little fun."

Harold, clearing his throat, again changed the conversation. "Hey, you guys got your fantasy football picks ready for this weekend?"

Since I didn't gamble, I was shut out of the conversation. I was about to leave when Vern said, "You know, lately I've been on a real lucky streak," which gave me a brilliant idea.

I knew exactly how I could finally get arrested!

Is anyone ahead of me? (Or perhaps *behind* me?)

You've heard of *The Full Monty*, right? For those who haven't, I'll give you a moment to Google it. (All others can sing along with me while we wait. *There was a farmer had a dog, and Bingo was his name-O. B-I-N-G-O! B-I-N-G-O! B-I-N-G-O! And Bingo was his name-O!*)

By the way, there's a misconception about who Bingo really is. Bingo is the *farmer*, not the dog. Just thought I'd clear that up. (Sorry if I've ruined things for anyone out there who named their dog Bingo.)

Okay, everybody back?

Well, instead of performing the full monty, I would go with the Partial Vivian, i.e., only half a monty, the upper half. (I do have some degree of decorum, after all.) I would go into the ladies' room, strip down to my panties, then streak around the restaurant. And if that didn't get me arrested for indecent exposure, I don't know what would! (Although for a woman my age, the exposure would actually be pretty decent, if you know what I mean, and I think you do.)

It wasn't as if there were many people still eating in the restaurant, and, after all, two of the Romeos had already seen at least a Partial Vivian (You don't need to know who. I'm not the kind of girl to kiss and tell—or anything else and tell.)

I stood. "I'll be right back. Don't you boys go away!" I couldn't help adding, "You're in for a treat."

I was moving in the direction of the bathroom when someone called my name. I turned to see Officer Cordona weaving her way around the tables toward me.

"Vivian, you need you to come with me," Mia said.

So, the police had finally decided to arrest me, at that! Either for driving without a license or petit theft or both. No need now to do the Partial Vivian, which was problematic, anyway, as chilly as it was in the restaurant.

I held out my wrists. "Are you going to cuff me?"

"No," Mia said with a slight smirk. "I have a hunch if I made an arrest, you wouldn't resist."

Her police car was double-parked out front, its lights flashing, and soon she deposited me in the backseat, behind the grill. We made the short trip to the station, where I was taken in through the back, led down the tan-tiled corridor, and dumped in a small, stark interview room containing only a table and two chairs.

Mia left, and I heard the door lock behind her.

I sat for a good five minutes, wondering why I

hadn't been booked, when finally the door opened and Tony bulled his way in. He was not wearing his usual office attire, but rather a casual ensemble of green sweater, jeans, and tennis shoes.

Surprised to see him, I burbled, "Why, Chiefie dear, I thought you'd left town!"

But I quickly realized he looked to be in no mood to be called "Chiefie."

He pulled the other chair roughly away from the table and sat, his eyes hard as bullets, his mouth a thin line, his chin set. "I *was* on my way, Vivian . . . but then got a call about you."

I shifted in the hard plastic chair. "Sorry, Chief Cassato. I really didn't mean to involve you."

"Well, now I am involved," he snapped. "Look, I know you're concerned about Brandy being inside with a felon who she helped put away—so am I—but I talked to the sheriff, who assured me your daughter's not in any danger."

"Oh, really? In season one of *Prisoner: Cell Block H*, Bella was attacked in the shower room by Martha. And in season six of *Bad Girls*, Frances was given poisoned coffee by Tanya. Not to mention that in *Orange Is the New Black*, season two, Red was knocked unconscious in the greenhouse by Vee when she hit her with a lock in a sock. Does *that* sound like Brandy isn't in any danger?"

"Vivian, those are TV shows. There's no greenhouse at the county jail, and there's always a guard in the showers with the women, and as far

as the coffee goes, well . . ." He smiled just a little. "It does taste a little like poison. It just won't
kill you."

Tony's weak attempt at humor did not placate me.

His eyes softened. "Vivian, you're not going
to help Brandy by getting yourself arrested."

"So, you refuse to book me for any of the
things I've done?"

"That's right. I refuse to let you manipulate
the system in such an obvious way. And if you try
anything else foolish, I've left instructions that
you're to be held here, in a holding cell at the
station, *not* in the county jail."

So much for the Partial Vivian.

He stood. Sighed. "If you really want to help
Brandy, Viv . . . find out who killed Camilla."

Had I heard him correctly?

I goggled at him. "You're giving me . . . *permission* to investigate?"

"Yes. I can hardly believe it myself, but . . .
yes."

"Do I have carte blanche to pursue my meth-
ods?"

Another sigh. "Within the confines of the
law."

That didn't sound like any fun.

I asked, "Is this a direct admission of the effi-
cacy of my extraordinary sleuthing abilities, as
exhibited in the past?"

"Don't push it, Viv."

"An implied admission, then?"

"Go," Tony said, pointing to the door like a

father banishing a soiled daughter. "Before I change my damn mind."

I went.

No one can say Vivian Borne doesn't know when to keep her mouth shut.

Mother's Trash 'n' Treasures Tip

Protect your antiques by installing a home security system. Our system is called Sushi.

Chapter Six

Alma Matters

As Three-Fingered Frieda advanced toward me, I backed up in the cell, looking over either shoulder and everywhere and anywhere for something to use to defend myself.

But I saw nothing.

In a fight, Frieda and I would be pretty well matched. Maybe I even had an edge, with my survival instinct kicking in. Of course, she had crazy on her side.

About three feet from me, TFF stopped, frowning a little. "Hey, dummy. I'm not here to hurt you."

"Mind if I decide that for myself?"

She held out her palms. "Nothing in my hands." She pushed up her sleeves. "Nothing up here, either." Then she turned the pockets of her slacks inside out.

"Nothing in there."

I still wasn't buying it. "So, then, what *do* you want?"

"Just to come to an understanding between us. Two reasonable women coming to terms."

I recalled the reasonable moment when she'd pointed an antique weapon at Mother and me.

Working to keep the tremor out of my voice, I said, "What kind of terms?"

Her smile curdled my blood only a little. "Oh, I think you'll be satisfied. Very."

"I'm . . . I'm listening."

TFF tilted her head. "You're going to have to testify at my trial, right?"

"Most likely."

"Well, when you take the stand, I want you to say you thought I was behaving, you know, crazily when I . . ." She stopped. "When those people died."

I squinted at her, trying to bring her into focus. "You *want* me to say you seemed crazy?"

"Haven't you heard, Brandy girl? I'm making a temporary insanity plea. I want you to back that up."

Telling a judge and jury that when Mother and I faced her down, TFF had seemed as nutty as a Baby Ruth wouldn't exactly be a challenge.

But I said, "Why would I help you?"

She stepped closer. Her eyes were wild, but her voice was calm. "Because I have information that might get you out of here. Or do you like facing a murder charge? I know I don't."

My eyes narrowed as my fear dissipated. "What do you know?"

"First, swear you'll help me."

I looked at those flaring eyes and had no problem with her request. You bet I would say she'd seemed crazy to me. Not that my testimony would carry any great weight. Last time I looked I wasn't a psychiatrist. Of course, I did live with Mother.

I said, "I swear."

"All right. First, tell me what you'll say on the stand."

"Following your attorney's lead, I'll say that in my humble opinion, you were completely and utterly out of your mind when you pointed that gun at Mother and me."

TFF smiled, as pleased as if I'd just given her a ringing endorsement. "Brandy, you're okay. Even if you are innocent of murder."

"Thanks. Now, what's the information?"

Three-Fingered Frieda glanced around, as if this small cell might have eavesdroppers lurking.

Then in a hushed, secretive voice, she said, "You know about those antiques I, uh, borrowed?"

That she, uh, stole.

"Yes," I said.

"Well, I used a local Serenity businessman to handle them for me."

Meaning she used a middleman to fence them.

"Be more specific," I said.

"Rodney Evans. Ever hear of him?"

"No."

"Well, he used to be small time, working out of a downtown pawnshop. But the last time I did business with him, he was driving a BMW and his wristwatch was a Rolex."

My eyebrows were high. "Sounds like he's moving up in the world."

"Yeah, by hanging onto somebody's coattails. He's got a big connection to unload that stuff now."

"Did he ever mention who that was?"

She shook her head. "No. These guys always play their cards close to the vest. But he specializes in antiques, so I gathered he came up in the world by making a fresh connection, probably an antiques dealer in Serenity . . . maybe somebody new to the game."

Which could have been Camilla.

Our conversation was abruptly cut short when the cell door seemed to fling itself open and Patty rushed in. The guard grabbed TFF from behind, twisted the woman's arms around her, then cuffed her.

As Three-Fingered Frieda shouted obscenities, I told Patty, "Hey, she wasn't bothering me or anything."

"Doesn't matter," the guard snapped. "This isn't your call."

"Where are you taking her?"

"Solitary. Sheriff's orders."

TFF said to me, wild-eyed again, "We got a deal, remember! I'm crazy, right?"

"Right," I said.

Then Patty hauled my new friend through the door, and I was alone again.

Had Frieda been on the level? Or had she just been playing me?

Flummoxed, I left the cell for the common area, where Jennifer, Carol, Tamicka, and Lupe were at the picnic table, playing cards. As I approached, their collective gaze rose to me, their faces unreadable.

Would they think I grassed on TFF? Was I now in danger from my fellow inmates? And by using a UK term like "grassed," had I been exposed by Mother to too many British crime shows?

Lupe spoke first. "Hey. Big props. Thanks for getting rid of that bitch. She made one mean top dog."

I was pretty sure, by the way, that Mother had introduced the "top dog" term into the local jailhouse vocabulary on her first stay here. (Not a UK show's fault, rather the Australian *Prisoner: Cell Block H* and its remake, *Wentworth.*)

"Yeah, nice goin', Brandy," Carol said. "And we're sorry we had to"—she gestured with her head toward Jennifer's cell, where they'd handed me over to their "mean top dog"—"you know."

"Yeah, our bad, Brandy," Jennifer chimed in sheepishly. "If we didn't do what Frieda said, she'd make our lives suck even worse. She'd come in, in the middle of the night, and threaten you with a shiv!"

"No kidding," I said. "A shiv?"

"Well, a spoon. That girl is crazy!"

Tamicka grunted. "You got that right, Jen. When Frieda don't get her way, she'd pick a fight just so we'd all go on lockdown."

Lupe asked me, "Did she try anything on you?"

Since they didn't know what had happened, I might as well boost my reputation. "Well, she pulled a spoon on me, but I knocked it out of her hand and told her who was boss. I could've handled her myself, without Patty sticking her nose in."

Jennifer gazed at me with newfound admiration. "You know, we could use a new top dog about now. Somebody smart and fair."

"Yeah," Carol said. "I nominate Brandy. She's her mother's daughter!"

That wasn't the best compliment I had ever got, and, anyway, I didn't want to be top dog, middle dog, bottom dog, or any kind of dog (Sushi, forgive me), and I was about to say as much when Tamicka objected.

"Wait just one minute!" the muscular thirtysomething said. "She's a newbie, and I been here *way* longer. What can she do that I can't?"

Suddenly the top dog position appealed to me.

"For one," I said, "I can land people who aren't nice to me in solitary. That's where Frieda is headed."

"Oh," Tamicka said, slumping a little. "Okay, good point."

"What *else* can you do?" demanded Lupe.

Jeez. Wasn't getting somebody stuck in solitary enough?

"Well," I said, "I can organize a play."

I *was* my mother's daughter, wasn't I?

Carol's eyes lit up. "As good as *The Vagina Monologues*?"

Mother had already had *Monologues* in rehearsal when her theatrical program got shut
down due to escape attempts.

"Better than that," I told them. "It's called
The Penis Papers." I figured Mother would work
with me on this.

That sent the women howling with laughter.

When they'd settled down, I went on, "This
play has three main characters, but they're all
male."

"I always wanted to play in drag," Carol cack-
led.

More laughter, and one yelling at her, "You
sure did!"

"All right," I said, shaking a supportive fist.
"Carol's in. Who else?"

Jennifer's hand shot up. *"Me, me!"*

"We need one more volunteer." I turned to
Lupe and Tamicka.

Tamicka flexed a bicep. "I'm more man than
most of these excuses for the male species."

To Lupe, I said, "Still need a stage manager."

"Cool," Lupe said. "What are you gonna do?"

"I'll direct, of course." With Mother's guidance. My biggest theatrical job to date had been
wrangling hats for Mother's one-woman version
of *Macbeth.*

Jennifer asked, "Do you think we could per-
form this penis play for the prison circuit, like
we did before?"

That was unlikely ever to happen again, after
she and Carol had so nearly escaped; but rather
than throw cold water on the notion, I said,

"Possibly. But we could certainly put it on for the men's cell blocks."

Every prisoner needs hope.

Eyes looked past me, and I turned to see Patty ambling up to me, exuding equal parts boredom and contempt.

She stopped to face me, eyes half-lidded. "Sheriff wants to see you."

If he thought I'd thank him for removing Frieda, Sheriff Rudder was in for a surprise. Who could say what further info I could have gotten out of her if he hadn't pulled the plug?

As Patty escorted me out, Tamicka called, "Tell that badge we want better food! That's job number one for a top dog!"

"Do my best," I growled.

Patty took me through several locked doors and then to a room I'd never been in before. A step up from an interview room, it had a nice conference table that sat six, with padded chairs.

Three other people were in the room: Sheriff Rudder, county attorney Jason Nesbit, and . . . Mother! No one was seated, which I took to mean this was going to be a short meeting.

Rudder's mouth started to work, but Mother beat him to the punch.

"You're free as a bird, dear!" she cried.

My eyes went from her to the sheriff. "I am? Is that true?"

"Yes," Rudder said.

"Bail?"

"No. Vivian is correct. You're free to go."

I looked to our hotshot county attorney, my

eyebrows raised. When you're wearing an orange jumpsuit, you can use a second opinion.

Nesbit was nodding. "The murder charge against you has been dropped, Ms. Borne."

As I slumped into the nearest chair, Rudder came over and rather gently said, "Some of your prints on the murder weapon were found *underneath* the other prints. That indicates that, as you said, you had picked up the tool earlier at the auction, and others had handled it subsequently."

Swallowing thickly, I said, "Thank you, Sheriff, for clearing me."

"Oh, he had nothing to do with it," Mother chirped. "Before he left town, Tony sent the tool to the CDC in Des Moines for further forensic evaluation."

My guy had come through for me!

Mother touched my shoulder. "There, there, dear," she soothed. "No need for tears."

I said, "You know what, Mother? The girls just made me top dog."

Mother said, "Ah! No wonder you're teary eyed! As a former top dog myself, I can well understand your disappointment in leaving such an honor behind."

As Rudder and the DA exchanged wide-eyed looks, I asked, "Can I go?"

The sheriff nodded.

Shortly—having traded my orange jumpsuit for a change of fresh clothes Mother had brought me (*not* a little black dress this time), and with my cell phone and Fitbit watch back in my possession—I was behind the wheel of the C-Max in the police lot.

I didn't ask Mother how the car had gotten here, or what the blond wig and an extra coat of mine were doing in the backseat, as the answers would no doubt disturb me.

I just wanted to get home, see Sushi, and crawl into my own bed.

When we entered the foyer, the little darling was so happy to see me that she piddled on the wooden floor, then leaped into my arms and licked my face ferociously.

Rocky, who I had forgotten was a houseguest, was more subdued, giving me a few welcoming barks, keeping clear of the puddle on the floor, making it clear that wasn't his doing.

"Are you hungry, dear?" Mother asked.

"Just tired," was all I could manage.

I put Sushi down and trod up the stairs. In the bathroom, I took a long hot shower to wash all the jailhouse smell off, then put on some comfy pajamas and tumbled into bed. Sushi and Rocky joined me. I pulled Soosh to me, while Rocky settled at my feet. Sleep beckoned, and I was ready to submit.

But first, I reached for my cell phone, which I'd put on the nightstand, and sent Tony a text. **Thank you.**

Mid-morning, I was awakened by Sushi licking my face with such determination that I knew Mother had sent her to get me up for breakfast—another clue to her mission: the tantaliz-

ing aromas of coffee and bacon—and the little creature understood she wouldn't get any of it until I came downstairs.

But such prodding was unnecessary: Brandy was starving.

Before I got out of bed, however, I made it first. (You read me correctly.)

HOW TO MAKE YOUR BED WHILE YOU'RE STILL IN IT

1. Lie flat in the middle.
2. Spread your arms and legs as if you're about to make a snow angel, and straighten the sheet and bedcover.
3. Fold back the top of the sheet and cover.
4. Plump up the pillows behind you.
5. Then slip out of the bed. Voilà!

WARNING: May not be acceptable for soldiers in a barracks.

Mother always said that going to sleep in a made bed made for pleasant dreams. I'll get back to you on that one.

I slipped on a robe, then—with an impatient Sushi leading the way—hurried down the stairs in my bare feet. After a night in jail, this felt like sheer heaven.

As I entered the fifties-style kitchen, Rocky greeted me, and I scratched his head.

Mother, at the stove, turned. "And how did we sleep last night?"

"I don't know about you, but I slept just fine,"

I said. I gave her my best Bugs Bunny impression: "Uh . . . what's cookin', Doc?"

"An omelet," Mother said proudly. "Just like the one my dear grandma-mah used to make for me."

As I mentioned before, Mother had always been a wonderful cook of indigenous Danish dishes. Her culinary skills were excellent, as long as she stuck to the recipe. Mine were spotty.

BACON AND EGG OMELET
(Flaeskeaeggekage)

(I can't pronounce it, either.)

½ pound sliced bacon
6 eggs
½ cup milk or cream
1 tablespoon all-purpose flour
1 tablespoon minced chives
½ teaspoon salt

Fry the bacon in a large skillet over medium heat until golden brown. Remove the bacon to a plate lined with paper towels and drain. Retain the bacon fat (no more than 3 to 4 tablespoons) in the skillet. Crumble the bacon and set aside.

Beat the eggs with the milk or cream, flour, chives, and salt in a medium bowl until well combined.

Heat the reserved bacon fat in the skillet over medium heat, and when it is hot, pour in the egg mixture. When the omelet begins to set,

sprinkle the reserved crumbled bacon on top.
Cook until golden brown. Fold the omelet and
serve hot.

Yield: *4 servings*

While Mother poured the egg mixture into
the hot skillet, I sat on our vintage red step-stool
chair to watch.

After a moment, I asked, "Did you speak to
Tony about the fingerprint evidence?"

Mother, vigilantly keeping an eye on the eggs,
said, "No, I didn't, dear. He was in route to New
Jersey but was keeping in touch with the CDC,
who told him of their findings . . . and that they
were forwarding the lab results to the county attorney." She used a spatula to fold the omelet.
"Of course, I hurried right down to the jail."

"Who drove our car there for you? Since
clearly, you're not allowed to drive."

"I plead nolo contendere. But, as it happens,
I essentially have been enjoying special dispen-
sation in that area."

I had no idea what she was talking about, and
had no desire to find out.

She scooped the omelet onto a dish and
handed it to me. "Here's a plate of heaven, dear."

"You're not having any?" I asked.

"I've already eaten. But I will join you in the
dining room for coffee. I have much to share
with you."

I sat at the Duncan Phyfe table, with a pot of
coffee, a pitcher of orange juice, crisp bacon,
toast, and the omelet before me, a virtual feast.

Mother, across from me, steaming cup of java in one hand, asked, "Did you learn anything in jail, dear? In regard to Camilla's murder?"

In between bites of the yummy omelet, I told her what Three-Fingered Frieda had told me, and my theory that Camilla might have been running a fencing operation with a man named Rodney Evans.

"Interesting," Mother replied, filing that away but making no further comment.

"What about you?" I asked. She'd said she had much to share. "Find out anything while I was doing hard time?"

"Well," she said cagily, "I had a most interesting conversation with the Romeos yesterday."

Mother had a love/hate relationship with those men. She loved them for giving her juicy information but hated that they knew so much information before she did.

She was saying, "Randall . . . You know which one *he* is, don't you, dear?"

"The pig-farmer guy?"

"Former farmer. Now, where was I? I'm afraid I've lost my train of thought. . . ."

Mother's preferred railway line was the Atchison, Topeka and Santa Fe, because she'd dreamed as a child of becoming a Harvey Girl.

"Randall," I prompted.

"Yes, Randall! He still lives on the farm next to Alma O'Grady, source of our infamous corn husker. He claims the old girl isn't the sweet innocent she appears to be."

"No kidding. What do we make of that?"

Mother took a sip of her coffee, then asked,

"Don't you think it's odd that the only prints on the corn husker belonged to you and Loretta Klein and Camilla? Shouldn't Alma's prints be on there, too? After all, she arranged the tools on the table."

"They'd been cleaned and oiled, remember?" I said. "Maybe she didn't want to get that stuff on her hands and wore gloves."

Mother grunted, not liking my answer—not liking any answer that contradicted her, actually. By way of revenge, she picked up an extra fork, leaned forward, and speared a piece of my omelet.

I asked, "Did Randall have anything else of interest to say?"

She swallowed the filched bite, then said, "Only that the corn husker was really his."

"What?"

"Seems Tom had borrowed it to show his tool club, and after his death, Alma neglected to give it back. In fact, *refused* to give it back. In addition, Randall has noticed strange comings and goings at her farm."

I snapped a slice of bacon in half and gave one piece to Sushi, the other to Rocky. "How so, strange?"

"That, my dear, is what we're going to find out."

"What? When?"

"Why, this morning, course."

Through a bite of omelet, I protested, "I'm in no mood! I just got out of stir!"

"Dear, it's off-putting when you speak with your mouth full."

"Look, give me a chance to relax under my own roof," I groused. "I don't want to go traipsing off on one of your wild-goose chases."

(Note to Editor from Vivian: *Can Brandy's use of the cliché "wild-goose chase" be changed in post? Sorry for the TV lingo. I mean, in editing? The girl simply can't learn to think outside the box!*)

I asked, "What about the shop?"

"Joe's on active duty until I give him his marching orders. And he's been doing a splendid job. Sales are doing fine."

"Good. Then I can stay here and relax after my ordeal."

Mother pushed back her chair and stood. "Dear, your ordeal has hardly begun. *Someone tried to frame you!* And that same someone attacked us both at Camilla's shop. Not to mention murdered your boyfriend's wife. Don't you want to catch that person, for what they put you, put *all* of us, through?"

"Of course," I admitted, then sighed. "When do you want to go to Alma's farm?"

"Soon. Very soon." She pointed a finger at the sky, or, anyway, the ceiling. "But first, let us repair to the incident room to fill out the suspect board."

The incident room, of course, was the music room/library/den; the suspect board—as previously mentioned—was the antique schoolroom chalkboard on wheels that she stored behind an old stand-up piano nobody played.

I sat in my usual spot on the piano bench, while Mother rolled out the board, then faced it, chalk in hand, a schoolmarm ready to write out a particularly tricky arithmetic problem.

A few minutes later she stepped aside for me to see what she had written.

SUSPECT LIST

Name	Motive	Opportunity
Alma O'Grady	?	?
Loretta Klein	?	?
Gerald Klein	?	?
Assailant	?	?
Phil Dean	?	?
Rodney Evans	?	?
The Mafia	?	?

"Well?" Mother asked.

"Well," I replied, "we've certainly had more to work with."

"Plenty of suspects, though!"

"Speaking of which, why is Mr. Klein on that list? *His* prints weren't on the corn husker."

"No. But we have to assume that if his wife is a suspect, he might be involved, too. Guilty until proven innocent, I always say."

"Not exactly the American way," I said, "but for our purposes, I'd have to agree. But, Mother, *Phil?*"

Mother relayed what Vern had told her about the mustached hundred-dollar bill that his bank teller niece gave to Phil—a bill only to be deposited a few hours later . . . by Camilla.

"All right. Leave Phil on," I said. "But the *Mafia?* Really?"

"Dear," Mother replied, "it would appear—based upon a snippet of conversation I overheard between Officers Shultz and Kelly—that a new drug connection has appeared in our fair city, despite the diligence of our esteemed chief of police."

"And you think *Camilla Cassato* might have been this connection?"

"It's within the realm of possibility."

The idea seemed far-fetched at best; at worst, Mother was padding her suspect list.

I was shaking my head. "Why would Camilla do business with the very people who caused the breakup of her marriage to Tony, forcing them into Witness Protection under threat of death?"

Mother shrugged. "Why, to get back at Tony, dear. He's got a new life, new job, new love, and she's been left behind. Why else would Camilla have moved here?"

"Because she still loved him."

"Did she, dear? Besides, love and hate quite often overlap. Two sides of the same coin." Mother replaced the chalk on the lip of the board. "Now, let us pay Alma a surprise visit!"

I went upstairs to get dressed.

It had snowed overnight, nothing substantial, just a nice sparkly dusting of white to decorate the dull brown of the landscape.

In the car we rode in silence for a while, but as I turned west, out into the country, I again expressed my doubt that Camilla could ever have been a conduit for Mafia drugs. Perhaps I just didn't want to believe her capable of that. Or perhaps I couldn't stand the thought of what it would do to Tony.

Mother shrugged and said, "Well, there's one way we can settle it."

"How is that?"

She removed her cell phone from her purse. "I'll call my friend, the retired don."

"You have the New Jersey *godfather* on *speed dial?*" I asked, eyes bugging at her.

Mother was tapping the screen. "Why not? We've kept in touch since New York. Watch the road, dear. It looks slick."

Through her phone I heard the voice of an elderly yet strong male. "Vivian! Is that you?"

"It is indeed. I hope my call finds you in fine fettle."

"My fettle is as fine as the next man's. And you, Vivian?"

"Top of the world, looking down on creation!" Her tone turned serious. "Don, my daughter and I could use your help."

"Of course! Shoot."

The godfather's response was a little unsettling.

"As it happens," Mother said, "we're playing sleuth on yet another murder case."

"The Camilla Cassato killing?"

"How ever would you know about that? A murder in a little backwater like Serenity!"

"I have my ways. And I've heard your daughter, Brandy, was charged, then released, as well. How can I be of help?"

"I'd like to know if Camilla was doing business with anyone in your, uh, former field of endeavor."

"Not family business, my dear, or I'd know. At least not immediate family."

"How about your . . . extended family?"

A pause. An unsettling pause.

Then "Let me make some calls to a few relatives, and I'll get back to you."

"Thank you, Don," Mother cooed. "You're a dear."

"Enjoying the Caddie?"

Before we left New York, the don had presented Mother with a 1960s black Cadillac convertible, complete with tail fins and a red interior, after our old Buick died on the West Side Highway. Unfortunately, the Caddie had had a run-in with a Learjet that was taking off and had lost (*Antiques Swap*).

"Oh," Mother said innocently, "we're not driving it this winter."

Not exactly a lie.

"Sure, sure . . . It's not convertible weather here, either. Say, when can you come and see me? I could use somebody who can give me a run for it, playing scrabble."

Mother blushed, then lowered her voice. "Perhaps after this case is put to bed."

He said something that I couldn't make out, and Mother giggled in a schoolgirl way, then ended the call.

I smirked. "Scrabble?"

"It's a perfectly fine game, dear."

"Strip Scrabble, maybe?"

"There's no such thing, that I know of."

"Anything else you'd like to share with me about your Sicilian game mate?"

"I don't believe so," she replied airily. "Ah, we're almost there."

The lane to Mrs. O'Grady's farm appeared, and I turned off the gravel road and onto it, the tires skidding a little on the frozen snow.

As the white two-story house with its quaint latticework came into view, I asked, "What's the plan? I mean, we're not exactly here to borrow a cup of sugar."

"I'll come up with something," Mother said. "I'm well trained in the art of improv."

"Well, you'd better come up with something wonderful right away."

Three vehicles were parked in front of the house: a dented Ford pickup, a rusted Jeep Cherokee, and an SUV with a mismatched side door.

I pulled the C-Max alongside the pickup and shut off the engine. "Well?" I asked Mother. "What wonderful thing did you come up with?"

"When Alma comes to the door," she replied, eyes narrowed, "I'll say we lost our way and need directions."

"That's it?"

"It's plenty!"

"She'll never believe that."

Mother turned over a hand. "Then I'll say we're knocking on doors for charity."

"What charity? Anyway, why didn't we just call

her first? Why any kind of ruse at all? Tell her we're looking into Camilla's murder and have a question or two. About the corn husker, maybe."

Mother twisted to look at me. "You're overly critical today, aren't you, dear?"

"Why knock on her door at all? If something odd *is* going on, why give her a chance to hide it?"

"What are you suggesting?"

I shrugged. "What's wrong with just peeking in a window?"

Mother smiled at me in pride. "You're becoming quite the sleuth, dear. Which window?"

"I don't know. One where we won't be seen."

"Splendid. Let's go."

We got out of the car, quietly closed the doors, and made our way in the snow around the side of the house to a first-floor window.

The shade was down, but not all the way, leaving a gap of about three inches. Mother and I were leaning in to peer through the window when a gruff voice behind us demanded, "What the hell do you think you're doing?"

We both jumped, then turned to face a bearded man of about fifty, wearing a stained canvas jacket, worn blue jeans, and a stocking cap.

He also had a rifle—pointed right at us.

"We're here to borrow a cup of sugar!" Mother blurted.

Something wonderful right away, huh? If I hadn't been so scared, I might have kicked her.

The man made a quick gesture toward the house with the barrel of the rifle. "You two better come with me."

A Trash 'n' Treasures Tip

When looking for an appraiser to value your antiques and collectibles, find someone who is an expert in that particular area. If said expert seems to be lowballing you and then gives you an offer, find another expert.

Chapter Seven

Blackboard Bungle

While the bearded man pointed a rifle at our backs, Mother and I—our hands up like we were outlaws this mountain man had rounded up—trudged glumly up the porch steps to Mrs. O'Grady's farmhouse.

When we reached the front door, he said gruffly, "Inside, you two!"

Mother glanced over her shoulder at him. "Just barge right in?"

"Do it!"

I turned the knob, and we were marched into an entryway that became a central hall, where the welcoming aroma of freshly baked chocolate chip cookies met us, seeming at odds with our dire situation.

"Alma!" the man called out. *"Alma!"*

From the back of the house came the scurry of the diminutive mistress of the house, drying her hands on a kitchen towel. "What in heaven's name is the hubbub, Carl?"

The apple-cheeked widow stopped short at the sight of Mother and me being held at gunpoint.

"Oh, my!" she said, the towel dropping from her hands, fluttering to the floor like a damp angel.

"Found these two peekin' in a window," Carl said, then gestured to me with the rifle barrel. "Ain't the young one who they sent to jail for murder? Must've escaped."

"The charge was dropped," I said defensively. "Call Sheriff Rudder if you don't believe me."

Mrs. O'Grady's eyes went questioningly to Mother.

"That's right, my dear," Mother said with a smile and a nod. "Brandy was released late yesterday afternoon. She's been cleared, believe you me."

"I do believe you, Vivian," the woman said.

But Carl didn't seem ready to lower his rifle just yet, demanding, "Then what was you two sneakin' around for?"

Fearful that Mother might repeat her sugar routine, I said somewhat lamely, "We saw you had company and didn't want to interrupt. I guess we should have knocked."

The sugar bit suddenly seemed to have merit.

"Just a couple of snoops, I'm afraid," Mother added, doing her best to look embarrassed (she doesn't really have the capacity to be embarrassed).

"Well, now that you're here," Mrs. O'Grady said, with a smile so sweet it seemed somehow sinister, "why don't you girls join our little group? We'll be having refreshments soon."

Chocolate chip cookies sprinkled with rat poison, perhaps?

Suddenly, to the right, the double doors to the parlor parted, and a face popped out, and the eyes in the face popped, too, in obvious response to the rifle.

Cora Vancamp, a retired high school counselor who once told me I'd never amount to much, said, "Alma, if you've been detained, I can take over the prayer group for you, if you like."

"If you would," our hostess replied with a nod. "I may be a few minutes at that."

Mrs. Vancamp gave me a mildly reproving look; then her head disappeared and the doors came together again. Maybe she was right about how I'd turned out.

Frankly, I wasn't sure which surprised me more: that Mother and I had mistaken a Bible group for a cabal of thieves, or that Cora Vancamp had so readily accepted seeing us being held at gunpoint.

"Carl," Mrs. O'Grady said kindly to our rifle-wielding escort, "thank you for your concern, but there's no real problem here. You can go now."

He frowned, head tilting like that of a dog

trying to understand its master. "You sure 'bout that, Alma?"

"Quite sure. Vivian and Brandy are old friends of mine."

Carl let out a skeptical sigh but finally lowered the gun. "Okay, then . . . but I'll be around if you need me. Just let out a scream or somethin'."

"I'll do that, Carl. Thank you."

Finally, he went out, grumbling to himself and casting suspicious glances at us over his shoulder.

Mrs. O'Grady told us, "Really, Carl's a peach."

More like the pits, I thought.

Mother said, "I'm sure he is. However, he doesn't present himself terribly well."

Mrs. O'Grady chuckled. "You know how these eccentric old farmers are. But he does odd jobs for me in exchange for hunting on my property."

Hence the rifle.

Mrs. O'Grady clasped her hands. "Now, what's on your mind, Vivian? I know you well enough to figure you didn't ride all the way out here on a whim. Must be important. Come have some cookies and tea."

She turned, and we followed her back to a cozy country kitchen, where wicker baskets displayed on cupboard tops seemed to be a passion, as did geese, an army of which were marching around the room on the border of the yellow-and-white wallpaper.

Mother and I sat at a rustic oak table, while

Mrs. O'Grady put the cookies on a plate. I'd let Mother eat one first.

"How do you take your tea?" she asked. We told her, and in a moment she was back with two steaming cups, placing them in front of us.

Taking the chair next to Mother, Mrs. O'Grady asked, "Now, what brought you girls out here to see me?"

Mother, shifting in her chair, demurred. "I'd rather not say. It would get a certain person in trouble."

I, not feeling demure-ish, blurted, "It was that pig-farmer neighbor of yours who sent us off on this wild-goose chase."

(Note to Editor from Vivian: *I will not protest the use of the cliché, since it fits in with the cliché decor. And, anyway, a cliché in dialogue is rather more acceptable. Just a word to the wise!*)

"Ah," Mrs. O'Grady said with a mild frown and a knowing nod. "And what unkind words did Randall have to say about me?"

"I would prefer not to repeat such things," Mother said, which was one of the most ridiculous things a gossip like her could say.

On the other hand, perhaps Mother was reluctant to jeopardize her friendship with Alma O'Grady (herself a possible source of gossip). Whatever the case, I decided to fill our hostess in.

When I'd finished, she said, a little stiffly, "Regarding the nature of the vehicles that come up and down my lane, our prayer group consists of older women who don't care to drive their expensive Cadillacs and Lincolns out in the country in bad weather, so they carpool in vehicles with four-wheel drive. I'm sorry their mode of transportation isn't more to Randall's liking."

Since I was stuffing a warm, gooey cookie in my mouth, Mother replied, "It was an unfair assumption on his part."

Of course, it was an assumption that Mother had accepted at face value.

"And as to his assertion that the corn husker in question was *his*," Mrs. O'Grady continued, chin up, "the operative word here is 'was,' since Randall gave the tool to my husband as a gift shortly before Tom died. So, naturally, when my 'good neighbor' asked for it back a few days after the funeral—a really offensive thing to do, in my opinion—I refused."

"Seems odd he would lie about it," I said as gently as possible.

The woman sighed. "Not when you consider that he's been angry with me ever since I complained to the EPA about the terrible stench emanating from his hog farm. Honestly, half the time we couldn't have our windows open! Well, those governmental folks paid him a visit and found all kinds of violations, which Randall refused to address . . . and, consequently, they shut him down."

Mother shook her head sympathetically. "And here Randall always claimed he walked away from the pig biz because he'd wearied of it." She reached for Mrs. O'Grady's hand. "Alma, dear, I do hope you'll understand our misplaced zeal. As you may suspect, we're investigating Camilla Cassato's murder and have to follow up every lead we get, however slim it might seem."

This was as close to an apology as I'd ever heard Mother make.

"I understand," Mrs. O'Grady said, then smiled, just a little. "But I'd appreciate it if you'd take me off your list of suspects."

Mother placed splayed fingers to her chest. "Why, Alma, dear, you were never on it!"

I hoped Mrs. O'Grady didn't come around to our house and peek through the window. She might see the blackboard, where she was first on the list.

Mother was saying, "You see, dear, we just needed to clear up some loose ends."

Mrs. O'Grady was frowning, in thought.

"Something on your mind, dear?" Mother asked.

She sighed. "As a matter of fact, yes. You mention loose ends. This might . . . just *might* . . . be pertinent to your case. . . ."

Mother sat forward, a cat that had spied a mouse. "Do proceed, by all means!"

Mrs. O'Grady raised a forefinger. "After you and Brandy left the auction on Sunday, I saw your producer—that out-of-town man with the beard?—having a somewhat surreptitious conversation with Camilla outside, by her car. I couldn't hear what they were saying, but it became *quite* heated."

Mother said, "That's Phil Dean. He was probably telling Camilla to stay away from the filming."

"I don't think so," Mrs. O'Grady countered. "Because they started out quite friendly, and one would think he'd have laid into her immediately if such were the case." She shrugged. "Anyway, for what it's worth, that was my impression."

"It may be worth a good deal, Alma," Mother replied. "Thank you for sharing."

Mrs. O'Grady let out a massive sigh. "Well, I must get back to the prayer group," she said. Then, bright eyed, she added, "Would you care to join us?"

I held my breath. Mother was capable of accepting, just to stay on Mrs. O'Grady's good side or, anyway, get back on it. And she was also capable of upstaging God Almighty, should the prayer meeting inspire her. Thankfully, she declined, stating we had an appointment to keep.

We thanked our hostess for the tea and cookies and took our leave.

Outside, by the car, I grumbled, "Well, she sure turned out to be a pickled herring."

"That's red herring, dear," Mother said, unperturbed by our (her) waste-of-time blunder. "Even the greatest detectives—Holmes, Poirot, Wolfe—go down the occasional blind alley. Anyway, we got a new lead out of it."

"Phil?" I grunted. "Don't be silly."

She swung toward me. "Dear, you must keep an open mind and a sunny disposition."

"I'll put you in charge of that." I turned to her. "Please tell me you were fibbing about having another appointment."

"No, dear." She checked her wristwatch. "Tilda is expecting us shortly."

Remember Matilda "Tilda" Thompkins? The New Age guru we'd had on our show, whose questionable talents Mother was convinced had helped crack several cases of ours?

I asked, "Why'd you set up a meeting with her, of all people?"

Mother raised a forefinger. "Because, my dear, Tilda should be able to regress me to the evening that we broke into Camilla's shop. Under her expert hypnosis, I hope to recall something about our assailant that has eluded us till now."

I rolled my eyes. "Okay. I'll take you there, but I'm not coming in for the floor show."

"But I need you to record what I say!" Mother protested. "You know that I never remember what I say or do while in a trance."

I might argue that she was in a trance more or less all the time, but I let it go.

I twisted toward her in the car. "Isn't it strange how every time you go under, out pops another one of your former lives! Just dripping with history!"

Mother, in addition to being Iras, Cleopatra's handmaiden, in 44 BC (in charge of the Egyptian queen's asps), had been around in 1615 AD as Matoaka, the younger sister of Pocahontas, with whom John Smith was *really* in love . . . or so Mother/Matoaka claimed. And who are we to contradict her?

"There will be no historical side trips, no matter how interesting they might be," Mother assured me. "This time I'll be able to give Tilda a specific date, time, and place."

"Well . . . okay. But don't expect me to buy it if you turn out to be Anne Boleyn's hairdresser or Davy Crockett's Indian guide."

"Understood . . . though wouldn't that be fascinating?"

I sighed and started the car. (You may think I report my sighing too frequently, but I assure you the bulk has been edited out.)

Tilda lived across from the Serenity cemetery, in a white two-story clapboard house that could nowadays be called shabby chic, though the emphasis here was on shabby. Mother's favorite guru/hypnotist might also be psychic, because she opened her door before we'd had a chance to ring the bell.

The slender, forty-something female, with long golden-red hair and translucent skin and a scattering of youthful freckles across the bridge of her nose, wore Bohemian attire, as she did no matter what the season: long madras skirt, white peasant blouse, and Birkenstock sandals (though she did add socks in winter).

We moved past Tilda's graciously gesturing hand into a mystic shrine of soothing candles, healing crystals, and swirling mobiles of planets and stars—much of it for sale. Incense hung in the air like a fragrant curtain, and from somewhere drifted the tinkling sound of New Age music. The room served as a living space, waiting area, and shop.

And did I mention she had cats? She had cats. Lots of them—perched on the couch (seat and back) and every chair, and on the windowsills. Nor were these your ordinary, run-of-the-mill felines, but rather reincarnations of dead humans.

Tilda sincerely believed that spirits from the

cemetery across the way who still had issues and hadn't "moved on" often floated across the street and took up residence in her assorted cats. She claimed that after a burial, a new cat would simply appear on her porch, and when she opened the door, it would trot right in, as if having lived there for years (and then would).

I knew some of the animals by name—Eugene Lyle Wilkenson, Constance Ruth Penfield, Franklin "Frankie" Carlyle, Cheryl Jean Steward—having known them in life. This didn't stop me from shooing them off the couch, even Frankie Carlyle, though he had been a bully and might bite.

"You've caught me at a propitious time," Tilda said, addressing us in her husky, sensual voice. "I can schedule you in between my tantric sex class and chakra session."

While I was trying to process that, Mother chirped, "How lovely when the stars align."

Would it be unkind of me to remind her that it was still daytime and the stars wouldn't be aligning for some time?

"So, ladies," Tilda asked, hands fig-leafed before her, "how may I be of service?"

Mother frowned. "Didn't I make myself clear on the phone? I need you to regress me again!"

Tilda sucked in air sharply. "Oh, dear! The last time we simply couldn't get rid of Madame Curie's talkative cook, and I am on a tight schedule."

(I forgot to mention Mother had prepared meals for the famous female scientist, including suggesting to the madam's husband the basic notion of pasteurization.)

Mother produced a paper from her coat pocket and handed it to Tilda. "I've written down just what you need to know, so that I go back only a week."

"That should be very helpful," Tilda replied, then raised a conditional finger. "But *should* a former life appear and refuse to move along, you and it will have to attend the pending chakra session. Come!"

We followed Tilda, who moved with ethereal, dreamy grace, back to the kitchen, off of which was a small, dark, claustrophobic room.

The single window had been shuttered, and the only source of light came from a table lamp, the revolving shade, with its cutout stars, sending its own galaxy swirling on the ceiling.

Mother stretched out on a red-velvet Victorian fainting couch, while Tilda took an ornate straight-back chair next to her. I sat on a little stool behind Tilda, cell phone in hand, ready to record Mother's every utterance.

Tilda, with Mother's handwritten instructions on her lap, reached for a long gold-chained necklace with a round, shiny disk, which was resting on the table next to the lamp. Dangling the jewelry before Mother's face, Tilda started to swing it like a pendulum.

"Watch the medallion, Vivian," Tilda said softly. "Consider its gentle motion. Surrender to its gentle motion. . . ."

Mother's eyes moved back and forth, as if she were viewing a tennis match.

"You feel relaxed . . . so very relaxed," Tilda cooed. "You're getting sleepy . . . so very sleepy."

As Tilda repeated this, every phrase progressively slower, ever more soothing, Mother's eyelids fluttered.

"Your eyelids are heavy . . . so very heavy . . . so heavy that you simply can't keep them open."

Mother's eyes closed.

"I'm going to count backward from ten to one. When I say 'one,' Vivian, you will be asleep, completely, deeply asleep. Ten . . . nine . . . eight . . ."

At "five," Mother's body went limp, but Tilda finished the count. At this point Mother proved she really was deeply asleep by beginning to snore. The kind of snoring that can riffle roof tiles.

To Tilda, I said, "She's had a busy day."

"No matter," the hypnotist said and withdrew the swinging necklace from in front of Mother's face and sat back, then consulted the notes in her lap.

"Vivian," the guru/hypnotist began, "I want you to go back to—"

But that's as far as Tilda got, for Mother, in a deep voice and her patented British accent, said, "*Greetings*! I am Myles Carter, personal attendant to King George the Third, defender of the realm, king of Great Britain, France, Ireland, and Hanover."

"Oh, for pity's sake," I muttered.

"I like to think of myself as more than a valet, in fact, as a trusted, valued confidant. Just today I was advising His Majesty to hold firm with these uppity colonists. Their threats of revolution are merely empty poppycock!"

At least she'd stopped snoring.

Tilda leaned toward Mother/Myles. "Mr. Carter, we need to speak to Vivian. Return Vivian to us, sir."

"Very good, madam," he replied stiffly. "I have a wig to powder, anyway!"

Mother's face relaxed.

I could hardly believe the guru/hypnotist had gotten rid of King George's manservant so quickly, but then, I guess, he was used to taking orders.

"Vivian?" Tilda ventured. "Are you with us?"

"I am," Mother replied in her normal voice.

"Last week," the hypnotist said, consulting Mother's paper, "you and your daughter were in Camilla Cassato's antiques shop, sleuthing. Suddenly a man appeared. I want you to recall the moment just before he pushed you. Can you do that?"

"Yes."

"He is standing very close to you. Can you see him?"

Mother, eyes closed, shook her head. "No. Too dark."

"What are you hearing?"

Mother frowned. "Heavy breathing. A *man* breathing."

"Anything else?" Tilda prompted.

"A paper crinkling."

"Can you see the paper?"

"No," Mother replied.

"What are you smelling?"

Mother's nose twitched. "Cologne."

"Is it familiar?" Tilda asked.

Mother nodded.

"Had you smelled it before?"

Mother nodded.

"Is it a common brand?"

Mother shook her head.

"Can you attach a face to it?"

"I think so. Yes. Yes, I can."

I sat forward on the stool.

Tilda asked, "Whose face do you associate with that cologne?"

"Our producer," Mother said. "Phil Dean."

A short time later, Mother and I sat in the car in front of Tilda's house while I played back the recording of her session on my cell phone.

After it concluded, neither of us spoke for several minutes; I was grappling with the idea that the mystery man who had attacked us was the producer/director of our show . . . and our friend. I imagined Mother was doing the same.

What she said, however, was, "Really? So I was Myles Carter, personal attendant to King George the Third, defender of the realm, king of Great Britain, France, Ireland, and Hanover?"

"Will you forget about that?" I said. "The question is, what papers was Phil after that night at Camilla's shop?"

Mother frowned. "Whatever they were, they must have been important enough for him to break in and try to get them."

"Could *Phil* have killed Camilla?" I asked, then said incredulously, "How could that even be possible? We're talking about Phil here, one of the nicest guys we know!"

"Dear," Mother replied, "how often do the friends or relatives or neighbors of a murderer go on television and say, 'So-and-so was such a nice person'? To which I say, if they murdered someone, apparently, they're not that nice!"

"If Phil did kill Camilla," I said, accepting that jarring possibility just for the sake of argument, "why didn't he take the papers, then?"

"Probably because he didn't have time after you came along."

"Oh. Right. Duh. Then . . . what now?"

"Now we go to the editing suite," Mother said, "and talk to Phil about all of this. Give him a chance to explain himself."

"I don't know about that, Mother. If our producer friend *did* murder Camilla, and we confront him, who's to say we wouldn't be putting ourselves in harm's way?"

Mother thought a moment. "We'll take some protection along."

"What? A rolling pin from our kitchen? We certainly don't own any guns."

"No," she said, with the kind of twinkle in her eye that could mean trouble, "but we do have Rocky and Sushi."

Actually, that wasn't a bad idea at all. Rocky was a trained attack dog who had once come to our rescue, and Sushi's little teeth were sharper than a Ginsu knife.

I started the car and pointed it in the direction of home, where we stopped only long enough to pick up the two dogs, who typically were both eager to be leaving the house. And I didn't collect a rolling pin or a Ginsu knife, either.

The editing suite where Phil worked was located in a residential area four blocks from the downtown proper, in a turn-of-the-last-century school that had originally been built for grades K through 12. Over the years, as the town grew, the austere three-story tan-brick school with bell tower had been appropriated as a middle school, then a high school, and finally a community college, and ultimately, it had been abandoned when a new complex of higher learning was built on the west side of town.

The old school, having fallen into disrepair, had been slated for demolition when Mother and her cronies from the Serenity Historic Preservation Society approached a few pillars of the community. They successfully made a proposal to turn the former school into office space using the original classrooms, thus saving the building's internal structure. Today, Serenity City Center, as it is now called, is home to a wide variety of small businesses, including a beauty salon, insurance agency, chiropractic office, music store, jewelry repair outlet, coffee shop, gift store, and, of course, editing suite.

The suite was on the second floor, room 202, and Mother and I, with Rocky and Sushi on respective leashes, climbed the wide wooden staircase, whose old floorboards creaked with our weight, echoed by the creaking of Mother's knees.

As we approached the room, Phil's voice could

be heard behind the closed door, and Mother, not standing on ceremony, walked right in.

Our producer/director, in his standard attire of plaid shirt, jeans, and running shoes, was seated at a station of high-end computer monitors, cell phone to an ear. One of the screens had a frozen picture of me shoving Camilla at the tool auction.

Startled by the intrusion, Phil ended his cell phone call with "I'll talk to you later," then came out of the chair, hands open in greeting.

"Brandy," he said with a big smile, "I heard you'd been released. Wonderful news!"

My eyes were still riveted on the computer screen.

Phil glanced back at it, then at me. "Ah . . . now that the charge against you has been dropped, we can use the footage . . . which, of course, makes the network very happy." He laughed, not terribly convincingly. "The suits were more than a little nervous after you were arrested. Really, I thought they might cancel us, like that crazy little beauty-pageant kid or that ever-growing family with the sex scandal. But now, well, we're in a good position to get picked up for a second season . . . especially with all the publicity we've been getting."

Phil had a lot riding on our show, which was the first series he'd produced after many years as a cameraman. His reputation was on the line. His career, too.

I forced a smile. "Lot's been going on. Kind of surprising you haven't been in touch."

He made an embarrassed face. "Well, I should have been, to show support, but I figured the show was the last thing on your minds right now." He took in the two dogs. "Well, Sushi! Our little star. And who's her friend here?"

"This is Rocky," I said, nodding toward Mother and the animal on its leash. "The chief's dog. We're taking care of him while Tony's away."

"The chief's away? Oh, of course . . . the funeral." Phil came over slowly and extended one hand down for Rocky to sniff, which the dog perfunctorily did. Sushi, meanwhile, was shamelessly pawing at the producer's slacks for the treats he usually gave her on set.

Phil bent down to pat her head. "Sorry, girl. Don't have any goodies for you here."

Sushi's lower lip went over her teeth, her loyalty tested.

The producer/director straightened. "You're uncharacteristically quiet, Vivian. Something troubling you?"

"Yes, dear," Mother said. "I was wondering exactly what papers you took from Camilla's shop. And I do think you owe us something of an apology for your loutish behavior."

Phil's eyes widened, and his mouth dropped open. "Excuse me?"

I said, "We know it was you the other night."

"You wear a most distinctive cologne," Mother told him. "Hugo Boss, isn't it? You should probably wear a little less of the stuff, dear. Particularly when you're pulling a caper."

Phil returned to his chair, sat heavily, leaned

back, and looked at us woefully. "I won't lie to
you. It was me, all right. And I do owe you an
apology, a big one. And I'm sorry I pushed you
two. I hope neither of you was hurt."

When we didn't respond to his apology, Phil
went on, "I really was going to tell you, you
know, come clean now that Camilla is . . . gone."

"You mean dead," I said.

He sighed, gestured with a hand. "I had to
get a document back that she and I had signed."

"What kind of document?" Mother asked.

He shrugged. "A contract. You see, after the
ratings of *Antiques Sleuths* turned soft, I needed
to jazz things up a little. So I hired the Cassato
woman to cause trouble . . . paid her to run bids
up on you and, you know, generally be the bad
guy."

Mother asked, "How much did you pay her?"

"Five thousand a week."

"That's more than you're paying us!"

He shrugged again. "Not total."

I wasn't concerned about that. I was angry
about something else. "You were afraid that contract would surface and word would get out that
our 'reality' show was faked!"

Phil straightened in the chair and said defensively, "Nobody thinks these reality shows are
really reality! Do people think wrestling isn't
fixed?"

Mother blinked. "Wrestling is fixed?"

Phil ignored that. "Look, ladies, I was just
doing my job, trying to make *Antiques Sleuths* an
entertaining program. We all have a lot riding
on this."

"Enough riding," Mother said, "for you to kill Camilla?"

He came out of the chair. "*What?* No!"

Rocky stirred.

Mother raised one eyebrow. "Didn't Camilla approach you after the auction and tell you she wanted more money? And didn't she threaten to go public about the contract if you didn't give her that raise? Didn't you then go to her shop, see the corn husker on the counter, pick it up, and hit her with it?"

"*No!*" Phil said. "None of that happened!"

Rocky, hearing the volume and tone of the producer's voice, emitted a low growl. Sushi was cutting Phil more slack, still hoping for a treat.

Phil reduced his timbre. "I was right here, in the editing suite, the entire afternoon she died."

"Can you prove that?" I asked.

"I used the restroom in the hall. Others in the building may have noticed me. And, also, I made a few calls."

"On your cell," Mother said. "There's no landline here. Which means you could have made those calls from anywhere."

Phil pointed a finger at us, then quickly withdrew it when Rocky again growled.

"Vivian, Brandy," he said softly, "I'm not the one who broke into Camilla's shop. You did. *I* had a key."

Mother harrumphed. "That doesn't make your actions any more legally acceptable than ours!"

Phil raised an eyebrow. "Really? What if I hold the lease on the shop?"

"You're bluffing."

"No I'm not. I pay the rent and utilities. And I furnished the shop with all those antiques."

Mother and I stared at him. So did Rocky and Sushi.

I sputtered, "Don't tell me that you . . . *you* . . . brought Camilla to Serenity?"

Phil shook his head. "She was already in town, looking to start an antiques business to rival yours. That much was true. But she needed capital, and she needed merchandise."

"And you," I said, "needed to boost our ratings."

He didn't deny it.

"We were doing all right," Mother insisted, more than anything offended by his disparagement of the show.

"Doing all right isn't enough in this business," Phil said. "Again, think about wrestling—the good guys and bad guys. Our show needed a conflict—someone for the viewers to hate. While rooting for you, of course."

Mother, eyes narrowed, was nodding. "Makes sense."

"Mother!" I said.

"Phil makes a good point, dear," she said. Then to Phil, she exclaimed, "What if for season two we intersperse solving Camilla's murder with segments about antiques!"

"I'm getting out of here," I said with disgust. "Come, Sushi. . . . Mother! Bring Rocky."

But when I glanced back to see if Mother was coming, she was giving Phil a "Call me" gesture.

On the drive home our conversation was limited, to say the least.

I said angrily, "I can't believe that after what Phil pulled, you still want to work with him!"

"Dear, I was merely trying to placate the man. At the moment, remember, he is our number one suspect! On the other hand, my idea for the second season does have merit."

"If I have anything to say about it, there won't *be* a second season!"

When we entered the house, Rocky and Sushi were the first to notice something was wrong. They began prowling around the living room, sniffing the air, the furniture, the rug, as if another dog had been here, encroaching on their mutual territory.

Mother, in the foyer, removing her coat, asked, "What's bothering those two?"

I gave the room a hard stare. Everything seemed to be there, but on closer look, a few things appeared to have been moved.

"Someone's been here," I announced.

Mother took a few steps into the room. "Good gracious, I think you're right! We've been burgled while we were gone."

For the next half hour we checked over the house to see what had been taken—me upstairs, Mother down—then reconvened in the living room.

Mother, hands on hips, announced, "The back door was forced open, but nothing seems to be missing down here. Well? Anything gone from upstairs?"

"All my good jewelry is still in the case—even

my wedding ring." Yes, I had kept it after my divorce. Only fools throw diamonds off bridges.

"I couldn't find anything missing, either," Mother said, puzzled. "Even our sterling silver flatware is secure."

"Something *was* destroyed, though," I said.

"Good heavens, what?"

"That large needlepoint picture hanging in your room, the one with the ornate frame. I found it on the floor, pulled apart, almost as if someone trashed it in anger."

Mother was frowning. "Dear, are you sure you don't remember seeing that frame anywhere in Camilla's shop? The one she bought at Klein's?"

"I'm sure it wasn't there." Then, "Why would the burglar think *we* had it?"

"No idea," Mother admitted. "But you *were* in her store that afternoon. Perhaps our intruder thinks you took it." She put a finger to her lips. "I wonder what's so important about that frame. . . ."

I glanced around at our mildly invaded home. "Mother, do you think we should call the police?"

"No, dear. This is *our* case, after all."

"But what if the burglar comes back?"

"We have the dogs. I'm sure we'll be safe."

Maybe so—but I kept the house lights burning all night.

A Trash 'n' Treasures Tip

When hiring an appraiser, tell him or her the reason for the appraisal and whether the item or items will be used for tax purposes, as a charitable contribution, or as a gift. The purpose of the appraisal can affect the outcome of the assessment, as certain rules and conditions apply. Mother's affection for a paperweight made from the ashes of Aunt Olive had little impact upon its appraised value.

Chapter Eight

Darkest Before the Don

Aside to reader from Brandy: Today I'll be helping Joe out at the shop, because Saturdays tend to be very busy. Mother, without a doubt, will be taking advantage of my absence to do her own investigating, which she's always been very secretive about, either leaving her cell phone at home or turning it off.

But today I'll know exactly where she goes!

Several weeks ago, I was looking for a little bathroom reading (if you'll forgive the indelicacy), and the only material I could find at such short notice was the current issue of Mother's *AARP* magazine, a periodical she claims not to be old enough to be receiving, but never mind.

Anyway, in the magazine was an article about

gadgets designed to assist "seasoned citizens," and among the gizmos listed was something called a PocketFinder. Basically, it's a little GPS disk that can be slipped into the pocket of anyone you wish to keep track of with the help of a computer or cell phone. This comes in handy particularly when a loved one with Alzheimer's or dementia might go wandering off. And while Mother certainly doesn't have Alzheimer's, she is clinically demented and, boy, does she go wandering off.

So I felt quite justified in sending for the device.

Last night, after she had gone off to bed, I sewed the two-inch disk into the lining of her coat, figuring she might find the PocketFinder if I slipped it in her pocket (even its name rather ambiguously suggests that result!). At any rate, now I'll be able to follow Mother's movements while I'm tending the till at the store.

I can't wait to spy on *her* for a change!

Dearest ones, this is you-know-who back at the helm, and with Brandy at the shop and out of my way, it's full steam ahead for the SS *Vivian Borne!*

When it comes to doing my own investigating, I've always believed in being an independent woman, relying on the kindness of strangers (or relatives) only when completely necessary. Therefore, when Brandy offered to drop me somewhere on her way to work, I declined. When I told her that *if* I decided to go anywhere today, I would get there myself, thank you, well . . . she had the tiniest self-satisfied smile on her face.

After the dear girl had gone her merry way (what was she so merry about?), and the sleeping dogs were happily entwined in a pool of sunshine on the living-room Persian rug, I shut down my cell phone, slipped it in my purse, grabbed my coat, hat, and gloves, and was out the door before you could say Jack Robinson—make that Jack Frost, considering the time of year. With my feet snuggled in a pair of Brandy's warm UGGs, I hurried along the sidewalk, boots crunching on a thin crust of overnight snow.

The traveling trolley, my usual mode of non-Brandy transportation, made regular stops about a block away and was due momentarily. The old gas-converted trolley car was provided free by the Downtown Merchants Association to encourage denizens of our fair city to shop with them, rather than their competition, the Serenity Mall. Since my investigations often took me downtown, the trolley was convenient indeed. But on the off-chance occasion that I needed to go elsewhere, I was usually able to convince the driver to veer off his or her main route by using (first) flattery, (second) pleading, and (third) blackmail. The third method was the least palatable, if the most effective, which is why I made it my business to know everything I could about the various drivers.

For a while I had been banned from riding the trolley after a freak accident had been laid at my feet—the trolley had swerved off the road and had hit a telephone pole, which had tipped over on a dry-cleaning establishment, whose roof had burst into flames. Since I am still in litigation with the owner of the dry cleaners, I cannot comment further on my supposed culpability, other than to say that if a person riding behind the driver suddenly burst into "The Trolley Song" (Judy Garland? *Meet Me in St. Louis*?), the songbird/rider's enthusiasm about the mode of transportation should not have unnerved said driver, however much clanging and dinging and zinging might have been involved. Anyhoo, thanks to the publicity and popularity of our TV series, the ban had lately been lifted off my trolley traveling.

The trolley arrived, and the doors opened to reveal a new driver (thankfully less nervous than the former one), and I was pleased as punch to see Vera Hornsby seated at the wheel. We're talking about a divorcée with so many skeletons in her closet, she could haunt a house . . . and easily be persuaded by yours truly to take me to the dreaded mall itself, without my even dipping into the A material. Or even the B.

"Well, hello, Vera," I said sweetly. "Lovely winter day, don't you think?"

Vera was a bottled blonde somewhere in the thirties range, whose attractiveness was sabotaged by an abundance of makeup.

Eyeing me warily, she said only, "Vivian."

Though this was hardly an answer to my friendly question, I headed past her toward the back of the trolley, where—should I have an uncontrollable urge to sing again—I would not likely inspire any alarm on the part of the driver.

I was the sole trolley rider at this hour of the morning, too late for downtown employees, who were at work by now, and too early for shoppers, who would find most stores not quite open yet and had no desire to wait out in the cold.

Taking a center-aisle window seat, I settled in for the relatively short ride downtown, then began to search my coat pockets.

You are correct if you have already deduced that I knew all about the PocketFinder and my dear deluded daughter's attempt to follow my tracks. When I recently perused a certain issue of the *AARP* magazine—why on earth do they insist on sending it to me!—I discovered that someone had circled the GPS apparatus with a pen. Since I doubted that Sushi had done it, that left little Brandy.

I, of course, didn't know when she might plant it on me, although just the other day I'd spotted her snatching a small package from the mail and spiriting it away. And then her little smug smile this morning provided all the confirmation I needed. (She telegraphs everything. It's a little late to mention this, but if parenthetical asides rub you the wrong way, you're reading the wrong book.)

I do have to give the girl credit for hiding the thingie in my coat lining, though I, of course, soon found and removed it, then placed the device on the floor beneath my seat. The PocketFinder would have a gay (in the traditional sense) old time riding the trolley around and around all day long! Let's see who's smirking now.

The trolley made its first downtown stop at the courthouse, a beautiful Grecian structure—Brandy has termed it rococo, but she's wrong—within which the people who work there all want air-conditioning and keep trying to get the building torn down and replaced with something modern. *Not on my watch!* (The courthouse employees have been quiet of late. Things always settle down in the winter months, when the old furnace is chugging along nicely.)

After tossing Vera a cheery "Toodles," I disembarked, then hoofed it over two blocks to Hunter's Hardware, which I knew would already be open, because farmers get up at dawn, while even the roosters are still snoozing, to head into town for supplies (the farmers, not the roosters).

Hunter's was a uniquely Midwestern aberration: the front of the elongated store, which hadn't been remodeled since women wore bustles, retained its original tin ceiling and hardwood floor, yet the business carried everything one might expect of a contemporary hardware store. But in the back of the place was a bar offering hard liquor to hardworking men who stopped in for hardware, plus some not so hardworking men who liked hard liquor, too.

Perhaps it's no big surprise that the best-selling drink at Hunter's was the screwdriver, which allowed guilt-ridden patrons to honestly tell their significant others that they'd stopped in for one.

The proprietors were a middle-aged couple named Junior and Mary, who bought the business some years back with money Mary got from something that happened that I'm not allowed to mention anymore, or even hint at. (But you can read our earlier books to find out, as those volumes predate the injunction that spoiled our fun.)

Where was I? Ah, yes—the proprietors. Junior ran the bar, and Mary took care of the hardware customers, but recently she had put her foot down, not the prosthesis one, (newbies will just have to go back and read those earlier titles) and told Junior to find someone to replace her: she was staying home to watch her stories and game shows.

Enter Vivian. I recommended fellow trolley traveler Billy Buckly, who I knew was looking for work. He is the town's most popular and most famous little person (also its only little person) and had married the widow Snodgrass after a romance blossomed on the trolley when it braked suddenly and he flew through the air and landed in her lap. (He *was* from a long line of acrobats on his mother's side, going back to the original Barnum & Bailey Circus, and there are those who suspect he'd hit his target.) Anyway, although the widow Snodgrass was comfortable (both her lap and her bank account), Billy craved gainful employment ("I'm not cut out to be a kept man," he would say), and Junior took my advice and hired him.

But two problems presented themselves for Billy while running the hardware section: he couldn't reach anything on a shelf higher than five feet, and his stature sometimes made it hard for customers to spot him. So when Billy suddenly appeared from around a display or popped up on the stool behind the counter, he would occasionally startle a patron. There were those with heart conditions who complained of Billy-inspired palpitations. (I suggested to my friend that he might wear jingle bells on his shoes, by way of warning, which didn't go over so well; for a while he stopped speaking to me.)

On the other hand, Billy was a good-natured whiz at his work, and a considerable step up (so to speak) from the sour, lackadaisical Mary.

My destination was the bar area, and I breezed through the front of the store, not seeing Billy, although that didn't mean he wasn't around somewhere.

I found Junior polishing tumblers behind a well-scarred bar that could have told more stories than even *moi.* He was a paunchy, rheumy-eyed, mottled-nosed man in his late sixties, who all too obviously had spent his career frequently sampling his own liquid wares.

Sliding up on a torn leather stool, I said, "Fine morning, don't you think? Brisk!"

"'Lo, Viv," he replied. "Yeah, nice 'n' brisk. The usual?"

My usual was a Shirley Temple, a result of my learning the hard way that hard liquor doesn't mix with my medication. (A case in point is Kalamazoo, where once I found myself with no memory of how I'd arrived. Or why.)

"*Too* brisk outside for that, Junior," I said. "Give me a hot toddy, and hold the toddy." Which was basically hot tea with honey and lemon.

While making my alcohol-free libation, he

said, "Glad to hear your girl Brandy is out of the clink. Nobody really thought she killed that gal, anyway. I bet you're working on the case, though. Any leads yet?"

"Nothing so far," I said as he set the steaming glass tumbler in front of me.

"Say . . . did you hear about that jewelry store robbery in the Quad Cities?"

Since I didn't want to know about that, I said rather curtly, "Not interested."

"Since when doesn't crime interest you?"

"Too far off my beat."

This might (or might not) have hurt Junior's feelings, but I was not here to converse with him. He made a decent toddy-less toddy and was the best Shirley Temple man in town, but otherwise, he was less a help and more a hindrance in any investigation. Junior had simply lost too many brain cells to be a worthwhile snitch.

That left Henry, the only other patron in the bar, seated three stools down.

Henry was Hunter's perpetual stool warmer. Pushing sixty, slender, with silver hair and a beak nose, he had been a prominent surgeon, but his career had come to an abrupt halt when he botched an operation after taking a shot of whiskey to steady his nerves just beforehand. The patient recovered but was missing a kidney instead of the intended appendix. Henry had lost his license and had even done a little time.

Over the years Junior and I had tried to get Henry off the sauce, sometimes meeting with success, other times not. Our most recent victory was having Junior serve him nonalcoholic beer (oddly, Henry's speech remained slurred). This success became a "not," when Henry got wise to the ruse and went back on the hard stuff.

And yet, on the wagon or off, Henry was always my go-to informant, seated as he was quietly at the bar all day, soaking up not just booze but information, as he took in all the conversation around him while others ignored his presence, since he seemed as much a fixture as the scarred counter itself. And a paucity of brain cells seemed not to be problem.

I slid down a stool, keeping a vacancy between us.

"And how is Henry today?" I asked cheerfully.

He looked my way with bloodshot eyes. "Henry's hunky-dory."

"And isn't that a wonderful way to be." Never paid to pepper the man with questions right out of the gate, so I just sat there, quietly sipping my hot drink.

"That was a real s'rpise," Henry slurred.

"What was, dear?"

"That she went in th' bidness."

"Who, dear?"

"Chief's wife. Antique shop, downtown." He shook his head.

Of course, Henry was unaware that Phil Dean had been picking up the tab.

"Th' bidness is reaaal bad," he was saying.

"Not that I've noticed."

"Show of yours." Henry talked in a kind of shorthand, but I could follow it.

I said, "Yes, I suppose the popularity of our

show has helped keep the customers coming into our establishment."

"Kill the Wagners."

"Yes, well, the Wagners went under after mixing in reproductions with authentic antiques. No one likes to be fooled, dear."

The practice of combining craft items with antiques, though acceptable these days, rubs me the wrong way, too. Be one kind of store or the other, I say!

Henry paused between sips. "Kleins just hangin' on."

I nodded. "I admit I thought Gerald and Loretta had bitten off more than they could chew when they relocated to that big building. But with their auction sideline, they seem to be keeping their heads well above water."

"Net."

All right, sometimes the shorthand was too much for me.

I asked, "What about a net, dear?"

"Innernet. Savin' them."

"Ah," I said. "I suppose one *must* change with the times."

I just hoped Brandy and I would never have to sell our wares on eBay or otherwise online. Neither one of us could wrap a package worth a diddly darn.

I asked Henry, "Say, has our producer, Phil Dean, ever come in here and warmed a stool?"

He shook his head.

"What about the chief's wife?"

"Not fit fer females."

Well, what was I? Chopped liver?

I let that pass, however, and asked, "Have any strangers been asking about Phil or Mrs. Cassato . . . or me?"

"Nope."

"What about a man name of Rodney Evans? Ever hear of him, Henry?"

"Nope."

I glanced at the eavesdropping Junior, who just shrugged.

Since Henry seemed to be a bust in the information department, and I had another matter to attend to, I downed the rest of my hot-sanstoddy, threw a five-spot on the bar, then slid off my stool.

"Nice seeing you, gents," I said with a farewell salute, though, frankly, they hadn't been helpful at all.

As I passed through the front of the store, I spotted Billy Buckly seated on a stack of catalogs behind the counter at the cash register, and took the time to breeze over.

Billy was about forty but always looked rather youthful, in part because he shopped in the children's section at JCPenney.

"Well," he said with a big smile. "There's my benefactress!"

He seemed over the jingle-bell suggestion.

"How do you like your new position?" I asked him cheerfully.

"Well, I love, I love it, love it. Everyone is so friendly!"

"Wunderbar!" It occurred to me that my friend might be of some use here, because even more than Henry, Billy had his ears closer to the ground than anyone else. (I mean that figuratively, not literally. PC Police, call off your troops!)

Billy was something of an antiques buff himself, or rather a collectibles enthusiast. His specialty was *Wizard of Oz* movie material, because of his family connection. But he liked thirties and forties pop culture items in general and was nicely tied into the local collecting community. He was no stranger in the antiques shops and secondhand stores of the area.

I told Billy that I was looking for a particular picture frame, one that Camilla had bought at Klein's the day she died, but that seemed to be missing in action.

"I could ask around," Billy said, with a shrug. "And let you know if I find out anything."

"Thank you, Billy, my boy," I said, then continued along my way.

I had arranged a clandestine meeting with Heather, my current police department snitch. Since many of my past informants at the PD had been either fired or relocated after giving me confidential information, I knew the woman would get skittish if I kept her waiting for long. So I shook, shook, shook my booty, making the three-block trek to the Serenity Public Library in record time. Or at least in record time for someone with two hip replacements.

Usually, Heather and I would meet in the south stairwell of the library's attached underground parking garage. I had dubbed her "Deep Throat" because of the Woodward and Bernstein movie, until Brandy enlightened me as to what that term actually referred to (I was shocked, if intrigued). Since Heather has a somewhat husky·voice, I changed her code name to "Sore Throat," but perhaps that wasn't any less of a double entendre.

With the inclement weather, the garage might be doing a booming business, so earlier I'd suggested that Heather and I converge on the library's second floor, in the seldom visited literary section (what a shame!).

I was to go to aisle 821F and stop at book 812.08, *Girl Sleuth: Nancy Drew and the Women Who Created Her,* while Heather would be in the next aisle, 821G, at 839.822, *The Collected Ibsen.* We would then remove the aforementioned books and talk through the space created in the bookcase.

Don't you just love the Dewey decimal system? Well, you should! It was developed in the 1870s by Melvil Dewey, a founding member of the American Library Association. Nowadays, some libraries have abandoned the DDS for other book classification systems—which I find overly complicated—and I have lobbied to make sure our library is not among the unfaithful.

Still, I couldn't do anything about it when a computer replaced the library's grand old oak card catalog. It used to be such fun perusing the little long drawers with their stiff white index cards, through which hundreds and thousands of people over the years, eager for knowledge, had riffled (admittedly, some left cold and flu germs behind, and you sometimes got more than just knowledge).

I had tried to buy that card-catalog cabinet

from the library, because it would be perfect for storing all my little trinkets in, but the library board wouldn't sell it to me—sour grapes, sez I, after I opposed and helped defeat their expensive proposal for a new library. (The current facility is only thirty years old, and that's practically a baby in my book of buildings!)

(Note to Vivian from Editor: *Vivian . . . does this have anything to do with anything?*)

(Note to Editor from Vivian: *I am painting a picture, of setting, of color, of . . . I know, I know. Get on with the story.*)

After arriving at our prearranged spot, I removed 813.08 from the shelf, and after a moment—I cleared my throat to clue my accomplice in that I was in place—Heather, on the other side, removed 839.822. But her volume was much thicker (Ibsen wrote a lot of plays in his time!), so I had to take out another book in order to create an even-sized hole.

The only problem now was that Heather was shorter than me, which I hadn't taken into consideration, and I could see only the top of her head. Since I didn't want to bend my knees and compromise my replaced hips—nor did I wish to aggravate those knees, since my doctor had been talking about replacing *them*, as well—I whispered for Heather to stand on a few volumes of Shakespeare, whose works were nearby. I felt sure he wouldn't mind.

The top of Heather's head disappeared, then returned a few moments later, and I could see most of her auburn hair and all of her red-framed glasses.

"What have you got for me?" I whispered.

Her eyes looked left, then right.

(You may wonder why a former dispatcher, promoted to forensics, would take such a chance consorting with me, but Heather had admitted she felt responsible for Brandy's incarceration by failing to discover the fingerprint evidence, which later the CDC had . . . and once I knew the woman felt guilty, I ran with it!)

Heather whispered, "Something else the CDC found."

"Oh?"

"There was an unidentified partial print on the corn-husking tool."

"Meaning . . . ?"

"Meaning somebody handled it besides Brandy or Mrs. Klein or Mrs. Cassato."

"Did the CDC run the print through AFIS?" I asked. Automated Fingerprint Identification System. "Did *you*?"

"No."

"Why not, dear?" The "dear" had a bit of an edge to it, I admit.

Heather shrugged with her eyes. "AFIS doesn't accept partial prints, because they aren't admissible in court."

"*Is* there a program that accepts partial prints?"

"Actually, yes. There's one designed to create an algorithm that fills in what the rest of the print *might* be—based on minutia points, chain-code contours, and other patterns. But the results wouldn't be conclusive."

I filed this new information away, then asked, "Do you have access to that program?"

She hesitated. "Yes. But I don't see how that could help."

"If there is a match—however tenuous—it could point to Camilla Cassato's killer." Then I added, "Of course, then it would be up to me to find further evidence that *is* conclusive."

Heather sighed. "Okay. Okay. I owe you and your daughter this much. I'll run the partial print."

"Thank you," I said. "How long will it take?"

"A day, maybe two. But that will be the last contact between us, understood, Vivian? On this matter or any other."

"No problem," I replied, as if I really meant it. The old acting chops always come in handy! Anyway, was she kidding? Having a snitch on the forensics team was like striking gold!

The hole in the bookcase closed as *Ibsen* slid back into place. That was a lot of plays! Depressing ones, too.

I was a little bit stymied about what to do with myself for the rest of the afternoon. Henry had been a disappointment, and I had yet to hear back from my New Jersey friend, the don, and now I must wait on a report from Heather.

Waiting is not my strong suit. Action, action, action! That's the Vivian Borne way.

I left the library and perambulated toward Main Street. The sun had come out, melting what little snow there was on the sidewalks, while tiny icicles clung to tree branches drip, drip, dripping to the ground.

On impulse and a hunch, I crossed the alley-way that ran behind the late Camilla's store, hesitated, then turned down it, avoiding pothole puddles as I walked.

At the back door to Yesteryears, I halted, then looked to my left, at the rear of the apartment house across the way. Something caught my eye.

In an open window on the second floor was a Hispanic youth of perhaps twelve or thirteen, perched just inside the sill, a cigarette in one hand, as he sent smoke into the outside. He was staring at me.

The youth took a drag on the cigarette, blew more smoke out the window, and made a gesture with his head to the inside of the apartment. When I pointed to myself, he nodded, then disappeared from the window.

Perhaps the young man wanted my autograph. It does happen!

I retraced my footsteps along the alley and walked around to the front of the large house, which had been divided into four apartments (hence four mailboxes) with one main entrance. Once inside, I climbed a badly stained carpeted staircase to the second floor, located the correct apartment, and knocked on the door, which quickly opened.

The youth, wearing a black shirt with a dragon, black jeans, and red-and-black running shoes, was perhaps five feet five, with dark hair and brown eyes. He was on his way to becoming a striking young man.

I said, *"Hola. Me llamo Vivian. Cómo está usted?"*

That was all the Spanish I knew, except for *"Dónde está el baño?"* And I didn't need a bathroom at the moment.

"I speak English, lady," the youth said.

"Thank goodness," I replied with relief. Realizing that might have sounded insulting, I added, "I didn't mean to infer that you didn't."

"Imply," he said.

"What?"

"You don't mean to imply I don't speak English."

"I certainly don't! But, let's face it, some of your countrymen don't, because you've just arrived in our wonderful country."

"Lady," he said, "you're only making it worse."

I tilted my head. "You're certainly an outspoken young man. But may I point out that *you* invited *me?* So, as my host, it's your responsibility to make me feel welcome."

"Okay."

He stepped aside, and I entered a living-room area that was comfortably furnished in the rich earth tones of brown, tan, and green, with splashes of red.

We appeared to be alone.

Closing the door, the youth said, "I'm Miguel."

I turned to face him. "And I'm Vivian."

"Yeah, I know. I saw you on TV before."

Perhaps he did want an autograph!

"Well, Miguel, what can I do for you?"

"It's what I can do for you." He smiled a little. "And *then* what you can do for *me.*"

I smelled blackmail in the air. I might have been indignant if it wouldn't have made me a hypocrite. I said, "Let's start with what you can do for me, shall we?"

"How about tell you who killed that woman?"

My eyes widened. "You *saw* who it was?"

"I sure did."

"Why didn't you go to the police?"

"The police look at a kid like me and think, *Gang.*"

"I see. Why did I think perhaps you didn't go to them, because you want *money* for the information?"

"Not money," Miguel said.

"What then? Ah, you'd like to be on my show!"

He shook his head. "I've seen it. Not my favorite."

The young man was outspoken, impertinent, and insolent. I liked him!

"Then what is it that you want?" I asked somewhat impatiently.

"I want to be in your next book. Me. Miguel Edwardo Garcia."

I gestured with an open hand. "Dear, our cases are not works of fiction. I can't just, well, shoehorn you in somewhere! The events—the people—are real and are used in the tradition of Dr. Watson chronicling the cases of Sherlock Holmes."

I took a breath, because I'd run out of air.

"Granted," I went on, "we *do* take some liberties—poetic license, they call it—and sometimes use false names for people to protect the innocent."

Or ourselves from libel suits.

"I'll sign off," he said, then set his jaw stubbornly.

"All right. Perhaps I *could* give you a small walk-on. Would that do?"

He just stared at me.

I tried again. "A secondary character with a few choice lines?"

Slowly, he shook his head.

We seemed to be at an impasse when suddenly the obvious occurred to me! Which occasionally it does.

"Dear," I said, "if you tell me who you saw, and that person is indeed the killer . . . well, naturally this entire scene between us—dialogue and all—*will* be in the book that my daughter and I write about this very case."

"I want my scene used," he said flatly, "even if the person I tell you I saw *isn't* the killer. Because it would still be a clue. A lead."

Outspoken, impertinent, insolent . . . and smart.

Since I wanted the name, I agreed. Anyway, this had gone on long enough to have the makings of a scene.

"Now," I said. "Who was it?"

"Not so fast," Miguel said. "I want to lead up to it."

So he wanted an *extended* scene!

"Very well," I replied, sighing. "But may we sit? My knees aren't what they used to be." And my bunions were killing me.

After we'd settled on the couch, the youth began, "I was home with a bad cough the day that lady got killed."

"It could be the cigarettes."

He smirked. "Okay, so I skipped school. I was ducking a test. Anyway, I was here, and my mom was at work. I was sneakin' a cig, blowin' smoke out the window, when I see this man come walkin' down the alley."

"Go on."

"This guy goes in the back door of that antique store about three thirty, then comes out ten minutes later in a big hurry."

"You're sure of the time?"

"Yeah. My mom comes home a little after four, and I wanted to make sure the smoke, you know, had cleared out."

"Can you give me a description of the man?"

"Don't have to. I recognized him."

"He was someone you know?"

"Not exactly. But that's another reason I didn't go to the cops. He was the chief of police."

My eyes popped. "Tony Cassato?"

"Yeah, I think that's his name. What? You don't believe me?"

I made a little scoffing sound. "Young man, it's highly unlikely the chief killed his wife. Maybe it was someone who *looked* like him."

"It *was* him!" Miguel said defensively. "Trust me, I know the guy when I see him. He came to talk to us at school about drugs—a day I *didn't* skip."

Could it have been Tony?

"Look," the youth said, "I heard him and her didn't live together, right? Him and that wife of his?"

"That is true," I said with a nod. "He and Mrs. Cassato were estranged."

"Well, my parents are 'stranged, too, and every time they get together, *they* want to kill each other."

"I don't mean to make light of your suspicions," I said, "but I *know* Tony Cassato quite well, and he wouldn't be capable of murder."

"He carries a gun around, right?"

"It's too ridiculous even to consider."

Was I trying to convince Miguel or myself?

"You're still gonna put me in the book, aren't you?" the young man was asking.

"I always keep my word." Unless my fingers are crossed, and I hadn't remembered to do that.

I checked my watch. There was just enough time to catch the trolley and make it home before Brandy, so I bid good-bye to Miguel, assuring him his scene would be included in the book (well, isn't it?), then scooted off to the courthouse.

With the trolley nearly full, I was in luck to find vacant the same seat I'd taken earlier. I located the little GPS button on the floor, slipped it back in the lining of my coat, pulled the threads tight, and made a knot.

Then I sat, my mind whirling.

Why hadn't Tony mentioned his late-afternoon Camilla visit to Brandy?

And if Tony *had* killed his wife, how could the man sit back and let *Brandy* take the rap? Or did he figure he could get her off at the last minute, if need be?

For now, I decided not to tell Brandy about my conversation with Miguel. No sense in getting her upset and causing a further fissure in the already fragile relationship between her and the chief.

I would confront him when he got back.

At home, I received a grand greeting from Sushi and Rocky, mostly because they wanted to go outside, so I accommodated them, then returned to the foyer to take off my coat. After retrieving my cell phone from my purse, I turned it on.

I had missed a call from my friend the don, who hadn't left a message. Quickly, I speed-dialed him.

"*Viv,*" he said gruffly, "where the heck've you been?" A man of his ilk was not used to being kept waiting.

"I do apologize for being out of reach," I replied but gave no reason. It takes more than a mob godfather to intimidate Vivian Borne. "Have you some information for me?"

"Yes," he said, not sounding so gruff. "I've talked to my extended family in New York, Chicago, Miami . . . and none of them are related in a business way or otherwise to the dead woman."

Camilla.

"I see," I said.

"But there is an L.A. branch of the family—once removed—that we don't see anymore at reunions, and that might have a recent connection in Serenity."

Did he mean Phil Dean? I recalled Officer Schultz's stray comment at the bakery. Could our esteemed producer/director be involved with distributing illegal substances?

"I appreciate this, Don," I said. "You've been most helpful."

"Good luck, Vivian. Don't be a stranger. And . . . be careful, young lady."

Charmer.

I let Sushi and Rocky back inside, then deposited dog food in their respective dishes, which they ignored in hopes of getting shares of whatever Brandy and I would be having for supper.

I heard the front door open, then shut, and in another moment or two Brandy tromped into the kitchen.

"How was your day?" she asked a little too eagerly.

Getting some leftovers out of the fridge, I said, "I met the most interesting people on the trolley. So interesting that I just rode around and around. And around."

Her eyes narrowed. "You stayed on the trolley all day?"

"That's right."

"And never got off?"

I gave her the same smug smile she had given me this morning. "Why, dear, you know people have said for years that I'm off my trolley."

Mother's Trash 'n' Treasures Tip

Very valuable collections need to be included in your estate planning; otherwise, heirs may have to pay an estate tax on them. I don't think, however, that I need to include my presidential-plate collection.

Chapter Nine

Staff Infection

Brandy here.

Have we lost anyone? If so, I feel your pain. A reader once tweeted that after she had read a chapter composed by Mother, she threw the book across the room and made a bull's-eye in her wastebasket (an expensive impulse, since it was a library book and she broke the spine).

Like pickled herring, Mother is an acquired taste.

Speaking of the grande dame, she must not have learned much on her solo investigative trip—and don't think for a minute that I believed she'd stayed on the trolley all day. . . . I know when I've been outfoxed. Usually, Mother can't wait to fill me in, while this time she was (for her) uncharacteristically reserved. Hence my deduction.

Possibly to avoid talking about her own day, she asked me how things had gone at the shop, and I told her we'd made a few nice sales, and rattled off the items.

"I thought we might *really* score," I said, "but it was a false alarm."

"How so, dear?"

"A great-looking guy came in, in a really sharp suit, Armani maybe, and with a haircut he didn't get in Serenity. He looked around the shop, took it all in. I asked him if he was looking for anything special, and he said no."

"A picker, maybe?"

"I don't think so. He just breezed in and out, looking like money."

She mulled that for a while. "What if he was looking for a certain picture frame?"

I sucked in a breath. "Do you think?"

"Would you recognize him if you saw him again?"

I nodded. "And I'd recognize his car, too—a silver BMW."

Mother's eyes flared. "I wonder if our almost customer is a suspect we've neglected—a name on my blackboard we haven't really looked into."

"Who would that be?"

"The fence Three-Fingered Frieda started telling you about before your two new friends were interrupted back at the jail—Rodney Evans. Didn't she tell you *he* drove a BMW?"

"She did!"

Her smile was a crooked thing. "And you know, dear, he may have already dropped by the house. Of course, we weren't in."

"You mean . . . Evans was our burglar?"

"Could be. And I believe he *was* looking for something special."

The next morning, Mother woke me up around nine to announce that we weren't attending church service this morning.

"Why not?" I asked. "Don't you think a prayer or two might help this investigation along?"

"Let's not be sacrilegious, dear. I want to go out to the Kleins' before they open at eleven, and inquire about that frame the late Camilla bought."

"You don't have to label her 'late.' She's the only Camilla either of us know."

"Not so, dear. The stage manager at my Off-Off-Off-Broadway play during my New York days was named Camilla Strulowitz."

"Well," I said, crawling out from under the covers, on which Sushi still slumbered, "I'll try hard to keep the two of them straight."

But I was fine with skipping church and checking out the Kleins. This was the first Sunday since my release, and I didn't relish answering any questions from the congregation about my jail time. Church gave prying snoops a patina of concern that I could well do without.

After a hearty breakfast, which I had insisted upon and had helped prepare, Mother and I headed out the door, leaving the dogs behind to deal with the table scraps (mixed in with their healthier dog food) I'd provided.

We found ourselves in the midst of an overcast day, a frigid winter wind attacking us, erasing any warmth we had brought with us from the house.

We climbed into the cold C-Max, me behind the wheel, Mother riding shotgun, and I grumbled shiveringly, "You know, we *could* have a warm car, if you'd just get rid of all that junk in the garage."

"Someday, dear," Mother said.

"You'd better not pass away and leave me with that mess."

"I'll do my best," she said cheerfully. "Ah, but think of the wonderful estate sale you would have!"

"Is it close enough to Christmas," I asked, "for me to say, 'Bah, humbug'?"

"Only if you're prepared to explain the derivation of the term."

"That's easy. It's from *A Christmas Carol.*"

"In fact, dear, it's likely from our own Nordic heritage and refers to suspicion—very apt, considering our situation, if not terribly Dickensian."

Her "reserved" phase appeared to be over.

As I backed the car out of the drive, Mother asked, too casually, "Have you heard from Tony?"

"Yesterday. He called me at the shop."

"Did he happen to say when he'd be heading back?"

We were tooling along Elm Street, which featured not a single elm. "He wasn't really sure. It depends on how he's getting along with his daughter. She still blames him for the separation . . . and, well, Tony didn't say this, but she may even blame him for her mother's death."

Mother's eyebrows rose above the big glasses, which was something of a feat. *"Really?"*

"Well, not 'really.' It's not like his daughter thinks he killed her mother! It's just that Camilla would never have come to Serenity if she hadn't wanted to try to reconcile with him."

I glanced at Mother—she was frowning. I asked her, "Something the matter?"

She shifted in the seat. "Dear, I hadn't wanted to mention this, but on my traverses yesterday—"

"Ha! I knew you hadn't ridden that stupid trolley all day!"

"Then why even mention it?"

"To let *you* know that *I* knew."

"Well, *I* knew *you* knew," she said. "So the point is moot."

"Really? Even if I knew that you knew that *I* knew?"

Such conversations are all too common between us, I'm afraid.

"Dear," Mother said, "do try not to be so infantile. Can't you see that I'm trying to tell you something? Something important?"

"Tell me, then." I turned onto the bypass.

"Yesterday," she said, "I spoke with a certain party who saw Tony leaving the back of Camilla's shop the afternoon she died."

"*What*? When?"

"About three forty-five p.m. Dear, had the chief mentioned this visit to you?"

"No!" I shook my head, hands tight on the wheel. "Mother, whoever you talked to must have been referring to his *morning* visit and gotten confused about the time."

"Oh, well, you're probably right, dear. Think nothing of it."

I shot her an incredulous glance. "What are *you* thinking?"

"Why, nothing, darling."

"Really, Mother," I scoffed. "Tony, of all people? He did *not* kill Camilla."

And we dropped the subject, though it hung in the air between us like Tilda's beaded curtain.

I turned off the bypass onto a two-lane highway, and then wheeled into the gravel drive of the auction house. No other vehicles were in the lot, so I drove around back, where a white panel truck with the Klein's logo on the side was parked.

Mother said, "'Twould appear Gerald is here, but not Loretta. That truck is his. His wife drives a black Lexus and is likely at church."

We exited the C-Max, then approached an entrance next to the closed roll-up door of a garage used for loading and unloading merchandise.

Finding the back entrance unlocked, we stepped into a large cement-floored, high-beamed room. A bank of high windows along the back wall provided the only source of light but was enough to reveal an array of packing materials—cardboard boxes of various sizes and reams of bubble wrap. In the center of the room was a long metal table with other mailing supplies—tape, labels, a scale—and a half dozen or so boxes that were sealed, stacked, and ready for shipping to Internet customers.

Mother was already moving toward the swinging double doors that led into the main area of the business.

I followed.

It was even darker in here, with no windows at all, and after a few steps, we froze. I tried using my little key-ring light, but it had finally run out of juice.

"See if you can locate a switch, dear," Mother said.

I felt around on the nearby wall but found nothing.

"I have a flashlight on my phone," I said.

"Good! Where is your cell?"

"In the car."

"Retrieve it then."

"Battery's dead. Do you have a flash on your phone?"

"I'm afraid not. You know, I really should upgrade my Jitterbug to a smartphone." Mother shrugged. "Never mind, dear. We'll go toward the light."

That sounded a little ominous, but she was referring to the front of the building, where a light emanating from the office was the only illumination at all in the vast space.

But as I began to move forward, Mother held me back. "Dear, let us exercise caution. I believe

Gerald is something of a gun enthusiast. It may prove prudent if we were to make our presence known, so we're not mistaken for miscreants."

"Anything that keeps us from getting shot at is my kind of prudent."

I expected Mother to holler Gerald's name a couple of times, but instead, she began to sing loudly "The Stars and Stripes Forever." Well, at least he would know we were patriotic miscreants.

Whenever she does something this embarrassing, I've found the only thing to do is join her. Only I sang the lyrics I'd learned at Girl Scout Camp:

> *Be kind to your web-footed friends,*
> *For a duck may be somebody's mother.*
> *Be kind to your friends in the swamp,*
> *Where the weather is very, very damp.*

(I pronounced "damp" in the British manner, of course.)

With this clash of lyrics, Mother stopped singing and turned to me. "Must you be so contrary?"

"You wanted Gerald to hear us, didn't you?"

"I'm sure he did," she huffed. "And he may very well shoot us, anyway!"

I moved out ahead of her, along an aisle of antiques, where in the darkness something as mundane as a wooden coat tree looked threatening, its spools like skeletal branches reaching out. A prim Victorian doll's sweet smile took on an evil cast, her glass eyes appearing to follow me as I passed, while a large stuffed toy lion looked ready to pounce.

I'd been in my share of spook houses in my day, but somehow none compared to this corridor of terror, and I couldn't wait to get out. I picked up my pace, then suddenly stumbled and went flat on my face.

Chagrined, I rolled over. There was just enough light filtering in from the still-distant office that I could see what I'd tripped over: the body of a man. He lay on his back, face glistening with blood.

I did not scream. I might have screamed, but I didn't. It was more of a yelp. Then I scooted back from him on my butt. Mother, always less squeamish, bent over the fallen figure.

"Is it . . . Mr. Klein?" I asked.

"It seems to be. In this darkness, it's hard to be sure. . . ."

She dropped to her knees, reached for a limp hand and, after a moment, said, "He still has a pulse."

She already had her cell phone out, calling 911, when I asked, "What should I do?"

"Get the ceiling lights on, dear, and see that the front door is open."

Now on my feet, I hurried up the aisle.

At the main entrance, I propped the door of a thousand notices open with one of the smaller nearby stoneware pots, then unbolted the main door and propped it open with a metal stand of brochures. On the main-entrance wall, I found a panel of switches and began flicking them on, one at a time, until every section of the store was lit up.

While waiting for the first responders to arrive, I went into the office, where I found the room ransacked—desk drawers pulled out, file cabinets emptied, papers scattered on the floor. Much the way Mother and I had found Camilla's back room.

Out at the checkout counter, in the newly illuminated space, I made an interesting discovery: the register had money in it, quite a bit, in fact, probably the starter cash for the day's business.

So this was a very specific robbery by a most specific miscreant.

Hearing sirens announcing themselves faintly, I headed back to the front doors, the scream of official vehicles growing in volume with my every step.

The paramedics were the first to arrive, two men quickly getting out of the emergency vehicle, its lights bathing the entrance with alternating blue and red. As they entered with their equipment, I said, "Middle aisle, halfway down," then yelled back to Mother, "Paramedics are here!"

Her faint reply, "Follow my voice," came back.

And then she . . . Oh, I just can't write what Mother did next. I just can't. *You* pick: (a) met the paramedics at the mouth of the aisle and calmly walked them to Gerald; (b) kept yelling, "Follow my voice," ever louder; or (c) once again sang "Stars and Stripes" at the top of her lungs. Hint: Not (a).

A police car arrived, adding its flashing lights to the mix. Mia was at the wheel, her squad car kicking up gravel as it came to an abrupt halt next to the emergency vehicle. Following Mia was Officer Munson in another squad car.

When the two officers entered, I quickly filled them in, and for once Mia gave me no attitude. Then, after they hurried on, I went to the checkout counter to stay out of the way.

After a few minutes Mother joined me, having been shooed away from the crime scene. Her calm manner was at odds with the blood smears on the front of her coat.

"How is Mr. Klein?" I asked.

She tsk-tsked. "It'll be touch and go, dear. He's been pretty thoroughly thrashed."

I told her the office had been ransacked, but that the cash register was flush.

"Interesting," she said. "So our intruder wasn't after money."

"Apparently not," I said. "But what was he or she after? This place is full of valuable antiques, but the entire focus was on the front office."

Mia emerged from the mouth of the center aisle, approached us, then positioned herself before Mother.

"Mrs. Borne, when you arrived? Were there any other cars in the lot?"

Mother glared at the officer. "Is that two questions or one?"

"What?"

"Good Lord!" Mother's eyes went up to the rafters, as if God alone might understand. "First the youngsters, then the Greatest Generation, and now those who protect and serve! Is there no end to this abominable affectation?"

Mia's eyes went to me, large but frowning. "Is she all right?"

"She has a thing about uptalking," I said.

"What is uptalking?"

"Skip it. Look, Mr. Klein's van was the only vehicle here when we arrived."

The officer nodded. "When was that? That you arrived?"

Mother moaned.

"About ten thirty," I said.

"And you were here because?" She was directing her questions to me now.

I said, "We wanted to talk to him before the store opened at eleven."

"Talk to him about what?"

"Antiques, naturally," Mother said brusquely.

Mia studied her for a moment, then asked us both, "Do you know where Mrs. Klein is?"

"Loretta is most likely at church service. New Hope," Mother told her. "We're members. Would you like us to go out there and bring her here or to the hospital?"

Mia's eyes were half-lidded now. "No."

"It's no trouble," Mother pressed, a little too eagerly. I knew very well that she wanted to question Mrs. Klein before the police had their chance.

"No," Mia repeated firmly. "Officer Munson will see to getting Mrs. Klein."

Mother added an inch to her height and peered down her nose, crossing her eyes a little to do so. "Very well, dear, but perhaps you're unaware that Loretta has a heart condition. Having a policeman show up at church service, looking for her, might well send the poor woman back into a-fib, necessitating another cardioversion procedure—which is no picnic, let me tell you!"

Mia's sigh was a long one. "I'll advise Officer Munson to exercise discretion."

"See that you do," Mother huffed. "Loretta's health, perhaps her very life, will be in his hands. Come, Brandy—that is, if you have no further questions, Officer?"

Just a tinge of uptalking from Mother there.

"You're quite finished here," Mia said, then raised a warning forefinger. "And, Vivian, don't even *think* about going to the hospital. . . . *Hold it!*"

We had started heading in the direction we'd come.

"Out the front way," Mia snapped, pointing in that direction.

"But our car's in back," I protested.

"I want to make sure you two leave?" she said. "I want to see you go?"

Mother groaned.

But we reversed our steps, and as we went past the officer, Mother sniffed, "The suggestion that we can't be trusted is wholly unwarranted."

Which garnered only a grunt from Mia. And it did sound a little like a question. . . .

Outside, in the cold, we lingered long enough

to watch the paramedics roll Mr. Klein—swaddled in a blanket, wearing a neck brace and an oxygen mask—on a gurney to their vehicle.

I turned to Mother. "*Does* Mrs. Klein have a heart condition?"

"It's possible. Can you say otherwise?"

"Let's go," I sighed.

We made the snowy trudge along the side of the building to the back, our teeth chattering by the time we climbed into the C-Max.

I started the engine, then backed up and slowly pulled away, Gerald's panel truck looking a little forlorn in my rearview mirror.

"Next stop," Mother said, nodding straight ahead, "the hospital."

I put on the brakes.

"Mother, you heard Mia," I reminded her. "Uptalker or not, she's a duly appointed representative of the law. You know, a cop? We'll get thrown out on our prying behinds—if not by the police, then the hospital staff."

After all, Mother was persona non grata at Serenity General. Her various antics, both as patient and visitor, were notorious topics of conversation from the lowest orderly to the highest administrator, and every doctor and nurse in between.

"Besides," I went on, "it's really beyond the pale to question Mrs. Klein, as upset as she'll be."

"That's the best time *to* question her, dear."

"How so?"

She shrugged. "It's self-evident, isn't it? The woman will be at her most vulnerable."

When I shook my head at her crassness, Mother

responded, "Dear, whether we're beyond the pale or not is beside the point. One person is dead, and another is at death's door. This is hardly the time to worry about someone's feelings. Now, drive on. *Mush!*"

As we came around the front of the auction house, the ambulance was just pulling out onto the two-lane highway, heading for the bypass, siren wailing and lights flashing. Following the paramedics was Officer Munson, presumably dispatched to collect Mrs. Klein, which left Mia behind to assist the forensics team.

At the mouth of the driveway, I'd just paused to check for traffic when a 1970s green Volkswagen van swung in and stopped alongside our C-Max.

Dexter Klein rolled down his window, and I powered down mine.

He leaned out, his face tight with concern. "Hey, did I see an *ambulance* just pulling out of here?"

I nodded. "Someone attacked Mr. Klein before the store opened. We happened upon him."

Dexter's concern turned to alarm. "Is he all right?"

"I don't know. He was pretty badly beaten. You should probably go out to the hospital."

"Oh, my God."

He put the van into reverse, backed out onto the highway, then sped off without another word.

Sped off in the opposite direction of the bypass and hospital, that is.

"That's a little . . . odd," I said.

"Everyone reacts differently to bad news," Mother philosophized. "Onward, dear!"

The hospital was two miles south, just off the bypass, a modern facility with exceptional care, if lousy cafeteria food (excepting the pies).

To avoid detection, Mother suggested we go in through a service entrance, which we did. She then led the way through a labyrinth of hallways before stopping at a door marked STAFF ONLY.

"Here's where they keep the uniforms," she whispered. "I think scrubs with little booties and caps would give us the best cover, don't you?"

"You can't be serious."

But she was.

I turned and left her there.

Vivian here.

After that rat Brandy abandoned me like a sinking ship—which, frankly, was just as well, as I doubted her acting chops were up to the job of impersonating a member of the medical profession—I ducked inside the uniform closet.

After locating on a middle shelf a suitable shirt and pair of pants (an unflattering shade of green, not in my personal color chart, but one puts on the costume a role requires), I put the uniform on over my slacks and blouse. Then I slipped the booties over my shoes and donned the shower-type hat, pulling it down jauntily low.

I exited, then traversed the corridors leading to the ER without being stopped and questioned.

If you live a role, the public accepts you. Apparently, the professionals, too.

Along the way I added some nice props to my costume: a stethoscope to hang around my neck, a doctor's clipboard to tuck under my arm (seemed Mr. Fusselman's temperature had returned to normal after his gallbladder operation), and a bedpan (clean) to fill my hands. *Perfecto!*

The ER waiting area had recently been reconfigured into two sections: one large room for those whose loved ones were not in a life-threatening condition, and another made up of several small rooms for those needing privacy due to some more serious situation.

So when I found Loretta in one of the small rooms, I knew at once that Gerald could not be in good shape.

Loretta, wearing her Sunday best, her face puffy, was alone, seated in a chair by an end table arrayed with ancient magazines. As I entered in my disguise, she looked at me with a mixture of hope and dread, anticipating news I might be delivering regarding her husband's condition.

I had to remove my cap before she recognized me.

"Yoo-hoo," I said and winked.

"Vivian?" she asked, confused. "What . . . ? Why on earth are you dressed like that?"

I settled into the chair next to her and balanced the clipboard on the bedpan on my lap. "Sorry, my dear. This was the only way I could be assured of getting past the staff to see you."

"You could get in trouble, couldn't you, for this?"

"A small price to pay for being of help to you. How is Gerald?"

Loretta drew in a quivering breath. "He's in a coma. They're running a CAT scan now."

I nodded. "To see if he has head trauma or, heaven forbid, brain damage."

That caused some tears to flow, and she dabbed at her eyes with a tissue. A medical man or woman can't pull any punches.

"Are you aware," I asked, "that Brandy and I found Gerald?"

"Yes, and I thank you for that. You may have saved his life. If he had been lying there much longer, well . . ."

"It was indeed fortunate that we came along."

Having gotten the niceties out of the way, I said, "Dear, we noticed that your office had been thoroughly tossed."

"Some damn thief looking for money, probably," she responded.

"That was my original thought . . . until Brandy told me there was quite a bit of cash in the register."

She frowned. "Is that right?"

"I believe the 'damn thief' was looking for something *other* than money."

"Such as?" A slight irritation crept into her voice.

"I thought you might tell me."

She shrugged. "Well, I don't know what that would be. And right now I don't care about the motive. Gerald is my main concern."

I backpedaled. "Of course, dear. I quite understand. But the sooner we investigate this crime, the better."

She goggled at me. "*We*? What? You and that daughter of yours? The police are already investigating. You need to stay out of this and let them do their job. Now, if you don't mind, I'd like to be left alone."

I patted her knee. "Certainly, dear. I didn't mean to upset you."

I gathered my bedpan and clipboard and stood. "Oh, by the by, do you know what happened to the picture frame Camilla bought the afternoon she died? It seems to have disappeared from her shop."

She whitened. "How does that frame have anything to do with this?"

"I thought perhaps you might have an insight to share." I sat back down. "Wasn't that frame sold for far less than it was worth?"

"How do you know that . . . ?"

"My daughter thought she might have seen Camilla switching price tags with another, presumably less expensive item."

Her eyes flared. "And she said nothing?"

I shrugged. "Brandy didn't feel she could risk another altercation with Camilla."

Loretta sighed. "Well, it was a costly mistake, that frame selling cheap. Particularly since it was being held for another customer. Our reputation could take a real hit."

"What customer?"

"I don't really know. Gerald . . . Gerald dealt with that." She swallowed, and her eyes were wet now as they fixed themselves on me. "Vivian, do you think this has something to do with . . . with what happened to Gerald?"

"I don't know, dear. But I promise you I will find out."

I patted her hand and left her there. Then I retraced my steps to the uniform closet, where I removed the borrowed clothes, a little disturbed that no one had bothered to stop and question me. I made a mental note to speak to the hospital board about the lackadaisical security around this place.

Brandy was waiting for me in the car.

"Well?" she asked as I climbed in. "Did you get caught?"

"Of course not."

"You were lucky."

"Dear, must you continuously underestimate me? I've played far more challenging roles."

Brandy smirked and started the car.

On the way home I reported my conversation with Loretta.

"She can't really think it was a robbery," Brandy said.

"Loretta seemed to think it might be, even after I mentioned the cash in the register. And I believe she knows more than she let on about that picture frame."

At home, both Rocky and Sushi danced as Brandy and I walked in the front door—whether happy to see us or needing to go outside, always open to interpretation. But Brandy was going with the latter, immediately moving toward the kitchen, calling the dogs along, while I removed my coat and hung it on a hook.

I was about to head in for a hot cup of tea when the doorbell rang.

Looking through the peephole, I saw Dexter Klein's face and opened the door.

The young man was sporting an old tweed coat with a velvet collar over a polka-dot shirt, plaid slacks, and wing-tipped shoes—a strange getup, but then who am I to talk? My generation invented the zoot suit.

Did I mention that he held in one hand a large ornate frame?

Mother's Trash 'n' Treasures Tip

If your collection has incurred sizable capital gains, consider selling off some of it and donating the proceeds to charity, which would decrease future taxation. Perhaps you'll consider the Vivian Borne Prisoner Players, the recently (re)established, tax-deductible theater group?

Chapter Ten

The Match Game

I returned from the kitchen to find Mother in the foyer with Dexter. My eyes somehow managed not to jump out of my head at the sight of the frame he was holding.

"Well, will you look at what this thoughtful young man has brought us, dear!" Mother said, as if he'd delivered a Christmas ham. "That *is* the frame Camilla bought, isn't it?"

I came over for a closer inspection. "Certainly looks like it," I told Mother, then asked Dexter, "Where, and how, did you come across this?"

Before he could answer, Mother said, "Let's not stand here in the entryway in a bunch. The young man is our guest. Shall we reassemble at the couch? It will be much more comfortable."

She had sat on that thing before, hadn't she? But I didn't argue.

"Dexter," Mother said, stepping into the living room and leading the way to our "comfortable" couch, "would you care for some tea?"

"Why not?" our guest said.

Mother smiled at me the way a queen does at a handmaiden. "Brandy, make us some tea, would you?"

Why am I always the last stooge in line, with no one left to slap?

"All right," I said. "Just don't start without me."

I dashed into the kitchen, grabbed the kettle off the stove, ran to the sink, poured some water in the kettle, rushed back to the stove with it, and turned on the burner. All in under one minute. Where is *The Guinness Book of Records* guy when you need him?

I returned to the living room, where Dexter had taken one end of the couch, and took the other, the ornate frame propped on a cushion in the middle, between us. Mother, knowing darn well how uncomfy that couch was, had taken the Queen Anne needlepoint armchair (also nothing to write home about comfort-wise), arranging herself rather regally.

"Before we discuss the frame," Queen Vivian said, addressing our guest, "tell me, how is Gerald faring? Is he still in a coma?"

"Actually," Dexter said, "I haven't made it out to the hospital yet."

Mother's eyebrows climbed over the rims of her large glasses, always an impressive feat. "Why not? Surely they haven't forbidden you entry to his room. You're a blood relative!"

"More like a distant relative," he replied. "But the thing is, I don't think either Gerald or Loretta would really want me there."

"Why's that?" I asked.

Dexter's head swung toward me. "Well, for one thing, they fired me the other day. Or I should say, Gerald fired me . . . not that Loretta made any effort to stop him."

Mother asked, "When exactly was this, dear, and why?"

"Last week, after I sold this stupid thing"—he gestured to the frame propped between us— "when it turned out it was already taken."

And of course I'd seen Camilla switch tags with another frame.

He was saying, rather defensively, "And it wasn't even my fault! Nobody told me it was on hold or sold or anything. Anyway, I'm pretty sure that Cassato woman who got herself killed? Switched tags with a different frame."

Mother, wincing only slightly at the uptalking, glanced at me, granting me permission to speak.

"I saw her do it," I told him. "But I didn't do or say anything to stop her—including tell you that day, at the front register."

He frowned. "Why not? You helped get me fired!"

"And I'm sorry about that. But I've had a thorny history with Camilla Cassato, so I just kept it to myself." I shrugged. "Really sorry. I'm afraid I've caused all of us trouble."

"Water under the bridge, children," Mother said.

The kettle whistled, and I answered its call.

Shortly, I was carrying in a tray with three cups of steaming tea, which I placed on the coffee table. I handed Dexter a cup and he took a sip, smiled politely, then never touched it again. Mother and I, however, sipped away.

"Tell me about your dismissal, young man," Mother said, settling back with her cup.

Dexter stroked the fashion-statement stubble on his chin. "Well . . . it happened that same day, after Gerald and Loretta came back that afternoon from an appraisal—"

Mother cut in: "About what time was this?"

"About . . . three o'clock, I guess?"

She nodded. "Go on, dear."

"Loretta went into the office to handle some bookkeeping, and Gerald started going through the day's receipts at the counter. Well, he noticed that the description of the frame I'd written up on the ticket didn't match the tag I'd taken off it. And, wow, did *he* go ballistic!"

I asked, "Does Gerald lose his temper easily?"

"Not really. Not that I ever saw."

"Go on," Mother prompted.

"Well," he said, then sighed, "Gerald said it was 'imperative' to get that frame back. That otherwise we'd be alienating an important customer."

"What customer is that, dear?"

"He didn't say. He just gave me a bunch of money—more than twice what that woman paid—and told me to go to her shop and buy the frame back. If she said no, then I was to tell her we had her switching tags on a security camera."

I asked, "Did you?"

"No," Dexter said. "They're just for show. Not hooked up to anything."

Mother asked, "Did you go to Camilla's shop?"

He nodded. "I went in the front, where I saw the frame kind of pushed off to one side, with no sales tag on it. The door to the back was closed. You know, the office area . . . ? But I could hear her and some man talking."

Mother frowned. "Did you recognize the man's voice?"

"No."

"Did their conversation sound . . . contentious?"

"Not really," Dexter replied with a shrug. "Their voices weren't raised enough for me to hear what they were saying. Anyway, after a few minutes I got tired of waiting, so I called out a hello. Then the door opens, and out she comes. She gives me a funny look, like 'What are you doing here?' I explain how I shouldn't have sold her that frame and how I need to buy it back, and I offer to give her double what she paid for it for her trouble." He made a sour face and shook his head. "No go. She says she won't sell it for even *triple* the price, and she isn't impressed by the security-cam threat, either. So where does that leave me? I guess you know—having to go back to the auction house, with no frame. And pretty soon no job."

I asked, "Did you leave the auction house right after Gerald fired you?"

"Pretty much. I had some things in a locker to collect, but . . . yeah. No reason to linger."

Mother asked, "So you don't know if Gerald left the shop and went off to see Camilla himself?"

"No. If he did, I was already out of there."

I asked, "And Loretta? Where was she?"

"Still in the office. Oh, she came out right after I got canned, and I sort of begged for mercy, playing the relative card. But she said something about how she couldn't contradict Gerald's decision, since he did all the hiring and firing, which I thought was pretty lame. Then she kind of scurried back in the office."

Mother placed her empty cup on the coffee table. "Now, dear, we understand that you lost your job over that picture frame. But what was it that made you think we might be interested in it?"

"Billy Buckly," Dexter said. "I've been brokering a deal between him and the Kleins to buy some *Wizard of Oz* movie memorabilia that his grandfather left him, which included a pair of ruby-red slippers."

"Impressive," Mother said. "Of the eight sets made for Judy Garland to wear, only four are known to exist."

"Yeah, that's what I understand," Dexter said. "Billy has a really valuable collection of *Oz* and other vintage show business stuff. But he got married recently, and the 'little woman,' as he calls her—not that accurate in this case, really—wants him to get rid of the stuff."

I said, "Sounds like an opportunity for you to make a nice commission."

"Yes, and get in solid with the Kleins. But that's out the window, so I got back to Billy the other day, to see if he'd let me represent the collection, even though I was on the outs with the Kleins. I figured I could find him a top buyer somewhere else. We were discussing that, and he mentioned, kind of in passing, that you were looking for a specific picture frame . . . one that sounded like the one Camilla bought that lost me my job."

Behind the big lenses, Mother's eyes were narrowed shrewdly. "Which brings us to the sixty-five-million-dollar question . . ."

She felt sixty-five thousand wasn't that much these days. Still sounded pretty good to me.

"Where did you find that frame?"

Dexter gave up a little dry laugh. "Well, that's kind of funny, you know, funny strange? I went to the Kleins' on Friday to pick up my last paycheck, and as I was leaving, I wadded the envelope up and threw it in the Dumpster out back . . . and there it was! The frame Gerald wanted so badly, that got me in trouble. Do you know why, after all of that, he'd just throw it away?"

"A good question," Mother admitted. "But another question comes to mind. How did he wind up with it?"

Dexter reached for the frame, then passed it over to Mother. "Here! You can have it. I don't want the stupid thing."

"We'd be glad to pay you for it, dear," she said. "A little something for your trouble?"

"Not necessary. I'm doin' okay. But thanks.

And thanks for the tea." Which he'd taken only one sip of.

He stood and gave us both perfunctory smiles. Mother and I rose, as well, and followed him to the foyer, and to the door.

Dexter was halfway out when he turned suddenly. "Oh, there is something else, something I forgot to mention. You asked me if I knew the man Camilla was talking to at the shop, and I don't. But I did catch a glimpse of the back of him when she opened the back-room door. He had on a plaid shirt, jeans, and Nikes. Not that that'll be much help. A lot of guys dress that way around here. You know . . ." He made a face. "Pedestrian."

I closed the door after Dexter and turned to Mother. "He's right. Lots of men around town wear plaid shirts, jeans, and Nikes. Let's not jump to any conclusions."

"Then why, dear, are we both thinking about Phil Dean?"

The dogs, who had been outside through all this, were barking impatiently, so I went to let them in. Moments later, I came back to the living room, trailed by Rocky and Sushi, and found Mother standing by the couch, holding the frame and looking into its emptiness, as if she might see something of interest there.

Suddenly, Rocky sprang toward Mother, almost knocking her over, but instead batting the frame out of her hands with that pair of big paws! The thing clunked to the floor, where the dog began sniffing it feverishly, as if it were the tree that the wood had once come from.

I had begun scolding the animal when Mother stopped me with a hand on my shoulder. "Dear! Didn't you once tell me that Rocky was trained for detecting narcotics?"

"That's right. Before Tony got him."

"Hold him back, dear."

While I hauled a whimpering Rocky away by the collar, Mother picked up the frame and scrutinized it.

"This is interesting," she said. "The side pieces are held together with little hinges instead of the normal nails."

Rocky was straining at his collar.

I asked, "So what?"

"So . . . that makes taking it apart easier. . . ."

Which she proceeded to do.

Holding the four wooden pieces out for me to see, she exclaimed, "Look! The insides are hollow!"

I really couldn't hold the straining Rocky back much longer; if he were a cat, that frame would be catnip. "Make your point, Mother, before Rocky yanks my arm from its socket."

"Think about it, dear! This frame makes a clever place for concealment of contraband! Illegal narcotics, for instance."

"If you want that for evidence," I said, nodding to the frame, still restraining Rocky, "you'd better put it somewhere up high—right away!"

Mother went over to a tall corner cabinet that held her collection of Hummel figurines, and placed the dismantled frame on its top just as Rocky broke loose from my grasp.

To the dog's credit, he didn't jump on, or

claw at, the cabinet, causing a Hummel earth-
quake; instead, he deposited himself before it,
sitting patiently while staring up at its top.

Mother said, "Dear, what do you think about
paying our friend Phil Dean another visit?"

"I'm with you."

A lot of evidence—granted, mostly circum-
stantial—was pointing to our producer: his own
admission that he wanted to keep his contract
with Camilla a secret; Dexter's description of
someone who was probably Phil talking to Camilla
shortly before she was killed; Mother's friend the
don's assertion about a recent L.A. drug connection in Serenity; and now the frame itself, a
vessel designed to transport illegal substances.
Had the narcotics, whose remnants drove drug-
sniffing dog Rocky wild, been intended for
Phil's distribution?

Mother was saying, "I believe we will find him
at the editing suite. He's nothing if not a hard
worker, our Phil! Otherwise, we should find him
at the Serenity Grand Hotel. Come along, dear."

"Should we take the dogs?" I asked, then
added, "Or at least Rocky? If Phil is responsible
for what we suspect, he could be dangerous."

"We should be fine," Mother said. "Anyway, I
just acquired a Taser gun, which could really
use some serious field-testing."

Why was I not surprised?

"A Taser," I said. "How much did that cost
you?"

"Two hundred dollars."

"Is it legal?"

"Oh, I haven't the slightest idea. But I assure

you, it's quite safe in the hands of a responsible person."

Now I *was* worried.

"All right," I said. "But I'm staying behind you."

"You'll have my back!"

I was more concerned with my front.

After all, I'd accompanied her once to the gun range, and her score was beyond pathetic. She did, however, score one bull's-eye . . . on her neighbor's target.

Mother went upstairs to get the Taser (likely from her sock drawer hideaway), while I went into the kitchen to make sure the dogs had water. Sushi, being diabetic, was notorious for draining both her water dish and Rocky's.

The canines had followed me, so I bribed them each with a treat since they weren't going; then I returned to the entryway to get my coat. Mother was already wearing hers, its right pocket bulging.

Anyone out there old enough to remember the song "Pistol-Packin' Mama"? Well, I couldn't get it out of my mind.

We headed out to the car.

On a Sunday afternoon Serenity City Center was relatively quiet, with the businesses and offices closed, though some music lessons and a dance recital rehearsal were under way.

Mother's knees seemed to creak even more than usual—how heavy *was* that Taser?—as we climbed the wide wooden staircase to the second floor, where we found the door to suite 202 unlocked.

As we entered, Phil, in another plaid shirt, jeans, and running shoes combo, swiveled in his chair away from the computer monitors.

"Hey," he greeted us cheerfully. "Glad you stopped by. I'm just finishing up." He rocked back in the chair. "I think we've got a terrific first season finale that should just about guarantee us a second season."

Mother moved toward him. "And I think we'll have a terrific second season opener when Brandy and I reveal who killed Camilla Cassato."

Phil leaned forward in his chair. "No kidding? You know who it is?"

"We believe so," Mother said.

"Anyone I know?" Phil asked.

"Intimately," she replied.

He frowned. "Who?"

From behind Mother, I said, "You."

Phil chuckled. But when we didn't join in, his smile faded. "You can't be *serious.*"

"I'm afraid we are," Mother said. "We have a witness who saw you talking to Camilla at the back of her shop shortly before she was killed."

Mother had taken a small liberty with that—the witness had seen someone who *might* have been Phil. . . .

"Who was this witness?" Phil demanded.

"Someone reliable," Mother answered coolly. "A most reliable witness indeed."

I said, "So much for you working here that entire afternoon."

The producer/director stood, and Mother's hand moved into her bulging coat pocket, while I took an extra step back.

"All right," Phil said, his face and shoulders slackening. "I did call on Camilla—at about a quarter to three, for half an hour. But I sure as hell didn't kill her. Come on, Vivian, Brandy. You know me better than that!"

Mother, all business, asked, "What was the purpose of this meeting?"

"To discuss the . . . ah . . . terms of a new contract."

I said, "By which you mean capitulating to her blackmail."

Phil raised his chin. "I prefer to think of it as a raise—and we *were* at odds over how big a raise, I admit—but her continued services were essential to the success of the series. Every good story needs a villain."

Were we looking at the villain of ours?

Mother asked, "And Camilla agreed to your terms?"

"Finally she did," Phil said.

I asked, "What happened next?"

Phil looked at me. "What do you think happened next? I left!"

Mother asked, "At what time?"

"I don't know exactly. . . . About three thirty, I guess. And yes, she was still alive when I left there! Come on, you two!"

Some crossness came into Mother's voice. "I don't see why you didn't share all this with us before."

Phil spread his hands; his expression was kind of pitiful. "Because I didn't want to get involved in one of your amateur sleuthing sessions, that's why! I had a television show to produce, in case you've forgotten, and I'm barely making deadline as it is!"

Mother shifted her stance, and focus. "What do you know about an antique frame that Camilla bought from the Kleins the afternoon she was killed?"

"A what?"

I said, "Large picture frame. On the ornate side."

Exasperation crept into his voice. "Why would I know anything about a picture frame? What are you two *talking* about?"

Mother said, "It was used to smuggle narcotics into Serenity. And I have it from an inside and most reliable underworld source that the origin of this contraband was California."

Phil's eyes showed white all around. "And because I'm from California, that makes me the bad guy? Do you really assume the drugs were for me because, hey, I'm from L.A. and everybody in the entertainment biz is hooked on *something*?"

"Dear," Mother replied, "I've seen you take pills on set that I don't believe are aspirin. I never commented before, because I'm not one to pry into the business of others."

Kind of amazing that she said that with a straight face.

The producer/director let out an angry sigh, turned abruptly, walked over to a desk, pulled open a drawer, removed something, and came back.

Thrusting a prescription bottle in Mother's face, Phil snapped, "These are for back pain. I used to be a stuntman before I was a producer."

That didn't mean he wasn't still hooked on them.

He was saying, "Do I have to tell you that I work long days, and sometimes these old pains recur? And sometimes *new* ones—a little lower down!"

Mother and I exchanged glances: had we been wrong about a trusted colleague?

Pocketing the bottle, Phil said, "Now, I've got a rough cut of our final episode of the season to send to the network . . . *and* a flight to catch. Or to put it in your terms, to make my getaway!" Fuming, he returned to the chair and the waiting screens.

"We may owe you an apology," Mother said.

Phil said nothing, his back to us.

"We'll let you know," she added.

And we left.

A few minutes later, Mother and I were seated in the car.

"Do you believe him?" I asked.

"Do you?"

"I think maybe." I shrugged, then started the car. "Where to now?"

"The library, dear. We have a rendezvous with Heather."

I couldn't believe that the former dispatcher, now a forensics tech, was still snitching for Mother. What did Mother have on her?

When we arrived in the south stairwell,

Heather was waiting for us and looking none too happy about it.

"I don't know why you insisted on this meeting," the woman said, directing her ire at Mother. "I told you there was no match for that partial print."

I looked at Mother. "What's she talking about?"

"There was an unidentified partial print on the corn husker. . . . Now, please, no more interruptions." Mother addressed Heather. "I don't mean to impugn your integrity, dear. But I suspect there *was* a match."

Her snitch's hesitance on answering gave Mother the opening to pounce. "Aha! I guessed right. Whose did it match?"

Heather's eyes went to me, with something akin to . . . what? Sorrow? Sympathy?

Why would she look at me like that? Unless . . .

I said, "The partial print belonged to Tony, didn't it?"

My heart was pounding.

Heather said, "Brandy, a partial-print match is not conclusive. It's nothing that would hold up in court. There could be *other* matches with prints that are not in the system."

But I knew, thanks to Mother, that a witness had seen Tony leaving the back of Camilla's shop around a quarter to four. I slumped down and sat on a dirty cement step.

"Dear," Mother said, bending down to pull me gently to my feet, "don't despair. It's within the realm of possibility that Tony may have quite innocently touched the corn husker when he saw Camilla either time."

I nodded, but my stomach was churning.

In the meantime, Heather was about to slip away when Mother stepped between her and the door. "Just one more question, dear." A stray thought distracted her. "Didn't you always love it when Columbo would do that just when a suspect was thinking he'd wriggled off the hook?"

Heather frowned. "Is that the question?"

"No, no! I'm wondering about a certain Rodney Evans, purported to be a fence of some kind."

The frown deepened. "What does *he* have to do with any of this?"

"That is the question, dear, as Shakespeare once said."

Heather sighed. "Well, he's a slick customer who, as you put it, wriggled off the hook plenty of times around here. But I doubt he's part of this."

"Why do you say that?"

"No local address anymore. Moved out of the area. I've no idea where."

Mother glanced at me, then said to Heather, "We think Mr. Evans may be back *in* the area. He may have broken into our house last Thursday."

"Really? Did you report it?"

"Well, no . . ."

"Then why do you expect police help?" Heather's lips tightened in irritation. "Vivian, we're done here. Not just done now, but hereafter. Don't ever contact me again. I'm not going to risk my career by giving you police information." She reached for the door handle.

"And about that topless party picture you have of me wearing a hands-free beer hat? Put it on the Internet, for all I care!"

The stairwell door slammed shut after her.

Mother sighed. "Now I'll have to find myself a new PD snitch. There has to be a better way for me to get inside information. That photo cost me twenty-five dollars!"

"Mother?"

"Yes, dear?"

"I want to go home. Right now."

"It's Tony, isn't it?"

"You drive."

"Happy to."

I was that upset.

As soon as I got in the house, I dropped my coat and purse on the floor and headed upstairs.

"Go have a good cry, dear," Mother called after me. "I'll call you when dinner's ready."

I didn't respond. I couldn't imagine ever eating anything again.

In my Art Deco bedroom, I stripped down to my undies, then crawled under the covers. Sushi had followed me upstairs and jumped up on the bed.

I'm a side sleeper, and normally, she positioned herself in back of my bent knees; but if Soosh sensed I was sad, she curled up against my stomach; and if she sensed I was really sad, she lay on my pillow, with her head in the crux of my neck, tongue reaching out now and then to lick my tears. (I'd like to believe Sushi was that perceptive, but maybe she just liked the salt.)

Anyway, for a long while I just lay there blubbering, thinking of Tony, and if this book were a movie, right now there would be a montage of our relationship: the day we first met as adversaries and he gave me his handkerchief and told me to stop sniffling and blow my nose; the time I was depressed, and as a joke, Mother made me a clubhouse out of a blanket and chairs, like she used to for little Brandy, and while I was under there, eating chocolate cake, Tony arrived and gamely joined me; the night at his cabin when he saved my life from an assassin's bullet that was meant for him; our secret rendezvous in a New York hotel after he went into WITSEC; our last romantic day together at his cabin, just before Camilla arrived on his doorstep. . . .

And now Tony and I were being pulled apart once again . . . perhaps for a very long time, if he really had killed Camilla.

But that just couldn't be possible! Could it . . . ?

I must have finally cried myself to sleep, because the room was dark when Mother gently shook me awake.

"Get up, dear," she said softly. "I need you to come downstairs."

As she left, I looked at the clock—7:46 p.m.— then crawled out of bed, put my clothes back on, and did as my mother had told me.

In the music room/library/den, Mother was standing in front of the suspect-arrayed blackboard, and she gestured for me to sit on the piano bench. A TV tray was in front of it with a steaming bowl of Danish *gule ærter* (split-pea soup), a grilled cheese sandwich, and hot coffee.

While I sat, Mother picked up the eraser from the lip of the blackboard, then, to my astonishment, wiped the board clean! She had never done that before during a case.

Then Mother turned and said, "Rather than listing motive and opportunity, dear, what we need is a time line—a time line of who saw Camilla, and when, on that fateful day. One other thing."

"Yes?"

"Eat your soup while it's hot."

I dutifully dipped spoon into bowl.

"When did Tony see Camilla that morning?" Mother asked, then added, "It's not really all that relevant, but we'll record it, anyway."

"He came to see me about ten thirty," I said, "so right before that."

She turned to the board, chalk in hand. "Let's see . . . Dexter went to her shop to try to buy the frame back about three that afternoon, with Phil still in back. Then Dexter left the shop about three fifteen." The chalk was squeaking on the board. "We don't know exactly when Phil got to Camilla's, but he said he departed about three twenty. Accepting that at face value, Tony must have arrived shortly after, around three thirty, and was seen leaving by Miguel at about three forty-five. Then you found Camilla a little after four."

"Who's Miguel?"

"My witness. Lives across the alley. A rear window, like in Hitchcock. Now . . ."

Mother stepped back from the board.

TIME LINE:

10:00 a.m. until 10:30 a.m. Tony
3:00 p.m. until 3:15 p.m. Dexter
2:45 p.m. (?) until 3:20 p.m. Phil
3:30 p.m. until 3:45 p.m. Tony
4:05 p.m. Brandy

Mother said, "Dear, twenty minutes elapsed between when Tony left Camilla alive and you found her deceased—time enough for any one of these people to have come back and done the deed . . . or someone *not* on the list."

"Like Gerald Klein maybe?" I asked.

"Like Gerald Klein maybe." Mother stepped closer to me. "Are you too downhearted to indulge in a little clandestine sleuthing with your mother this evening?"

"Let me guess. You want to break into the auction house? Again?"

"Yes," she said, nodding. "That's where it all began—and perhaps that's where it all will end. In any event, I think it's about time we found out what was going on in that place."

"Okay. But how do we get past their security system? Their cameras may be for show, but their alarm system isn't. We'll need their code."

Mother smiled slyly. "When we were there this morning, I noticed that four numbers on the security pad were fainter than the others."

"That's a lot of combinations to punch in before the alarm goes off."

Mother said, "The numbers happen to be the last four digits of the phone number there. I feel confident that's the code. A chance worth taking, don't you think?"

"I hope so. Otherwise, you'll be directing and I'll be stage-managing *The Penis Papers* in stir."

I went upstairs to get into my burglar clothes (that I have such an outfit waiting on a hanger says way too much about me), and as I finished dressing, my cell, on the nightstand, rang.

"Hi," Tony said.

"Hi."

"I'm on standby for a flight but, with any luck, should be in Serenity around ten. Mind if I drop by?"

"Make it in the morning, okay?"

"Sure." Pause. "Everything all right?"

"Can I ask you something?"

"Anything."

"I need the truth."

"Well, of course!"

I waited a beat before asking, "Did you see Camilla around three thirty the afternoon she died?"

Silence.

Then: "I did. To ask her again for a divorce, but she wasn't having any, so I left. I should have told you, but I didn't want to upset you any further."

"Didn't exactly work, did it?"

"Honey, I'm sorry. I did tell Mia about it—it's in her report—and also that I may have touched the corn husker on the desk. It was just you I was protecting."

I couldn't help sighing with relief.

"Brandy? Brandy, you didn't really think *I* might've killed Camilla, did you?"

"Don't be ridiculous," I lied. "Did you think *I* might have killed her?"

"No."

Sometimes not being totally honest is a good thing.

"Brandy . . . I love you."

"I love you, too. See you tomorrow."

I sat on the edge of the bed, tears running down my face, happy ones this time. Sushi came out of somewhere and licked my face, enjoying the salty repast. Then I wiped my face on my burglar sleeve and went downstairs.

Mother was waiting in the foyer, coat over her own black ensemble. "I've got everything we'll need, dear. Are you ready?"

I nodded. "Let's go."

A Trash 'n' Treasures Tip

If you intend to have your collection go to your heirs, make them aware of its value and how best to dispose of it when the time comes. They may not be into collecting Buster Brown shoes memorabilia. The dog's name is Tige, by the way.

Chapter Eleven

Cuckoo Ha-chew!

By ten at night, it was dark enough outside that Mother didn't feel it necessary to wait until the witching hour before we broke into the Kleins' auction house, though she did bemoan losing the mood the "witching hour" term brought.

As I turned into the gravel parking lot, I cut the car lights so we wouldn't be seen driving in, though at this time on a Sunday night it seemed unlikely anyone at the business would be there to see us. Even so, precautions were always worth taking, and I made my way slowly around to the back.

The graveled lot did not extend around to the other side of the building, but I parked the

C-Max there, anyway, on the grass, nicely out of sight, should a patrolling squad car swing by. Mother in her basic burglar black and I in the gray sweatshirt and jeans I'd been arrested in not long ago, we exited the car and made our way in the dark to the back door. There she retrieved two small Mag flashlights from her fanny pack, handed them to me, then from a little pouch extracted two metal picks. While she worked her magic on the lock, I kept a sharp lookout.

When the bolt clicked, Mother whispered, "Easy peasy, dear! Be ready with the flashlights, now."

As the door opened, a high, shrill warning sound—not loud—emanated from somewhere, indicating that we had about a minute before the alarm would go well and truly off.

Quickly, I closed the door, then aimed a flashlight on the nearby security keypad as Mother played her "educated hunch" (as she called it) and entered the four last digits of the Kleins' business phone number. I hoped she was right—no female wants to get arrested in the same outfit twice.

The high-pitched noise ceased. I smiled to myself. Seemed there would be no jailhouse production of *The Penis Papers* in my immediate future, after all!

I handed Mother her flashlight, and we both beamed our dueling shafts of light around the packing room *X-Files*-style (much cooler than cell-phone glow).

"What exactly," I asked, whispering for no good reason, "are we looking for?"

She had moved forward and was now edging along the long mail table, where the half dozen sealed cartons we'd seen previously awaited being sent out to buyers.

Mother said, "Let's have a look inside these packages," panning her flashlight over them. "It'll be better than Christmas morning."

"Is it legal for us to do that?"

She gave me an unblinking stare. "Why, dear, is it legal for us to be in here?"

Good point.

She circled to the rear of the table, put down her flashlight, and picked out one of the smaller boxes.

What the hey. I joined her, providing the light while she opened the carton with a box cutter, then folded back the cardboard flaps.

We peered inside.

On top was a letter, typed on auction-house stationery, thanking the buyer—one Richard Wong in San Francisco—and invoicing him for one thousand dollars, hoping he'd be satisfied with the item and service.

Beneath the letter lay said item, swaddled in bubble wrap; Mother withdrew the object and proceeded to unwrap it. Shortly, Mr. Wong's purchase was revealed to be a rather ugly cuckoo clock. Even for a cuckoo clock.

"How is that thing worth a thousand bucks?" I asked.

"Let's see," she replied.

Then, to my astonishment, Mother began to destroy the clock, pulling out its inner workings, ripping off the decorative headboard, and yanking the sides apart. She even unceremoniously plucked out the little cuckoo bird from its nesting hole.

What exactly, I wondered, would the stage manager's duties for a production of *The Penis Papers* actually entail?

Meanwhile, the antique clock lay in pieces. No contraband. No nothing but clock parts.

"You could stuff all those pieces back in the box," I said, "but I doubt Mr. Wong will pay the thousand-dollar fee."

Mother ignored that and asked, "Where's the rest?"

"The rest of what?"

"The workings—weights, chains, pendulum."

I checked inside the box. "They're in here, wrapped separately. Why?"

"Hand me the two weights," she ordered.

I passed them to her.

Mother held one metal pinecone-shaped weight in her right hand, the other in her left, and hefted each separately.

"Dear," she said, a spike of excitement in her voice, "I believe one pinecone is significantly heavier than the other."

"Why would that be?" I asked. "Aren't they both supposed to be the same?"

One eyebrow lifted high above her glasses. "I suspect we're not dealing with a manufacturer's defect." She placed the two weights on the table. "Find me a hammer."

With a shiver, I wondered what kind of props *The Penis Papers* stage manager might have to handle.

I flashed my light around, spotted a wrench on the end of the table, and snagged it.

"Will this do?" I asked.

"Nicely," Mother said approvingly, then gripped it and, using the flat side of the wrench, whacked one weight really hard. But the wrench bounced off, with the only result being Mother shaking a sore hand as she shifted the wrench to her other hand and extended the thing to me.

"You try the other one, dear," she said.

I picked up a piece of the bubble wrap, wrapped it around the handle of the wrench, then smacked the second weight.

This pinecone cracked open, splitting into two natural halves . . . *and spilled out a gleaming array of gems.*

"Diamonds," Mother said, eyes glittering back at the stones. "Emeralds too. And sapphires. Beautifully cut."

For a while we just stood there staring at the shimmering treasure.

"Not all contraband is narcotics," Mother pointed out.

She scooped up the stones and held them in a palm for a closer look. "I'll bet these are from that recent Quad Cities jewelry store robbery."

"I read about that in the paper," I said. "But I don't get it. Mr. Klein robbed a jewelry store? That rates a big 'huh?'"

"No, dear, actually it might explain—"

But what it might explain would have to wait,

because Mother was cut short by the motorized grind of the garage door going up.

"Cut the flashlights," Mother whispered.

She pocketed the gems, while I doused the lights, and together we frantically stuffed all the clock parts back into the box. Then, taking the cuckoo carton along for the ride, we dropped to the floor just as the garage-door opener completed its cycle and the whirring motor stopped.

We had some concealment, thanks to the stacked supplies that were stored beneath the table—as long as the overhead lights weren't turned on, anyway—but there were spaces between those supplies that allowed us to see who had unexpectedly arrived.

In the open garage doorway, a figure was silhouetted against the headlights of an idling vehicle, but it took that figure moving out of the bright lights before I made him out as Dexter Klein.

Dexter paused, perhaps listening for the warning shrill of the security system, which didn't happen, then walked quickly to the security pad, stopped, stared at it, and shrugged, obviously concluding the system hadn't been set. Dexter turned, and as he strode toward us, I nudged Mother, putting a finger to my lips.

We could hear one of the sealed boxes getting lifted from the tabletop above us as Dexter picked the package up. Then we saw him, with the medium-sized box in hand, returning to his idling van, where he slid a side door open and deposited the box inside.

As he returned, presumably for another package, I felt a tickle in my nose from the dusty supplies and clamped both hands over my mouth like a speak-no-evil monkey. Mother, aware of the impending sneeze, put her hands over mine, one simian helping out another.

Time froze while Dexter selected another box and I struggled to contain the achoo that would be our undoing. As he began the trek back to the van, I couldn't hold it any longer, and behind all four clasped hands came a little piglike squeal.

But Dexter kept moving, the sneeze blotted out by the Volkswagen's running engine.

Mother and I sighed with relief, but that relief was short lived. A silver sedan appeared, skidding on the gravel as it came to an abrupt stop behind the van, blocking it in, and from an open window of the car came an extended arm and then . . . *the sharp reports of a gun firing*!

Dexter, by the side of his van, holding the latest box, tossed it inside, slammed the door, ran around the front of the vehicle, and jumped behind the wheel. After throwing the van into reverse, he smashed into the front of the sedan with a crumpling crunch, pushing it back far enough so that he could maneuver out.

As he did, Dexter's taillights washed red over the face of the shooter: a *familiar* face. . . .

I said, "*That's* who scoped out our shop yesterday."

The sedan was familiar, too—the silver BMW I'd seen him park in front of our shop! He probably wore a Rolex, too, since Three-Fingered Frieda had been right about him all the way. . . .

"Our likely home invader," Mother was saying. "Rodney Evans."

The van sped off, and the BMW, despite its crunched-in nose, took immediate, gravel-scattering pursuit.

While this unexpected drama played out, Mother and I had gotten to our feet.

"And now we follow them!" she said excitedly.

"What? No! And now we call the *police*."

She gave me a long-suffering look. "Dear, we simply must determine where they're going, before bringing the police into the picture."

That did sort of make sense. Mother sense, but sense.

"Okay," I said, "but we lay back. We're spectators on wheels, not participants joining in on the chase."

"Agreed."

I ran to get the C-Max.

Mother, in the meantime, went to the corner of the building, where I picked her up.

"They headed out into the country," she said, buckling her seat belt.

"Then we don't have to follow them."

"But they could turn off in any number of places," Mother protested, her eyes a little wild behind the big lenses. "Hurry, or we'll lose them!"

I hurried. At the mouth of the parking lot, I turned left onto the two-lane road; well up ahead, two sets of red taillights were flying into the night. From the car in pursuit came occasional firefly flashes of orange gunfire, making little pops at this distance.

"Perhaps I should call the sheriff," Mother said, cell phone in hand. "We're on his patch now."

In another moment, she was saying, "Sheriff Rudder? Good evening. Vivian Borne speaking . . . Yes, I know you can tell it's me from caller ID. I'm just being punctilious. . . . What? Look it up! Sheriff, if you'll just curtail your ranting, I'll *tell* you what this is about! Perhaps you'd like to take notes. . . . Well, that remark was wholly uncalled for. . . . What do we think we're doing? We *know* we're following Dexter Klein in his van, which is being trailed by an unknown gunman in a BMW, who is periodically firing at him, and if you want to retire on a high note, you'll get out to County Road G, going west of the bypass, ASAP!"

She ended the call, then said to me, "It's about *time* he retired!"

During Mother's conversation with Rudder, I closed the distance between us and the two vehicles—not that I wanted to or was driving with a heavy foot, but because that vintage Volkswagen van didn't seem to be able to go any faster than about sixty.

In a few more minutes, we were about a quarter of a mile from the pursuing BMW, which was riding the van's back bumper, and I let up on the gas.

"Don't fall back, dear!" Mother said.

"Evans has a gun, remember?" I reminded her.

The BMW zoomed alongside Dexter chariot race–style in an attempt to force the van off the road.

But instead, Dexter swerved violently into the side of the BMW, the car taking the full brunt of the big vehicle, forcing it onto the shoulder. Obviously, you shouldn't get into a chariot race with a bigger chariot.

The battered BMW lurched back onto the highway, but the driver had overcompensated the maneuver, causing the car to slam back into the van, sparks flying on contact from the metal of the old Volkswagen.

The two vehicles seemed locked together in fierce battle as they barreled down the highway, taking up both lanes, when abruptly they veered off the road, slammed into a wire guardrail, broke through, and careened side by side into a deep gully, disappearing into the dark.

I eased the C-Max onto the shoulder. Mother and I got out, walked to the break in the rail, and gazed down.

Both vehicles lay at the bottom—the BMW upside down like an overturned beetle; the van on its side, a felled behemoth.

There was no movement from either.

Mother was already calling 911, reporting the two-car accident to the dispatcher, going into more detail than perhaps she needed to.

When she finished, I asked, "Should we do something other than stand here? Maybe try to help the drivers out of their vehicles, before there's an explosion?"

"Not when one of them, as you pointed out, is armed. If we go down there, we could end up as hostages, with our car commandeered, if either of those two should be playing possum. Anyway, exploding vehicles? That's strictly for TV and the movies."

So we waited in the cold by the C-Max, alternately watching for signs of life below and for help to appear on the horizon.

Finally, multiple lights began flashing in the distance, accompanied by the faint but building sounds of sirens.

A rather gleeful Mother said, "You know, despite all this excitement, I'm somewhat disappointed I didn't get to use my Taser!"

She had withdrawn the electrical deterrent from her coat pocket and was regarding it when the Taser discharged, its tentacles flying hungrily toward me.

The searing pain in my skull announced the loss of all my motor skills, and my body went rigid. When the shock mercifully ceased, I flopped to the ground and passed out.

The last thing I heard was Mother saying, "Whoopsie!"

Vivian stepping in, because at this point, Brandy was somewhat incapacitated for the nonce and recovering in the ER, and we must not let our narrative lag! While I'm always pleased to have the opportunity to add my storytelling skills to the mix, this instance is one I do not relish.

But first, I would like to assure you, dear reader, that the firing of my Taser was entirely unintentional—an unhappy, unfortunate accident.

That said, I am pleased to have seen, and experienced, the weapon in action. A good writer dealing with the world of crime must be knowledgeable in the ways of firing a weapon, in this case a Taser. Otherwise, how can one write about such a thing convincingly? Of course, the same is true of a gun, which is why I recently went to the firing range . . . scoring a bull's-eye on my very first visit!

At the moment, Brandy was stretched out on one of those uncomfortable examination tables, while the doctor—a polished gentleman of Indian descent (the South Asian variety, not Native American)—was tending to her. Simultaneously, a nurse was taking her vitals (Brandy's, not the nurse's own).

I leaned over the table. "Dear, speak to me. Are you all right? How terribly clumsy that was of me!"

Brandy couldn't seem to focus on my face. "I . . . I can't see you, Mother. Come closer."

Oh, my! I hoped the darling girl hadn't gone as blind as little Sushi before the cataract surgery.

I bent down farther, and Brandy's hands came up and caressed my throat . . . then tightened! She shook me a few times, but I was fortunate that the girl's strength was so hampered. She might have accidentally choked me to death.

Drawing away, I coughed a few times and managed, "Now, dear, you *know* I didn't do that on purpose! I would rather it had happened to me."

"That much," she snapped, "we agree on!"

"You needn't be surly," I replied, stroking my throat. "The doctor said you'll be fine in a few hours, and in the meantime, at my suggestion, they'll be giving you that full checkup you haven't had in years. Win-win! By the way, what did it feel like to be Tasered? It's good to know these things."

"Someday, Mother, when you least expect it, I'll show you."

"Very droll, dear."

But just in case she wasn't jesting, I made a mental note to keep the weapon somewhere where the dear girl would never find it. The sock drawer just wouldn't do.

Sheriff Rudder appeared at my elbow. "Vivian?" He gestured with his head to the hallway. "A word?"

As we stepped into the corridor, I asked, "How did Dexter fare from the crash?" The young man was in another exam room.

"Broken arm, leg, fractured pelvis. No air bags in the van."

Still, he should soon be in shape enough to stand trial for murder, if necessary.

I asked, "And how's the driver of the other car doing? Rodney Evans?"

"He'll live." The sheriff's head bobbed back. "You *know* who he is?"

"Certainly. Don't you?"

"Yes, *I* know who he is! Law enforcement has been trying to get Evans on fencing stolen property and illegal substances for years. We just haven't been able to get the goods on him."

I smiled. "Well, I may have just the goods you need. Or rather, the goodies."

I reached into my coat pocket and withdrew the handful of gems, then held them out in a palm piled with glittering, reflecting cut stones—diamonds, emeralds, sapphires, and more.

Rudder's eyes popped. "Good Lord, Vivian. Where did you get those?"

"Not in a box of Cracker Jacks," I said. Sometimes I crack myself up.

Then I told him.

But can you imagine, dear reader, what that ungrateful man said? That he was going to have Brandy and me charged for breaking into the Kleins' auction house!

Another non–Native American Indian doctor approached, gesturing down the hall.

"Sheriff," he said, "Mr. Gerald Klein is no longer in a coma, and he requests to see someone in authority."

Rudder said to me, rather pompously, I thought, "Excuse me, Vivian. This is official business. Perhaps you can get that ancient lawyer of yours on the phone. You'll be needing him."

The doctor gestured down the hall again. "Mr. Klein said that if Mrs. Borne was still here, he would like to have her present."

I said to Rudder, "Well, he may very well talk to you *not* in my presence. Yes, you go on minus *moi*, Sheriff, and see how you do. I'll find a phone to call my attorney."

Rudder said nothing, just pawed at the air in front of me by way of invitation.

We followed the doctor down the hall to the ICU, through the double doors, then into one of the private rooms, where Gerald Klein, beneath a thin white blanket, lay hooked up to a variety of beeping monitors.

The once robust man was barely recognizable.

In a chair next to the bed was wife Loretta, wearing a navy blazer and slacks, a geometric-print silk scarf tied around her neck, her eyes red, face puffy.

The doctor crossed to the bed and leaned over. "Mr. Klein . . ."

Behind closed lids, the auctioneer's eyes moved back and forth.

"Mr. Klein," the doctor repeated. "The sheriff is here . . . with Mrs. Borne."

Gerald's eyelids fluttered open; his eyes found Rudder, then me; and, with great difficulty, he began to speak. "I . . . I want to confess."

"That's wise," the sheriff said. "We already have evidence of stolen property being moved through your auction house."

"Thanks to me," I said.

"Not that," Gerald said, shaking his head, just a little, but noticeably. "I want to . . . to confess to killing . . . Camilla Cassato."

"*You!*" I blurted. On the suspect blackboard of my mind, Dexter Klein had moved to the top of the list.

Rudder gave me a "shhh" frown, then asked the patient, "Are you fully aware of what you're saying?"

Gerald Klein nodded.

"You do know you're entitled to a lawyer," the sheriff went on.

Sometimes I could have just kicked that man!

"No . . . there may not be time for that," the auctioneer rasped. "Let me speak."

"First, I have to read you your rights."

Gerald nodded, swallowing thickly. After his rights had been read to him, and had been said to be understood, Gerald began, "I went to the Cassato woman's shop to get . . . to get back a frame that our . . . our clerk Dexter mistakenly sold to her. . . ." His eyes found me. "You . . . you understand about the frame . . . don't you, Vivian?"

"I do. Do you know when this was, Gerald? What time?"

"About . . . about ten minutes to four. I had to wait until her husband left . . . the police chief? And then I went in."

From the sidelines, Loretta Klein said coolly, "Darling, why don't you leave it there and let me call our lawyer?"

I could have kicked *her*, too!

"*No!*" He paused, struggling for breath. "I . . . I offered Camilla more money . . . quite a bit more . . . than she had paid for the frame . . . but still she refused."

The doctor stepped forward and said, "I think we will have to leave it here. Mr. Klein is overexerting himself."

Was there anyone in the room I *didn't* want to kick?

Ignoring the doctor's advice, I prompted Gerald: "What happened next?"

"I saw . . . saw that corn husker on the desk . . . picked it up. I don't know what came over me, but I . . . I hit her with it. She fell to the floor . . . and I just took the frame and left."

Loretta was crying quietly into a hankie.

Gerald's hand with the IV reached toward me. "I'm sorry, Vivian, about Brandy being charged for my crime. I was a . . . a coward, not coming forward. You will tell her?"

"Yes, dear. She's a forgiving child." With the blush of her hands still on my neck, that was something of a stretch. But Gerald seemed to need the exoneration.

"Now about the frame," I continued. "The drugs inside—they were meant for Rodney Evans?"

"*What* drugs?" Rudder asked.

The sheriff, like the doctor, really wasn't being all that helpful.

I asked, "Was Rodney Evans the person who attacked you? Gave you this terrible beating?"

Gerald nodded. "When I . . . gave him the frame, and the drugs weren't there, he . . . he went crazy." He squeezed my hand. "Loretta had nothing to do with my side business. You *must* understand that."

"And Dexter?" I asked.

"Not him, either. But I think . . . think he came to suspect something of what had been going on . . . after I fired him."

Loretta said, rather plaintively, "Gerald, why did you get involved with that Evans creature? Our business was doing just fine!"

Her husband's voice was but a whisper. "No. It wasn't. Bankruptcy . . . around the corner.

Without the secondary business, we . . . we were . . . going . . . to lose . . . *everything.*"

The hand that had been clutching mine went limp, as did the man's body, head lolling to one side. The monitors began beeping their warnings, while a directive of "code blue" came over the intercom.

As a team of doctors and nurses descended on the room, Sheriff Rudder and I slipped out. Nobody had to prompt us.

A Trash 'n' Treasures Tip

When leaving a collection to heirs, none of whom want it, stipulate in your will to have it sold and the proceeds divided between them. Someone not terribly interested in a baseball card collection might enjoy cash just fine.

Chapter Twelve

On the Fence

Late Monday morning, Mother, Tony and I were seated at the Duncan Phyfe table in the dining room, enjoying a lovely brunch. Tony had come here from the police station, where the sheriff had briefed him on the events of the night before, including, of course, Gerald's deathbed confession to killing Camilla.

Frankly, distracted by my Taser hangover, I was a little surprised that Tony had accepted Mother's invitation to join us—he had to know she would pester him with question after question. But I hoped that he would want to see me badly enough that he'd put up with her.

And he did. Want to see me, *and* put up with her . . .

Rocky, who hadn't seen his master since Wednesday (forever in dog time), had gone bonkers, jumping on Tony and pawing at him the moment he walked through our door. Pleased as I was to see my guy, somehow I had restrained myself from pawing at him. Sushi had sat on the sidelines, pouting because she wasn't the center of attention, jilted by both Rocky and Tony.

Back to the table. Mother was wearing Christmassy green slacks and a red top, yet another outfit of hers from Breckenridge. I was in not at all Christmassy black slacks and a purple cashmere sweater. As for Tony, he was in his standard work uniform of light-blue shirt, navy- and white-striped tie, and gray slacks.

Mother had prepared her delicious *Hof Pandekager* (a pancake recipe available in *Antiques St. Nicked*, an e-book novella), which was served with warm cinnamon applesauce and sides of German sausage and fresh fruit.

"Well," Tony said, taking a break between pancakes, "I clearly can't leave you two alone for even a few days without you getting yourselves in a jam with my colleagues. You'll both have to answer for the break-in at the Kleins', you know." He paused and looked sternly at Mother. "I distinctly remember telling you to stay within the law."

Mother lifted the coffeepot. "Strange . . . I have no memory of that, beyond the rear door having been left open, which, of course, might make proving breaking and entering a hard go for that ambitious, young county attorney of ours. Refill, dear?"

Tony's only answer was a grunt, but when he held out his cup for her to fill, I detected the ghost of a smile. Then he sat back, knowing what was to come: payment for the brunch.

Mother replaced the pot on its coaster, leaned forward, and tented her hands. "I believe I know how Rodney and Gerald ran their operation, but I would appreciate your take on it. I mean, you are an expert on this kind of thing."

"It's relatively simple," Tony said with a shrug. "Rodney was a fence for stolen property. He collaborated with Gerald to use the Kleins' antiques business to ship those items—hidden inside various relatively worthless items, like that cuckoo clock that held the gems—to buyers in other parts of the country."

That might seem relatively simple to Tony, but I was confused. "How does drug smuggling fit into that?"

"Well, right now this is theoretical. There's digging that we have to do. But it appears that Mr. Evans is a versatile and ambitious man. In addition to shipping stolen goods around the country through Gerald Klein, Evans also had controlled substances shipped to himself via Gerald Klein."

"Quite ingenious," Mother replied. "A new twist on an old game, dealing all kinds of contraband by going through a respectable conduit. Gerald could even provide what appeared to be a legitimate receipt!"

Tony was nodding. "Or be on the receiving end of one. We found the receipt indicating that picture frame was shipped to the Kleins, with Rodney Evans the intended buyer."

I asked, "How long has this been going on?"

"We don't know yet. Probably only since things got tough for the antiques dealers in the area, and the Kleins' legitimate business got in danger of going under."

Mother said, "Well, whenever it began, I think the scam could have thrived for quite some time . . . if Dexter hadn't sold that frame to your late wife. Do you think that young man was aware of what was going on? Or possibly even a part of it?"

Tony raised a cautionary palm. "I really can't comment on Dexter Klein, Vivian. He's the subject of an ongoing investigation."

"Well, can you at least tell me whether the young man is being cooperative?"

"He isn't. He's indicated he'll be lawyering up."

"Well, then," Mother went on, "can you comment on the packages that were found in his van? Have they been examined?"

"Yes."

"Anything of interest found?"

Tony considered the question.

"Come, come," Mother said. "I did discover the stolen jewels, after all. That should give me *some* capital here."

"All right," Tony sighed. "One package was stuffed with packets of counterfeit twenty-dollar bills."

"Stuffed where?" Mother asked.

"In a teddy bear."

Mother clapped once, delighted. "Clever! What else did you find?"

Tony sighed again but answered, "Fake gift cards."

"In?"

"The spines of several books."

"I hope those books weren't valuable."

"No, though the receipts included would indicate they were."

I said, "Mother, I think probably all the merchandise used was junk—like the cuckoo clock—as Tony said."

"Well," Mother said, "Gerald certainly was an ingenious middleman. Unless his wife, Loretta, was involved, as well . . . or do you believe Loretta was innocent in all this, as Gerald stated?"

Tony shrugged. "Deathbed testimony carries considerable weight. I'm willing to take her husband's word that she didn't know what was going on—for now. But that, too, is part of our ongoing investigation."

I asked, "Does Mrs. Klein say she knows Rodney Evans?"

Tony looked my way. "She claimed to have seen him only a few times, when she came back early from church on Sundays. Apparently, that's when Evans and Gerald conducted their business. As far as she knew—she says—Evans was just another customer."

Mother said, "And you buy that?"

Tony shrugged, then pushed back his chair and let out some air. "Well . . . I should get back to the station. Vivian, thank you for one fine brunch."

"You're most welcome, Chief." Mother slapped her hands on the table. "I guess that just about wraps everything up, doesn't it? In a nice neat bow."

Very soon, I would come to regret missing the oh-so-slight sarcasm in her voice. But at that moment I was focused on Tony, who was saying as he stood, "Oh, and, Vivian, one embarrassing photo isn't going to cost Heather her job. But if you ever ask her for inside information again, I *will* have to fire her . . . and charge you with obstruction of justice."

Mother's chin came up. "I have not the faintest idea what you are referring to."

I accompanied Tony to the front door, with Rocky tagging after. As we stood facing each other, I asked, "Do you, uh, mind clearing something up about Camilla?"

"If I can."

"She didn't know there were drugs in the frame when she bought it." I posed that as a statement, not a question, to help take the sting out.

His expression was utterly blank. "Are you wondering why Camilla refused to sell it back at twice the price?"

I nodded.

"I don't really know. I can't imagine she knew anything about the drugs. She wasn't perfect, but that? That just wasn't her." He shrugged. "Knowing her, she probably simply liked the frame. Wanted to keep it no matter what. She was stubborn that way."

Wasn't she?

Mother's face popped around the corner. "Sorry to disturb your little tête-à-tête, but, Chiefie . . ."

Uh-oh. He was "Chiefie" again.

"Who do you think will take over Sheriff Rudder's position when he steps down?"

"The voters will decide that this summer, Vivian."

"Hazard a guess."

"Well, it'll likely be Daryl—Daryl Dugan."

Rudder's second in command, a not very smart, strictly by-the-books man. Mother and I called him Deputy Dawg, though not to his face.

"Thank you, sir, for the insight," Mother said and disappeared.

He was frowning, looking past me at where Mother had gone, when I said, "Tony?"

His attention was on me now. "Yes?"

"Did you ever think that maybe I . . . I had killed her?"

I couldn't bring myself to say "Camilla" or "your wife"—"her" was the best I could manage.

"Not for a moment did I think that," he said. "Did you really ever think that I might have done it?"

"Never!"

If one or both of us were lying, it didn't matter. We had moved past that terrible moment.

"Then," I said, "we're all right? You and me?"

A powerful arm wrapped around me and drew me to him, and his mouth was on mine.

Right answer, I thought.

When we parted, he asked, "How about a take-out dinner at the cabin tonight?"

"Sounds perfect."

"You can bring Rocky then. Sushi too. I'll pick up Thai food after work."

Rocky, expecting to make an exit with his master, seemed confused when Tony commanded, "Stay, boy." After Tony left, the dog ran to the livingroom picture window to look out, making a sad little whine, which upset Sushi, who had trotted in and started to yap.

I knew how Rocky felt. I always hated to see Tony leave, too.

I barked, "Who wants to go outside!"

Both "go" and "outside" were hot-button words for the dogs, who instantaneously forgot their angst and started leaping in the air.

I put on my coat, hat, and gloves, slipped on a pair of waterproof boots, and retrieved a well-chewed Frisbee from the top shelf of the closet. Then we three went to the back door through the kitchen, where Mother was doing the dishes.

She asked, "How long will you and the little angels be out there, dear?"

"Depends on how cold it is," I said. "But at least fifteen minutes. Why?"

"I'll have some hot cocoa on the stove for you when you come in."

"That sounds perfect," I said.

"Have fun, dear. You know what they say? It's a dog's life!"

The dogs had a great time (me, too) cavorting in the new-fallen snow, Rocky hurling himself into the air, catching the disk, Sushi acting as his cheerleader. But then my fingers and toes got cold, and I started thinking about that hot cocoa.

Inside, Mother was no longer in the kitchen, and I called out to her to ask if she wanted me to bring her a cup. When I got no answer, I went into the living room, and that's when I noticed that her coat was gone and her purse and my UGGs.

And the car keys.

Oh rapturous joy! Oh heavenly days! For the very first time, I get to *end* the book! Not only that, but this time around, I have written the equivalent of three and one half chapters—a new record for me. I'm sure our sales on this title will skyrocket! (This is Vivian, if you hadn't already figured that out.)

After Brandy went outside to entertain the hounds, I took the car keys from the stand by the front door, got on my coat and her snugly UGGs, grabbed my purse, and—hoping the order not to arrest me remained in force—drove off in the C-Max. Destination: the hospital.

Rather than repeat my scrubs-outfit ploy, I entered through the lab/radiology entrance, circumventing the front information counter, where I might be questioned by a well-meaning volunteer as to the purpose of my visit. That was my business!

After going directly to the central elevator, I rode up to the third floor, where I expected Dexter would likely be in residence with his broken arm and leg.

After stepping off the elevator, I proceeded to the nurses' station, behind which I knew would be the staff's schedule board, giving detailed information regarding each patient—their doctor, day nurse, night nurse, case manager and, most importantly, room number.

Finding Dexter to be in room 317, I traipsed down the hallway to that number, prepared to tell any police officer on the door that Chief Cassato had approved my visit. But perhaps not surprisingly, there was a lack of security on Dexter's door. After all, where would he be going in his condition, anyway?

With the corridor empty, I quietly opened the door and slipped inside.

Dexter had a private room with the standard fare—recliner, bed, retractable table, TV high on the wall, small bathroom.

He was in the half-raised bed, asleep, one leg up in traction, his broken wing in a cast by his side.

When I rolled the recliner up to the bed, the young man's eyes jumped open in alarm.

"Good morning," I said, sitting. "Or is it afternoon already?"

He was studying me curiously. "Why . . . why are you here, Mrs. Borne?"

"Just to have a friendly little chat, dear."

"About?"

"About the poor judgment that put you in that hospital bed."

He shifted a little, which made him grimace a tad in discomfort. "No offense, but I really shouldn't talk to anyone about this until I see a lawyer."

I nodded. "Probably wise. Then consider this a friendly visit, just to see how you're doing. How lucky you were to walk away from a crash like that!"

"I . . . I didn't really walk. They cut me out of there and carried me."

"I meant that more or less as an expression— that you survived where you might not have. Lucky for you, Brandy and I were on hand to call nine-one-one posthaste." I sat back in the recliner. "It's nice that you have a private room and don't have to share your television with anyone. What are the odds of landing a hospital roommate with the same tastes in entertainment?"

"I, uh, never thought about that."

I sat forward with some enthusiasm. Or perhaps I was just acting. . . .

"You know, dear, the other day, I saw a terrific *Columbo* on television. A rerun, of course, but then they're all reruns now, aren't they? The guest villain was Robert Culp. Did you know the producers liked him so much, they used him in three different episodes? The only other guest star they had more times was Patrick McGoohan. He was in four. You know, *The Prisoner*? *Secret Agent*?"

"I don't watch old TV shows."

"But did you ever see *Columbo*? As a child? That is, when *you* were a child, not Peter Falk."

He was getting irritated now.

"Well," I went on, "in this particular *Columbo* episode, Robert Culp was the killer, of course, but someone made the ill-advised move of trying to blackmail *him*. Isn't that foolish? I mean, really. What's one more murder to a killer? With that said, how long do you think Robert Culp's blackmailer lasted?"

"No idea."

"Just past the fourth commercial."

"Really."

I gestured with an open hand. "My point is that blackmailing a murderer is a perilous exercise. Suppose, for example, that Gerald wasn't Camilla Cassato's murderer. . . ."

He sat up a little, which made him grimace in discomfort even more.

"But that you know who *is*. And you are contemplating blackmailing that murderer, just like that foolish associate of Robert Culp did. Unless, of course, you already *have*—but more likely it will be later, when you're back on your feet, though possibly with a crutch."

His expression was blank, yet somehow it spoke volumes.

I continued: "I don't think you were involved in Gerald's shady business. Otherwise, you would have known not to sell that frame to Camilla. But you may have suspected something was going on, after Gerald's reaction to the frame being sold. So you decided to go to Camilla's store to take a closer look at the frame in question, which you did. While she was in back, you had a close enough look to find the smuggled drugs . . . and take them." I paused. "But when Rodney

Evans beat Gerald within an inch or two of his life, you got scared. You knew Evans was no one to fool around with! So you gave the hot-potato frame to us."

Dexter wasn't looking at me at all, but rather straight ahead and up, his eyes just missing the TV.

"Where *are* those drugs, dear? In your apartment? Somewhere hidden in the remains of that ancient Volkswagen of yours? Unless you were able to market them with incredible speed, so to speak, the police will almost surely find them. They already have the packages you stole and put in your van, which you clearly suspected contained more contraband."

Dexter turned my way quick as a blink. "Look, Mrs. Borne, I took those packages only because I was unfairly fired. Didn't I have *some* kind of compensation coming?"

"Not a brilliant move, dear. That only makes it look like you were in on the operation."

"But Loretta says that Gerald exonerated me!"

"Ah! Then she's been to see you already. Did she make a preemptive offer?"

He swallowed. "I don't know what you're talking about. What kind of offer—"

"For you to keep quiet, of course. You see, I think it's likely that after you were fired, you were around long enough to happen to see that it was *Loretta* who left to retrieve that frame from Camilla Cassato—*not* Gerald. What has she promised you for your silence? A partnership in the business, perhaps? Not a good offer, now that the fencing operation has been shut down."

The young man's eyes turned frightened. "Suppose she did make me an . . . an offer. What should I do?"

"What's *right*, dear. Come clean."

His eyes flashed. "Then I'd come out of this with nothing! And still end up in jail, charged with what? Accessory after the fact, possession of drugs and stolen property?"

His uptalking could be forgiven in this stressful circumstance.

"Dear," I said, "however it plays out, you'll have your life—which, if you try to blackmail a murderer, will almost certainly not be the case. Perhaps you will be granted immunity for your testimony. If not, the right lawyer will work out a plea bargain for you, and you'll more than likely be free and clear. Have you secured an attorney as yet?"

"No."

Somewhat proudly, I said, "I can get you Wayne Ekhardt himself."

"Isn't he . . . dead?"

"Not that it shows," I said. "And he's still the best criminal defense lawyer this side of the Mississippi."

"I don't know how I could afford him."

I gave the boy a big smile. "Do the right thing, and it will be my treat, dear."

"You would do that?" he asked dubiously.

"To bring a killer to justice, absolutely." I put a finger to my lips. "But the police will need more evidence than just you saying you saw Loretta leave around the time Camilla was killed."

His eyes flashed again. "What if I could tie Loretta to the fencing business?"

"How?"

"It's . . . it's possible she keeps a separate set of accounting books in the safe."

"Well, if she hasn't destroyed them, that would be highly helpful."

I got out of the recliner and looked down at Dexter. "I don't sense that you're a truly bad individual, dear. . . . You're just a young person who's made some rather unfortunate, impulsive choices. You know, I understand the frustration of millennials. You're the first generation to discover that you're worse off than the previous one . . . but that doesn't give you any rights of entitlement. The world does not owe you a thing, Mr. Dexter Klein. However, you're clever and smart, and I'm sure you'll go far. . . . Just make sure it's in the right direction."

I left him there to mull that over.

At home, I found an angry Brandy in the kitchen, unloading the dishwasher.

"You took the car!" she yelped. "Where on earth have you been?"

"I'll give you chapter and verse in a while, dear. But right now I have something to tell you."

"What? Did you hit another mailbox?"

"Don't be silly," I said. "I just want to share with you an important decision I've made."

"This should be good." Brandy was holding a stack of our Fire-King dishes, and she shifted their weight in her hands.

"I've decided that we should decline to do another season of *Antiques Sleuths*."

Her mouth dropped, but fortunately, the dishes didn't. "Why? I mean, I personally don't think we should sign on again, not after what Phil pulled on us."

"I agree wholeheartedly. How can we trust Phil at this juncture? How can we work side by side with someone who betrayed and manipulated us?"

"You're saying you don't want to be on TV anymore," she said, dazed.

"Some other day perhaps," I continued, "in some other venue . . . but for now, I'm going to have my hands and schedule full in the upcoming months."

"Doing what? Producing *The Penis Papers*?"

"No, dear. Campaigning for the new sheriff."

Her eyes disappeared into slits. "You mean, supporting whoever's running against Deputy Dawg?"

"Spot on, dear!"

"Well, who? Who's *your* candidate for sheriff?"

"Well . . . me, dear."

This time the dishes did shatter to the floor.

See you at the polls!

To be continued . . .

A Trash 'n' Treasures Tip

Your investment in a collection will lose its value if you—and the heirs who may receive it—do not care properly for the items, such as keeping them safe from sunlight, moisture, overhandling, and harmful alloys. Mother once hung a valuable watercolor, which the sun reduced to a frame with a blank piece of paper in it.

About the Authors

Barbara Allan is a joint pseudonym of husband-and-wife mystery writers Barbara and Max Allan Collins.

Barbara Collins is a highly respected short story writer in the mystery field, with appearances in over a dozen top anthologies, including *Murder Most Delicious, Women on the Edge, Deadly Housewives,* and the best-selling *Cat Crimes* series. She was the coeditor of (and a contributor to) the best-selling anthology *Lethal Ladies,* and her stories were selected for inclusion in the first three volumes of *The Year's 25 Finest Crime and Mystery Stories.*

Two acclaimed hardcover collections of her work have been published: *Too Many Tomcats* and (with her husband) *Murder—His and Hers.* The Collinses' first novel together, the baby boomer thriller *Regeneration,* was a paperback best-seller; their second collaborative novel, *Bombshell*—in which Marilyn Monroe saves the world from World War III—was published in hardcover to excellent reviews. Both are back in print under the "Barbara Allan" byline.

Barbara also has been the production manager

and/or line producer on several independent film projects.

Max Allan Collins in 2017 was named a Mystery Writers of America Grand Master. He has earned an unprecedented twenty-two Private Eye Writers of America "Shamus" nominations for his Nathan Heller historical thrillers, winning for *True Detective* (1983) and *Stolen Away* (1991).

His other credits include film criticism, short fiction, songwriting, trading-card sets, and movie/TV tie-in novels, including the *New York Times* best-sellers *Saving Private Ryan* and the Scribe Award–winning *American Gangster.* His graphic novel *Road to Perdition,* considered a classic of the form, is the basis of the Academy Award–winning film. Max's other comics credits include the "Dick Tracy" syndicated strip; his own "Ms. Tree"; "Batman"; and "CSI: Crime Scene Investigation," based on the hit TV series, for which he also wrote six video games and ten best-selling novels.

An acclaimed, award-winning filmmaker in the Midwest, he wrote and directed the Lifetime movie *Mommy* (1996) and three other features; his produced screenplays include the 1995 HBO World Premiere *The Expert* and *The Last Lullaby* (2008). His 1998 documentary *Mike Hammer's Mickey Spillane* appears on the Criterion Collection release of the acclaimed film noir, *Kiss Me Deadly.* The current Cinemax TV series *Quarry* is based on his innovative book series.

Max's most recent novels include two works begun by his mentor, the late mystery-writing legend Mickey Spillane: *The Will to Kill* (with Mike Hammer) and *The Legend of Caleb York*, the first western credit for both Spillane and Collins.

"Barbara Allan" lives in Muscatine, Iowa, their Serenity-esque hometown. Son Nathan works as a translator of Japanese to English, with credits ranging from video games to novels.

Don't miss the next zany, irresistible
Trash 'n' Treasures mystery

ANTIQUES WANTED

Coming soon from
Kensington Publishing Corp.
Keep reading to enjoy a delightful
sample chapter . . .

Chapter One

Support Your Loco Sheriff

Where to begin? Well, how about with the fact that Mother is running for county sheriff?

What!?! (you might well ask). Is that even possible? I thought the position was appointed by the mayor with the approval of the city council.

So did I! But voters have always picked the sheriff. And now that the current sheriff, Peter J. Rudder, is stepping down due to health concerns, there's going to be a special election in a couple of months—and you know how many friends Mother has.

Didn't you try to stop her?

What do you think? I told her that she had no

experience, no aptitude, no qualifications whatsoever.

And what did she say?

She said, "Dear, lots of people hold office who aren't qualified."

Who could refute that? But surely there are some qualifications.

Surprisingly little! For our county, the candidate must be at least twenty-five years old, been a resident here for no less than one year, and have a minimum of 160 hours of law enforcement training at an accredited law enforcement school—which Mother got several years ago taking night classes at the community college, after solving her first murder case.

Oh, brother . . . Maybe you should contact her psychiatrist for his help.

I did.

And?

He refused to talk to me on grounds of patient confidentiality. And *my* therapist's advice to me, before you ask, was to stay on my antidepressant.

Wow. Maybe you should just get out of town. You know, on the next stage.

That's your solution? Leave town? And I'll handle the sarcasm, thank you very much.

Leaving out the back door is what I'd do if she were my mother.

Not helpful!

Hey, you came to me. You seemed to want my opinion, and I gave it.

Sorry, you're right—I'm just a little stressed.

Look, the voters aren't stupid—they care about who's serving and protecting them. So you can be outwardly supportive while inwardly secure in the fact that she'll never win.

You think?

Sure . . . but keep a suitcase packed and ready.

The *she* in *she'll never win* (for you newcomers) is Vivian Borne, midseventies, Danish stock, attractive despite large, out-of-fashion glasses that magnify her eyes, widowed, bipolar, legendary local thespian, and even more legendary amateur sleuth.

She-Who-Is-a-Little-Stressed is me, Brandy Borne, thirty-three, divorced, blond by choice, Prozac-popping prodigal daughter who came home from Chicago, postdivorce, to live with her mother in the small Mississippi River town of Serenity, Iowa, seeking solitude and relaxation but instead finding herself the frequent reluctant accomplice in Vivian Borne's escapades. Did I mention reluctant?

The third member of our household (and possibly the smartest) is Sushi, my diabetic shih tzu who once was blind but now can see, which sounds oddly spiritual for a dog, but really just means she had successful cataract surgery.

On what appeared to be just another Monday morning, Trash 'n' Treasures—the antiques shop Mother and I run together—was closed for the day. That left us pajama-clad, lingering leisurely over breakfast at the Duncan Phyfe table in the dining room.

Because the meal Mother had made was better than our usual fare—egg casserole, homemade hash, crisp bacon, sausage patties, and giant frosted cinnamon rolls—I suspected the elder Borne had something more in store for me that was not so palatable.

Finally, unable to munch down another morsel, I sat back and sighed, being far too ladylike to burp (as far as you know).

"Well," I said, "let's have the check."

Mother, seated opposite, gazed at me with a dewy-eyed innocence right out of a silent movie. "The check, dear?"

I gestured to the dishes around us. "All that couldn't have been free. Has there been a murder? Do you need me to stage-manage your next one-woman show? Let's get it over with."

Mother lay a splayed hand to her chest. "My darling girl, your mistrust and suspicions cut me deep."

Darling girl? This was going to be a rough one. A grunt of a response was all I could manage (sort of a half grunt, half burp). (Okay, so I'm not so ladylike.)

"Still," she went on, at once casual and grand, "I do have something in mind for today. Shall we retire to the library?"

Bedlam would have been more like it, but the library was—in addition to being a music and TV den—Mother's incident room when she and I (did I mention reluctant?) were on a case.

Mother stood from the table and smoothed the front of her 1940s pink chenille robe with shoulder pads, apparently on loan from Joan Crawford, an item of apparel she'd refused to give up even after I'd bought her a nice new robe for Christmas. (Once, I tried throwing the ratty old thing out with the trash, but she managed to retrieve it before the garbage truck came by. For someone with glasses that thick, she has sharp eyes.)

I followed Mother into the library/music/TV/incident room, which was redolent of ancient moldy books, smelly old brass instruments (mostly cornets), and air freshener—a lethal combination to inhale on a full stomach.

She gestured for me to sit on the bench of an antiquated stand-up piano that neither of us could play. Oh. Reminds me. For about a month there was another smell added to the room's fragrant bouquet: a dead mouse, which had gotten strangled in the piano wires. Accident, suicide, or murder—that one we never solved.

(**Note to Brandy from Editor:** *While I understand you are going through a difficult time with Vivian, readers come to these books for a good mystery and some lighthearted chuckles, and a mouse strangled with piano wire does not fit either category. Please adjust your tone.*)

(**Note to Editor from Brandy:** *Yes, ma'am. But it did happen. And we really never did solve it.*)

From behind the stand-up piano, Mother rolled out the old schoolroom blackboard she always used to compile her list of suspects, and stood before it, hands clasped beneath her bosom.

"No murder today, darling," she said. "Nor pending theatrical event. No. What I need is your help deciding upon my campaign slogan."

From incident room to campaign headquarters, in a blink!

Mother went on, "Something catchy like *Tippecanoe and Vivian, Too!*"

"Huh?"

She gave me a mildly cross look. "*Tippecanoe and Tyler, Too?* William Henry Harrison's presidential slogan in 1840?" She sighed. "How soon they forget. . . . Tyler was his running mate, and Tippecanoe was a battle Harrison won against the Shawnee nation."

"Okay, first, nobody knows that today; and second, you don't have anything to do with Tippecanoe or Tyler, too; and third, even if you did, bragging about beating Native Americans only works if you're running for sheriff in the 1800s."

Mother's eyes behind the large lenses studied me suspiciously—was I being helpful, or just obstructive?—I'll never tell.

"What other slogans have you come up with?" I asked, realizing my sarcasm had been showing, adding, "And stay away from any presidential ones—you're running for sheriff, remember. *Present-day* sheriff."

"Excellent advice, dear. Although I did rather like Goldwater's *In your heart, you know he's right,* only with a *she.*"

"Maybe so," I said, "but you don't want to remind voters of somebody who lost." Anyway, they might just think, *In your head, you know she's wrong.*

"Good point, dear," Mother replied.

See? I *was* being helpful.

Mother furrowed her brow, then brightened,

a lamp with its switch thrown. "How about . . . *A clearer vision for the future!*"

"With those glasses?" Okay, obstructive.

"*Qualified, experienced, and dependable?*"

"Wouldn't go there." Helpful.

Hands on hips, Mother huffed, "All right, Little Miss Smarty-pants—why don't *you* come up with something?"

So much for Her Darling Girl.

I got up, walked to the blackboard, plucked a piece of white chalk from the wooden lip, then wrote in block letters, *VIVIAN, BORNE TO BE SHERIFF.*

Mother clapped her hands. "Oh, I *do* like that, dear! Very clever. Now, let's talk about promotion."

Since this confab apparently was going to go on for a while, I returned to the bench. Sushi trotted in from the living room and jumped up on my lap. She looked at Mother in a *This-Is-Going-to-Be-Good* fashion.

Mother, resuming her teacherly stance before the blackboard, said, "I have a few notions that I came up with in the middle of the night."

Middle-of-the-night notions were never her best, but at least were frequently entertaining. I waited with bated breath.

With a smile only slightly edged with mania, Mother asked, "Why don't we print leaflets and drop them from an airplane all over town?"

Gulp.

She continued, "And while the plane is up there, it can sky-write my new slogan. Like *Surrender, Dorothy* in *The Wizard of Oz?*"

Pay no attention to the woman behind the curtain.

I took a deep breath, then said slowly, so it would sink in, "I'm pretty sure dropping leaflets from a plane would be considered littering, and you could be fined, which doesn't suggest to the populace that you'd make an ideal sheriff. As for sky-writing, the cost is probably prohibitive."

Mother's face fell like a cake when I opened the oven door too soon. Not that I ever did. Lately.

I shifted on the bench. "By all means, print up leaflets . . . but hand them out instead, you know, wherever you go. Door to door. On street corners. That kind of thing."

Mother made a face. "That's so dull! Not a Vivian Borne–style showstopper."

The last time Mother stopped a show was in *Hello Dolly* when she ("Goodbye!") danced off the stage into the orchestra pit.

She was asking, "What if the plane doesn't sky-write, but merely drags a banner?"

"Again, that depends on the price . . . but it can't be cheap."

Mother frowned, then brightened. "Here's an idea that won't cost too much—you drive me around town while I proclaim my slogan from a bullhorn!"

I shook my head. "Now we'd be disturbing the peace. Look, who's going to pay for all this promotion, once we decide what we can do that won't cost too much, or get you arrested?"

A forefinger raised in declamatory fashion. "A super PAC?"

"You can't form your own super PAC," I said, "and anyway, who are the big money boys that'll line up to back you?"

"How about a medium PAC?"

"No, not even a teensy-weensy PAC. Mother, you're going to have to get donations the hard way—by going around town and begging your friends for money."

Mother touched a finger to her chin. "I do have friends! Not to mention a few enemies who might contribute, knowing what I have on them."

I sighed. "Blackmail may not be the best way to start your law enforcement career."

She shrugged. "It's worked for many who came before me."

"Be that as it may, the people who donate won't want to see their hard-earned money wasted on any looney-tunes antics like sky-writing."

She sighed. "I suppose you're right, dear. Any suggestions on other ways to raise some campaign funds?"

I thought for a moment. "What about collecting items for a white elephant sale?"

Traditionally a white elephant sale was a step up from the usual garage or rummage varieties because "white elephants" were things of value that had fallen out of favor over time, or were too hard to maintain by an owner but still desirable by others.

Mother exclaimed, "Excellent idea! We could make a good deal of money."

"And look fiscally responsible, trying to self-fund your election, which in turn will encourage supporters to make cash contributions as well."

"Dear, you're a genius," Mother remarked. "What a wonderful campaign manager you'll make!"

"Wait . . . *what?*" I stood, spilling Sushi to the floor like a furry drink. "Let's get this straight. . . . I'm *not* going to be your campaign manager!"

"But you already *are*, dear," Mother said. "You volunteered!"

"I did no such thing."

"It was implied, in the context of all your wise counsel. Anyway, I need you. You can see that. Just look at the unrealistic promotional ideas that *I* came up with without your grounded guidance!"

Her midnight notions really had been pretty bad.

Her expression turned pitifully pleading. "Please say you will? Pretty please?"

My sigh came all the way up from my toes. "Stop. Don't add *with sugar on top.* I'll do it. I'll hate myself in the morning, but I'll do it."

Mother's pitiful countenance suddenly evaporated. "Thank you, dear. Now, get dressed. Places to go, things to do, people to see."

As she darted past me on her way out, I thought I caught a tiny, smug smile.

Had I just been had?

Had I been played, like one of her smelly old cornets? With nutsy talk of Tippecanoe and leaflets dropping from a plane and sky-writing and a bullhorn and super and medium PACs?

What do you think? (That's rhetorical. We don't need to reopen our conversation.)

Half an hour later, about a quarter to ten, I was behind the wheel of our C-Max, having become the de facto chauffeur in the family since Mother lost her driver's license due to various infractions; she was riding shotgun, while Sushi was left at home holding down the fort.

I've had a few complaints from readers about detailing what Mother and I are wearing in these narratives. If you prefer to think of us as flitting about in the nude, skip the rest of this paragraph. For those of you without dirty minds, I was wearing a floral cotton shirt by Madewell, my favorite DKNY jeans, and a pair of Sam Edelman sandals; Mother was in a pink sweater and matching slacks by Breckenridge, and white shoes custom made to accommodate her painful bunions.

Our destination on this sunny spring morning was the fittingly named Sunny Meadow Manor, an assisted-living/nursing-care facility situated in the country off the bypass—or as Mother calls it, "The Treacherous Bypass," due to the lack of stoplights needed to insure safe cross-traffic passage.

Mother had always enjoyed visiting nursing homes, and would sometimes drag along a reluctant Brandy, who didn't want to face the final stage of life—especially as depicted by the at-risk patients in wheelchairs lining the hallway, many of whom were forgotten souls.

"Why," I asked, "are we going to Sunny Meadow? You aren't thinking of changing addresses, are you?"

"Unfunny and unkind, dear," Mother replied. "No, my intention is to solicit items from the assisted-living residents for our white elephant sale."

"That doesn't seem very likely to succeed."

"Why do you say that?"

"Well, anybody living there has left their homes behind and most of their belongings."

Mother twisted toward me. "Dear, have you ever been *inside* any of those apartments?"

"Well . . . no."

"If you had, you'd know that the units are indeed rather small, but are usually crammed with more possessions than the residents should ever have brought along with them."

"Not to be crass," I said, "but what makes you think you'll get anything of value?"

"Because, dear, only the very well-off can afford to live in those apartments, with all of the extended services. So they've undoubtedly brought along their *best* things—things that have meaning, but might by now have become burdensome."

"Like a silver tea set," I reasoned, "that needs constant polishing."

"Bingo." Then she lowered her voice: "I really should avoid saying that, since that particular game is almost certainly going on in the commons area."

I took my eyes off the road momentarily. "So

your plan is to weasel these well-off senior citizens out of their best things?"

Mother's laugh was musical, if irritating. "Oh, my, no. They'll practically *beg* me to take them."

I remained skeptical, but in such matters, she was usually right.

I turned off the bypass, then drove west into a countryside of Grant Wood–esque rolling hills comprised of freshly planted fields dotted with the occasional oak or maple tree. Sunny Meadow Manor itself was perched on one of those hills, up a sharp incline, and surrounded by evergreen trees whose boughs gently swayed in the breeze.

I had been to Sunny Meadow Manor several times, having visited Mother there when she was recovering from her double hip replacements—that went back about eight years, when I was still married to Roger and living in a Chicago suburb.

So I was familiar with the layout, which hadn't changed any—the first floor devoted to assisted-living apartments, the second given over to usual nursing home fare, with the third the Alzheimer's Unit. Any higher floor than that would have pearly gates.

As I drove up the incline, Mother said, "Now, I'll do all the talking, dear."

Which I'd planned on, anyway. I was willing to aid but not abet.

I wheeled into the front parking lot, and we exited the car. A wide cement walk took us to double glass doors, which we passed through. To the left was the visitor waiting area, unchanged since Mother's stay: same couches, chairs, and wall prints in soothing pastel colors. The decor did seem a little shopworn now—the fabric on the furniture threadbare in spots, wall prints faded, fake floral arrangements outdated. Still, the section was pleasant enough.

To the right yawned a hallway leading to the administrative wing, muffled voices emanating toward us from various offices. Straight ahead was a reception area consisting of a mahogany desk and chair, the kind of setup a concierge might have in a nice hotel.

No one was behind the desk at the moment, but Mother moved toward it anyway, then bent and picked up a pen tethered to its holder (did the residents here have kleptomaniac relatives?) and proceeded to sign us in to the register.

She had just finished and straightened when a voice rather sternly called, "*Mrs. Borne!*"

We turned.

Rushing toward us from the administrative hallway came a rotund man, pushing fifty, with thinning brown hair, mustache, and wire-framed glasses. He wore a navy business suit, white shirt, plain blue tie, and shiny black shoes. (Or would you prefer to imagine him naked? To each his/her own.)

Planting himself in front of Mother, he said, "Mrs. Borne, I hope you're not on these premises with the intention of collecting *more Vivian-Borne-for-sheriff* signatures from our residents! I've received several complaints from relatives whose loved ones are in the Alzheimer's Unit."

"Oh, goodness, no," Mother gushed. "I've

collected all the signatures I needed to file for my candidacy. We're here just to visit." She gestured to me. "This is my daughter, Brandy. Brandy, this is Mr. Burnett—the new managing director of this lovely facility."

"Nice to meet you," I said, and smiled.

Burnett acknowledged my presence with a curt nod. Then he said, "Fine . . . as long as you two really *are* here *just* to visit."

"We are," I said. Which was true in a way.

The manager nodded again, then turned and headed back to the administrative wing, a chugging little engine minus its train.

I gave Mother a hard stare.

"What, dear?" she asked.

"You filed your intent-to-run papers with signatures from *Alzheimer's* patients?"

She shrugged. "Only a few. And only when they really did recognize me. The temptation was to use them more than once."

"That's not funny, Mother."

She patted my arm. "I know, dear. I'll most likely get the disease myself—it runs in the family."

So I had that to look forward to, too, along with bad hips, glaucoma, and bunions. Heredity is such a wonderful thing.

We headed back to the wing of apartments, which totaled twelve in all, where I was soon to discover that Mother had been correct about the residents having brought along too much stuff with them.

Mother's MO for each stop was a cheery ten-minute visit spiced with juicy gossip, followed by a sales pitch for unwanted items for her white elephant sale to finance her campaign for sheriff. Then, when an item was offered, she got an assurance that said item was not on the wish list of any of the giver's relatives.

So as not to take up pages detailing these many visits, here is a recap of what was collected over the next few hours.

Mrs. Rockwell gave Mother a large vintage 1960s sun-burst clock by Welby, about two feet across with alternating brass and wood rays, and a black-and-gold face. The reason the woman unloaded the clock: the dial had become too hard for her to read. Interest from relatives: none. Reason for their rejection: the clock didn't fit their decor; the clock was ugly. (It was. But a discreet check on my cell phone turned up a similar clock for sale on eBay for four hundred and fifty dollars.)

Mrs. Goldstein donated a Louis Vuitton suitcase, circa 1980, medium-sized (the suitcase, not Mrs. Goldstein), brown, with the famous LV logo. Reason for unloading: she didn't travel anymore. Interest from relatives: none. Reason for their rejection: not a complete set; too large for baggage carry-on; too small to use for a long trip; might get stolen at the airport. (eBay value for similar suitcase: between five and eight hundred dollars.)

Mr. Fillmore—to our astonishment—offered to give to the cause his ten-year-old Buick Century with tan leather interior, and mileage of only fifty-plus thousand. Reason for unloading the car: after several near accidents, he had stopped driving, yet was still paying for a parking spot at the facility. Interest from any relatives: none, although a sixteen-year-old grandson who had just gotten his driver's license had expressed interest until he saw the car. Reason for grandson's rejection: he'd never get a girlfriend driving a "geezer car." (Internet value: three thousand to five thousand dollars.)

Not all of the donations were treasures; some were more in the trash area—like a collection of mostly broken and glued-back-together Hummel figurines, and costume jewelry missing stones. Still, Mother accepted these offerings with the same effusive gratitude as the good stuff.

All in all, it had been a highly successful trip to Sunny Meadow, and I had gotten my daily exercise making multiple trips to and from the C-Max with our loot. (Mr. Fillmore's Buick I would pick up later, as he had to find the title to the car.)

After my final foray outside, I rejoined Mother just after she'd exited the Hummel lady's apartment.

She burbled, "I'd call this a bona fide success, wouldn't you?"

I gave her a simultaneous shrug and nod. "You were right about coming here."

We were heading in the direction of the front entrance when we passed an apartment whose name-plaque read: MRS. HARRIET DOUGLAS.

"Hey, you missed her," I said.

"I didn't miss her, dear."

"She's not a friend, huh?"

"No, Harriet's a *good* friend, but she happens to be the aunt of Deputy Daryl Dugan, my only competition in the race for sheriff."

"Ah," I said, eyebrows flicking up. "Best not to put her on the spot."

"Quite astute, dear."

We were moving away from the apartment's door when it suddenly opened, startling us both into a little dual jump.

Framed in the doorway was a diminutive, plump woman with short, permed, white hair and wire-framed glasses. She wore a blue cotton housedress with white bric-a-brac trim, and tan slippers. Standing slightly behind her, a constant companion, was an oxygen tank on wheels, a thin plastic tube running up and around the woman's head to both nostrils.

Harriet clasped her hands and said to Mother, "Oh, good! I've caught you. I was afraid you'd leave without seeing me."

Mother replied, "Harriet, darling, I didn't want to impose upon you because—"

"Yes, yes," the woman interrupted impatiently, "I know why you're here. All of us oldies but goodies text each other. But, please, come in—I'd like a word."

She and her tank moved to allow us passage, and I followed Mother inside.

We were in another cramped living room, which might have been otherwise were it not for all the furniture. The decor was formal in nature: floral chintz couch and matching chair, leather recliner, large tube television, cherrywood accent table with a Tiffany-style lamp, coffee table, big corner hutch displaying collections of antique plates, glass paperweights, and small crystals (probably Waterford) running on the religious side, like angels and crosses, but with a few animals thrown in.

The air had a strong scent of room freshener, beneath which I detected cigarette smoke, and I hoped Harriet wasn't lighting up around her companion, Mr. Oxygen Tank.

Our hostess said cheerily, "Please, sit."

Mother and I moved to the chintz couch while Harriet took the recliner, parking the tank alongside.

"How *are* you doing with the emphysema, my dear?" Mother asked sympathetically.

"Getting worse all the time, I'm afraid," the woman sighed.

And yet she still smoked.

Harriet seemed to have read my mind, saying, "I only smoke occasionally, when I'm upset, and then I go outside . . . *without* my tank." Our hostess began to cough, and we waited awkwardly for the attack to end.

Then Mother asked, "Was there something in particular that you wanted to see me about, Harriet?"

"Yes," Harriet said, as winded as if she'd just run a race. "I wanted to tell you that—while you and I *are* old friends—I'll be supporting my nephew in his run for sheriff."

"Well, naturally," Mother said. "I wouldn't have expected otherwise." She added graciously, "You must be *very* proud of him."

That was her best piece of acting in some time.

Harriet made a face. ". . . Yes. I guess I am. Blood being thicker and so on. Still, I *do* cherish our long friendship, Vivian, and so I'd like to quietly, anonymously contribute to your white elephant sale."

Mother smiled, pleased. "How wonderful, dear. And my lips will be forever sealed on the subject."

Harriet gestured to the accent table nearby. "I'd like to give you this Tiffany lamp—it's not an original, of course, but a replica made by the Dale Tiffany Company."

I knew about that company, founded in the late 1970s, and their reproductions were highly respected and sought after. And this particular lamp was exquisite: the glass shade showing ruby red peonies, with green, yellow, and blue accents, and an Art Nouveau bronze base.

I could tell the lamp had Mother excited, too, by the way her eyes sparkled behind her lenses.

I asked, "Are you sure you want to part with it?"

Hand on her heart, Mother said, "Yes, my dear, are you *quite* sure?" But I knew she wanted to kick me.

"I am," Harriet said, nodding to each of us in turn. "I can't read by it, so it's no good to me. And before you ask if anyone in my family wants it, the answer is no."

"Does that include Daryl?" I pressed. I didn't

want any further conflict between Deputy Dawg and Mother.

"Especially Daryl," Harriet laughed, which got her coughing again. Then she added, "Daryl and his wife, Candy, have contemporary tastes—besides, I bought the darn lamp, and I can do with it as I please. But if you don't *want* it . . ."

"We want it!" Mother and I said in unison. Perhaps a little too eager.

"Good," Harriet said. "That's settled. Now. There's something *else* I'd like to give Vivian."

Mother and I glanced at each other, in shared wonder about what fabulous treasure might be bestowed upon us next.

Harriet was waving a bony hand at the corner hutch. "It's in the first drawer, right on top."

When Mother started to rise, the woman snapped, "Let Brandy get it—that's what daughters are for."

Brother. Would I be that crabby at her age? Probably, if I were tethered to a tank. Who wouldn't be?

I got off the couch and crossed to the hutch, opened the top drawer, and looked in. Staring back at me was a toothlessly grinning bearded old goofball in a floppy hat.

Gabby Hayes. An autographed photo of the old-time sidekick to cowboy stars in the movies of the thirties, forties, and fifties. The signature had a surprisingly flowing flourish to it.

I picked up the framed black-and-white photo, and turned to Mother and our hostess. "Is *this* what you mean?"

"Yes, yes!" Harriet said. "Give it to your mother!"

I did, then sat back down.

Mother studied the studio still with delight. "Oh, and it's *signed*, too."

"Yes," Harriet said, nodding, "and there's a letter of provenance in the back of the frame."

Mother looked from Gabby to Harriet, whose smiling expressions were similar, although the latter was wearing dentures. "How did you *know* George Hayes was my favorite cowboy character actor?"

Harriet smiled. "You once mentioned to me that you'd learned a lot about acting watching Gabby Hayes display his dramatic skills. It made an impression, and I never forgot it."

Now I could never forget it, either.

Our hostess went on, "But you must *promise* to *keep* the photo, and not sell it in your white elephant sale."

"Why, I wouldn't *dream* of doing such a thing!" Mother exclaimed.

And she meant it, too.

"Good," Harriet said. "Because I got it from Daryl—he has quite an impressive collection of western memorabilia—I don't want him to know that I asked him for it to give it to *you*. It would hurt his feelings. It was from the Judd Pickett collection!"

I said, "Ooooh," as if that meant anything to me.

Mother crossed her heart. "I promise to keep and cherish it, and never to tell."

Antsy to leave, I said, "Well, uh, we should get going. Thank you, Mrs. Douglas, for the lovely lamp."

"And the fabulous photo!" Mother added.

"You're welcome, girls," Harriet replied, then told me where I could find newspapers and a box. Since packing things up was what daughters were good for.

While I wrapped up the lamp, and Mother and Harriet were saying their good-byes, Harriet suddenly said, "There is *one* thing I would love to have from you two."

"What's that, dear?" Mother asked.

"One of your books."

"Which one?"

"Oh, the latest, please," Harriet replied.

"Hardcover or paperback?"

"Hardcover."

"Regular or large print?" Mother asked.

I was holding the box now, and it was getting heavy.

Harriet said, "Large print would be better."

Mother said, "We keep copies in our car for just such requests, and I'll send Brandy back with one."

"Thank you, Vivian. I'll leave the door unlocked."

We made our exit.

In the reception area, the sign-in desk remained vacant, and we didn't bother to sign out because I was holding the heavy, oversize box, and Mother was staring admiringly at Gabby Hayes in her hands, who stared back at her with a rakish, toothless grin.

Outside, the sunny sky had been replaced by ominous dark clouds, the air heavy with the smell of rain soon to come.

In the car, I found a place in the backseat for

the box while Mother retrieved our current tome from the trunk. As I hoofed it back to the main entrance, large drops of rain started falling, but I made it to the overhang just before the downpour came.

I stood for a moment watching the deluge, wishing I'd grabbed an umbrella from the car. Then I entered the building, went by the unattended desk, and proceeded down the hallway to Mrs. Douglas's apartment.

I was reaching for the doorknob when an explosion within blew the door off its hinges, and flung me back against the corridor wall like a rag doll.

A Trash 'n' Treasures Tip

Celebrity autographs are easily forged, so buy only from a reputable dealer who will assure its authenticity with a money back guarantee. My heart sank like the *Titanic* when Mother pointed out to me that the signature on my Leo DiCaprio eight-by-ten was spelled *DeCaprio*.